W9-AUR-281

TWIGS

ALISON ASHLEY FORMENTO

To Brooke,
Follow your own path!
A Formento

MeritPress
F+W Media, Inc.

Published by Merit Press
an imprint of F+W Media, Inc.
10151 Carver Road, Suite 200
Blue Ash, Ohio 45242
www.meritpressbooks.com

ISBN 10: 1-4405-6565-1
ISBN 13: 978-1-4405-6565-6
eISBN 10: 1-4405-6566-X
eISBN 13: 978-1-4405-6566-3

Printed in the United States of America.

10 9 8 7 6 5 4 3 2 1

Library of Congress Cataloging-in-Publication Data
Formento, Alison.
Twigs / Alison Ashley Formento.
pages cm
ISBN-13: 978-1-4405-6565-6 (hard cover)
ISBN-10: 1-4405-6565-1 (hard cover)
ISBN-13: 978-1-4405-6566-3 (ebook)
ISBN-10: 1-4405-6566-X (ebook)
I. Title.
PZ7.F766Tw 2013
[Fic]--dc23

2013015535

This is a work of fiction. Names, characters, corporations, institutions, organizations, events, or locales in this novel are either the product of the author's imagination or, if real, used fictitiously. The resemblance of any character to actual persons (living or dead) is entirely coincidental.

This book is available at quantity discounts for bulk purchases.
For information, please call 1-800-289-0963.

For Dan, my forever radio guy.

Acknowledgments

My wonderful and persistent agent Courtney Miller-Callihan and uber-supportive, insightful editor Jacquelyn Mitchard of Merit Press have made my debut novel a reality. To say I'm grateful to these believers in *Twigs* is an understatement, but yes, I am forever grateful to them both. Special thanks to writing and critique friends Laurie Boyle Crompton, Cynthia Sherwood, Shari Berger Maurer, Wendy Mass, Cyndy Unwin, Tracy Brown Walton, Lauren Monahan, Ann Malaspina, and the entire KidLit Authors Club. Added thanks to Critcasters, NJSCBWI, and Verla Kay's Blueboarders—especially Kip Wilson Rechea, Deena Lipomi, Janel Rodriguez, Marissa Doyle, and Kate Messner. A writing exercise at the Mahwah Library Writers group began the journey that became Twigs's story. My sincere thanks to those early readers, particularly Judith Faulkner for her support from page one.

Chapter 1

I doodled my real name in big loopy letters all over the brown cardboard. I'd emptied forty cartons of Winstons from that box and stocked the cancer case behind the register. It still reeked of tobacco. I should've tossed it in the bin after I flattened it and gotten back to stocking shelves, but instead I'd grabbed a black marker and spent the last ten minutes making letters. All kinds. Block letters. Swirling ones. I'd grown bolder with each attempt.

Madeline Henry

I switched from the marker to the cheap plastic Uptown Pharmacy pen people used to sign their credit card slips, and scribbled a row of small tight letters. This time I added my middle name.

Madeline Annette Henry

Something about seeing my full name in print made it truly mine, even though I'd never used it except on official documents. The more times I'd written it on all of the college forms, the more I knew I wanted to use it from now on. Why not? It was my first and only time starting college, right? No better time to be a new me, even if the old me was stuck in Titusburg.

The bigger I scribbled the letters, the better I felt.

"Who the hell is Madeline, Twigs?"

I jumped and turned to see Chad Bell putting a medicine bottle on the counter. The empty box fell to the floor under my feet. My face got hot. I'd been so caught up in writing my name that I'd forgotten that he'd come in the store to fill a prescription. I rubbed my nose. Even though his overalls looked clean enough, Chad always smelled like oil from working at his dad's garage.

"Hey, Chad." I smiled at my brother's buddy and stamped down the box. "Did you get your thyroid pills?"

I began rearranging the ChapStick display, as if the little tubes could rescue me from Chad's eye lock.

"Yep, Twigger girl." He grabbed a handful of beef-jerky sticks from the jar on the counter and tossed them next to his medicine.

My throat tightened and I dropped a ChapStick tube. Chad enjoyed teasing me with annoying names, like some doofus big brother, unlike my sweet real one, Matt. It was bad enough being referred to as a part of a gun, but Chad had known me forever. He knew I couldn't stand being called a girl. Now I'd hit eighteen, I was determined it would stop.

I gave Chad a little tap on his arm. "You know I'm starting college this week."

"So who's Madeline, Twigster? Some secret cousin?"

Chad wouldn't let it go. He hadn't been known as "the Mule" for nothing when he'd played defense for Titusburg High. Matt said Chad had been so stubborn with the football that he'd never given ground to any other players, even on his own team.

I cleared my throat. If I wanted to use my real name when college started, then I had to own it. No better time to start than the present. "It's me."

Chad stared at me for a few seconds and then brayed out a laugh that fit his nickname. "Ha!" He spoke my name syllable by syllable, "Mad-e-line!" and laughed again. "That's a good one. Does your big bro know about this, Twigsy?"

The Mule trampled my Madeline name-high the way he used to plow down opposing football players. I slapped the counter. "Stop, Chad. I'm not Twigger, Twigsy, or Twigster. I'm Madeline. And Matt's a little busy fighting a war right now, so don't bother him with stupid e-mails."

Chad held his hands up, like I might hit him. "Ooh, this Madeline is one tough chick."

"Go stick your head under a car, okay?"

Chad laughed and gave me a fake salute. "Whatever you say, Madeline."

I grabbed his jerky and medicine and rang him up without another word. Half an hour after he'd left the store, I was still annoyed at myself for letting him get to me. But at least it helped pass the time.

I shoved a stack of *National Enquirers* into the display stand and grabbed one for myself. The gorgeous blonde-of-the-moment had gained two pounds, and the blurry cover photo caught her in the act of eating a double-scoop cone. Even with the extra weight, she was a goddess, something I'd never be. I read what the eighteen-year-old starlet would earn on her next film and nearly choked. "No fair," I said to the picture. "Same age as me—you make ten mil and live in Movie Land; I make minimum and live in Arkansas." I stared at the photo, half-hoping the goddess might pop to life right here at Uptown Pharmacy and console me. "Hey Twigs, er . . . Madeline," she'd say, "I've got a walk-on part for you in my next flick." Then she'd give me a once-over. "But you'll need some enhancement surgery first."

Maybe I'd buy this issue, since reading it might be my only entertainment now everyone I knew had left for college. Turning the page, I noticed a photo with the caption, "I'm Grace Kelly's Love Child." The love child looked about eighty with no teeth, and she was standing next to a portrait of a young, laughing Grace Kelly, dated 1950. I gasped at how much it reminded me of Mom when Dad used to tickle her. I quickly turned the page, pushing that memory away. I continued thumbing through the rag mag when something crashed on the other side of the store.

I took off running and stopped short at Aisle 7. Holy crap! Hair clips, brushes, gels, assorted dyes, and hair-spray bottles littered the floor around a sobbing woman slumped there. She really wailed, like someone had just died or something. She looked about my mom's age with hair dyed the color of mustard. Boxes of L'Oréal and Clairol hair dye filled her lap.

"Ma'am? Are you okay?" The woman looked at me, midsob, and threw a box of Ebony 14 at my head. "Hey!" I barely swerved out of the way in time. Then the howling woman cried even louder.

A buzzer sounded, alerting me that a customer needed service up-front. Dink had made a bank run, so except for Mr. Franks in the pharmacy, I was in charge. Nothing like giving authority to someone people rarely noticed.

"Um . . . I'll be right back." I tore myself away and rushed to the cash register, where a couple of tweener boys were pounding on the buzzer.

"Okay, okay. Can I help you?"

"Pack of Marlboros," said one—the taller boy. He stared over my head at the glass-front shelves filled with cancer sticks.

His serious I'm-old-enough-to-smoke face cracked me up. "Funny, boys, funny." Grabbing a long red licorice stick from the huge jar on the counter, I held it like a cigarette. "How about a Twizzler instead? Much healthier."

"Marlboros," the jerk demanded, while the other boy nodded in agreement, a real-life Bobblehead.

"Look, I've got—" I shut my trap. Why should I explain anything to these brats? "You're underage." I tapped on the faded "No Sale to Minors" sign, and both boys shuffled their feet. "Pick out something else or leave. I'll be right back."

"We want cigarettes." Jerkboy crossed his arms defiantly and Bobblehead mimicked his every move.

I had a crisis to deal with and it didn't include these jerk-offs. I hurried past them. "See that?" I waved at a camera mounted on the wall. "Hi, Casper." I plastered an eat-crap smile on my face. "Casper is watching us right now."

I had done this before, whenever leaving the register—which should never happen, but Dink had a habit of taking megabreaks. If the camera had actually worked, every move the boys made would have been taped, but it had been busted since I started working at Uptown Pharmacy right after I graduated in June. On my first day, Dink announced that Casper was the security guy and encouraged me to give him a big wave. So I grinned and flapped away at the camera.

"Practically invisible, Twigs, but nice. Casper's a friendly ghost, right?" Dink had laughed so hard at his own dumb joke that the ends of his greasy moustache wiggled.

I approached Aisle 7 and peeked around the corner, in case lethal hair products began flying again. The woman had opened a bottle of hair dye and sat holding it over her head.

"No!" It just popped out. I even surprised myself, but I wanted to stop her and save myself a big mess to clean. She looked up at me, red-eyed, with the saddest face I'd ever seen besides my own in the mirror.

"Get away, little girl." The woman's words were garbled, like she was chewing on marbles.

I felt sorry for her, but "girl" irked me. "I'm eighteen," I said, needing to keep things straight with this stranger. Okay, maybe I'd just turned eighteen, and at four-foot-nine, I'm not tall, but I'm a grownup now. Mom had written that on the 18th birthday card she'd given me last month. *You're a grownup now, Twigs.* If something is written down, it's true, right?

The woman screamed, "I said, get away!" Teardrops dripped into her cleavage and she pointed the dye at me as if holding a gun.

"Uh, ma'am . . . just put that down, okay?" I inched closer, holding my arms and hands out in front of me and wishing I had something—even a broom—for protection. I could yell for old Mr. Franks, the pharmacist, but he would never hear me. He had a hard enough time hearing people shout for their prescriptions.

"Stay back or I'll . . ." The hair-dye woman paused, as if making a huge decision that would change both our lives forever. "I'll dye you, little girl. I mean it. I'll dye you with this—"she glanced at the bottle—"Clairol Born Blonde! You wanna look like me?"

My fingers twitched at my side, like Gary Cooper in *High Noon*. I'd only seen that film eighty or so times with Dad. I hadn't been able to watch it since he'd left, but I still remembered every scene.

"You look just fine," I lied.

"You lie." Her voice cracked and she wailed, "He left me for a blonde!"

I shouted over her, "You're blonde, too!"

Okay, her hair looked more like a clown's wig—bright grade-school yellow—but it would be considered blonde. Her crying abruptly stopped and an uneasy silence fell over Aisle 7. I felt more nervous now than when she'd been bawling like a baby.

"What's wrong with her?" Another voice snapped the quiet in half and I spun around to see the cigarette boys standing a few feet behind me.

"I'm no blonde!" the woman screeched. She thrust the plastic bottle of dye straight out and squeezed the middle. A shot of Born Blonde sailed through the air right at me.

"Whoa!" Bobblehead jumped back and fell into his tall Jerkboy friend.

"Get off me, ass-wipe!" Jerkboy pushed Bobblehead and he crashed into me, sending me face first into the spray of Born Blonde.

Gloppy beige liquid splattered across my face and neck. Some even landed in my gaping mouth. A sour taste combined with a tart pickle smell made me gag and spit. What didn't reach my face covered the front of my white Uptown Pharmacy smock.

"Aaackk!" I sputtered.

Dad, or my brother, Matt, would've definitely handled this better than me. The Henry men always kept their cool, like real cowboys.

The cigarette boys scrambled backward. "What a whack-job!" yelled Jerkboy, and Bobblehead nodded. They hauled ass when the woman screamed and hurled another open bottle of dye. This time, it caught me. Not the bottle, but a spewing wave of dye. Bright orange liquid hit my left shoulder and splashed up, soaking part of my hair.

"Stop!" I'd had enough.

I rushed the woman, kicking bottles of hair dye out of the way, and quickly grabbed her hand before she could throw again. Though short, I'm strong for my size. I wrestled the woman's wrist down hard onto the ground and she released the bottle, which twirled across the linoleum floor like a hockey puck.

"Let go of me!" she cried.

She sobbed, dripping saliva into her cleavage, her neck wobbling as much as her heaving breasts. I weighed probably a quarter of this woman, but sheer willpower helped me keep her slammed to the ground.

"Come on, let's calm down and talk." I kept a lock on her throwing arm. "What's your name?"

The woman stared at me, breathing raggedly. I felt a little triumph when, after a moment, she answered, "Helen. Helen Raymond."

"Okay, Mrs. Raymond. I'll let go if you promise to stop throwing hair dye. It's not nice." Helen Raymond bent her head and shook with more sobbing. I felt the hand under mine go limp and it frightened me. "Mrs. Raymond?"

"I'm never going to be Mrs. Raymond again!"

Just then, the store speaker clicked on, whining with irritating feedback. Mrs. Raymond and I both flinched. Mr. Franks always turned the volume full up—blasting everyone in the store. He thought no one could hear him unless he shouted.

"Dink and Twigs! I'm going to lunch now!"

Twelve on the dot. Mr. Franks had taken his lunch at the same exact time every day for the last forty-three years. When I'd been hired, Dink had told me that nothing could change that. If a person needed medicine to keep from dying and ran in at noon for a prescription, they'd be out of luck.

"Dink and Twigs?" Helen Raymond muttered.

Where had Dink gone? Must be flirting up the new cashier at the bank and forgetting about the time, as usual. Dink's baldness and personality equaled big-time dork in my book, but being part owner of Uptown Pharmacy and one of the only eligible bachelors in Titusburg somehow made him attractive to the single women in this pathetic town.

"Twigs is me," I told Mrs. Raymond. "Or it was. Now I'm Madeline."

"Oh." Mrs. Raymond had that confused look most people got when they heard my name.

The theme from *Rocky* blared from the huge pink purse next to her. She took out an expensive pink bedazzled phone and tapped it on with fingernails that were the same vivid color. She let out a fresh wail at the name that appeared, and then, just as suddenly, pressed her lips to the end of the phone.

"Get your ass out of our house, Stu! I mean it!"

This beat anything on reality TV, or the time when Mom calmly toppled Dad's pyramid of beer cans right before he left home. I didn't want to be too obvious as I listened, so I began picking up some of the boxes. Mrs. Raymond stood and paced while she talked, leaving hair-dye footprints wherever she walked. Somehow, though, she seemed more together now than before. I quickly began shoving boxes back on the shelves, just to get them off the floor. If Dink saw this mess, he'd have a coronary.

"Walk Sly before you leave." Mrs. Raymond's voice was flat. "No, Stu," she continued. "If you take him with you, I swear I'll kill you."

Mrs. Raymond leaned against the shampoo-bottle shelf, ignoring them as they teetered and crashed to the floor at her feet.

"Get your whore another dog!" Her voice raised an octave. She flung her phone, Frisbee style, and it clattered down the aisle. It landed at Dink's feet.

He rubbed his shiny head. "Twigs?" Dink's eyes surveyed the mess—wet dye, boxes, and bottles everywhere. "What's going on?"

"Dink, I—."

He let loose on me before I could finish.

"Two kids were hauling out of here holding something under their shirts. Don't tell me you left the register unattended!" Dink had that I'm-Your-Boss-and-You'd-Better-Listen tone that he used when he wasn't making stupid jokes.

"Did you stop 'em?" Mrs. Raymond's shrill interruption caught Dink off-guard.

"Ma'am, this is not your business. I'm speaking to my employee." Dink's eyes focused on Mrs. Raymond's ample cleavage, and he crossed the line with his blatant stare. She grabbed the large bottle of Pantene shampoo I'd been holding and heaved it at Dink, knocking him to the ground.

"Keep your eyes to yourself!" Mrs. Raymond stepped over Dink as she marched toward the exit.

Seeing Helen Raymond flatten Dink like that made me feel a lot better than I usually did at work. I stood stock-still, savoring the moment, and then rushed to Dink, where he lay stunned. He looked up at me and rubbed his cheek where the Pantene had made contact.

"Make her pay."

"Pay?" I asked.

"This." Dink sat up and pointed at the mess filling Aisle 7.

The buzzer sounded. I jumped, jolted back to reality, and Dink waved a dismissive hand at me to go help whoever had buzzed.

Helen Raymond stood at the register, holding a pack of breath mints. "I'll take these," she said, acting as if she'd just walked in and had never had a hair-dye meltdown. It was the complete opposite of anything I'd ever seen at home. "Can't let the heart run your life." Dad had said that more than once when one of us got upset over something, as if trying to convince himself, too. I'd thought about that a lot since he'd left. Most of those old movies we'd watched together were all heart, full of "Save me, help me, love me" angst.

Feeling uneasy, my fingers trembled as I rang up the Certs for Mrs. Raymond. "That's ninety-five cents." I tried to mirror her sudden calmness.

"Fine." Mrs. Raymond pulled out a Visa. "Charge a thousand."

"A thousand dollars?" I wondered if I'd heard right.

"That's what I said." Mrs. Raymond slid the Visa across the counter.

I hesitated, afraid of taking the card. Could I get fired for this? Helen Raymond reached out and I flinched, half expecting something to fly at me. She grabbed my wrist and forced the Visa into my hand.

"Just swipe it . . . " Her eyes flicked side to side until she remembered. "Please, Twigs—now—Madeline."

The way she said my name felt like a splash of ice water in my face. Brisk and fresh. So different than the way most people usually spoke to me. I smiled at Mrs. Raymond, probably the most real smile

I'd given in a long time, and actually felt my heart bounce a couple of times as I pressed in a one and three zeroes on the machine.

I swiped the credit card and waited for it to process. The raised name printed on the Visa was Stuart Raymond. I passed the receipt to Mrs. Raymond. She smiled a crooked smile as she signed off on the thousand-dollar payment.

"Can I get coffee somewhere around here?" she asked.

I pointed across the street. "They have free coffee at the bank." You know this kind of stuff when you're always broke.

Mrs. Raymond shoved the Certs and receipt into her pink bag and pulled out a tissue. She reached out again and gave my name tag a good wipe, removing most of the dye. "Thanks for all of your help."

"Help?" I watched Helen Raymond strut like a fashion model toward the exit. I had a weird urge to follow her, and strut, too, but my feet held fast to that worn spot behind the register where I stood each day.

Mrs. Raymond turned and gave Dink a wave, as he rounded the corner, dirty mop in hand.

"Hey, wait! Lady!" Dink yelled, about to chase after her.

"Dink, it's okay. She paid."

I tossed him the copy of the receipt and Mrs. Raymond walked out, bright sunshine glinting off her yellow hair. In spite of her hair and husband problems, I wished I could be Helen Raymond, or let it all out like her—especially at home. Especially with Mom.

Chapter 2

Dink's sour mood ruined the rest of the day at work for me. He always rode my ass, but didn't seem to get it that the dye-tossing Mrs. Raymond had just forked over a thousand bucks to the store—well nearly, after subtracting the loss of a pile of cheap hair products.

"Dink, your uncle will see the profit, right?" I asked, as we topped off a trash can with empty Clairol bottles. "Maybe he'll give you a bonus or something."

Dink ran the store for his semiretired uncle, who spent more time on his fishing boat than anything but came in once a month to check the books.

"That's not the point, Twigs," Dink said, in his typical you-know-nothing way. "We can't have people coming in here and tearing down my shelves. Or stealing cigarettes."

Dink had glared at me on that one, since we discovered Jerkboy and Bobblehead had taken a carton of Marlboros. I decided not to remind Dink that if he had been in the store instead of flirting at the bank, then none of this might have happened, or at least, I would have been able to stay at the register. Still, Mrs. Raymond had been the most interesting thing that had happened since I started working at Uptown Pharmacy. She'd shown more emotion than my entire family put together. Mom had barely shed a tear the day Matt left for Iraq. "Be tough for your brother," she'd said to me and Marlee, even though I often thought I heard her cry late at night. No, I didn't want to be tough. I yearned to scream and cry like Helen Raymond and then plop a thousand bucks down just because. It might even get Mom's attention or bring Dad back.

After work I so wanted to get home to shower and change. Born Blonde dye had dried in globs on my white smock, making it look like I'd been playing in mud or something much worse. The smock I could wash, but my hair? Mrs. Raymond's aim had been good enough to splash dye all over most of the hair that hung loose over my shoulders. I hadn't cut it for a few years and had made a little pact with myself that I wouldn't even trim it until Dad returned. But if the dye had created orange stripes, making me look like a demented tiger, I might have to rethink my no-cut oath.

I pulled my lime green Geo into the driveway at the house, turned off the ignition, and pulled out the key, listening as the engine did its *putter-putt* drumbeat shutdown for a solid minute. I waved at Mr. Platton sitting in his usual spot on his porch next door. Getting out of my car, I couldn't help but notice the difference between our yard and his. Yard work wasn't at the top of anyone's list in the Henry family since Dad left. Mom spent most of her free time searching for the next man in her life. With Matt in Iraq and Marlee working full-time at being the most popular fourteen-year-old in town, mowing our lawn was up to me.

I had mowed it a few times, but I hated when Mr. Platton or some other in-your-face neighbor remarked that maybe I was too little to mow. Besides, brown grass and weeds didn't matter much, especially when Brady had just left town. He'd only been gone one day, but when you're used to seeing someone nearly every free moment since you met in eleventh grade, that day seems endless.

Mr. Platton seemed to read my mind as I walked toward the front door. "Hey there, Twigs. How's life with the boyfriend away?"

He lowered the afternoon *Titusburg Standard* he'd been reading and removed his reading glasses. I really didn't want to talk, even to explain that I wanted him to call me Madeline, so I ignored his question. I knew he missed Mrs. Platton since she'd gone on one of her antiquing trips, because he'd mentioned it about a thousand times.

"Gotta get inside, Mr. Platton. I'm expecting a call."

Mr. Platton knew a lot, but I wondered if he knew that I was hoping Brady had left me a sexy-want-you message. I'd forgotten to take my cell phone to work that morning and hoped it was loaded with Brady calls.

"Sure, sure. I know how it is." Mr. Platton raised his eyebrows a little. I nearly gagged thinking about him talking to Mrs. Platton the way Brady did to me.

"Oh, Twigs. A black car stopped at your house earlier—well, it slowed down in front of it. Might be important."

What the hell? I thought. Another UFO tale, maybe? Mr. Platton had nearly caused a neighborhood riot a few years ago when he said a giant metallic disc had landed in the empty lot across the street. There was a big hole, but there had been some rain. Half the neighbors believed the UFO story and half didn't. My dad always believed Mr. Platton, especially after a few beers.

"Okay. Black car. Thanks, Mr. Platton." I hustled into the house before he dragged me into a conversation about spies and espionage. Or before he asked again if I had heard from Matthew or Dad. Matthew, yes. Army life is tough. Iraq sucks, but not as much as Titusburg. Just his typical e-mails. News from Dad? Nope. Not a peep. Silent as when he and Mom used to have their I'm-not-talking-to-you marathons.

I dropped my keys in the coffee tin next to the door. Quiet house. Always refreshingly quiet if Marlee and her friends weren't around. Cheerleaders scream about everything. New jeans—eeek! French manicure—aaah! An e-mail or a call from a cute boy, or even a dorky one, always brought an eruption of screams—the piercing, painful kind, highlighted by giggles. "Oooohh, hee, hee, hee. Aaaaah, hee, hee, hee . . ." Marlee can outscream all her friends; she'd been the only freshman to get on the senior cheerleading squad because of it.

And she's smart, too. When your younger sister helps you with senior math, it makes her that much easier to hate.

My cell phone sat next to the coffeepot in the kitchen where I'd left it, fully charged. I had five messages waiting. Bless you, Brady.

"Hey Twigs, miss you."

That made me smile. I sure did love the way Brady half-whispered my name. He'd forgotten that I'd asked him to call me Madeline now, but I was so happy to hear from him, I could let it slide.

Next message: "Hey, they've got grits in the student caf. Made me think of you." I laughed. Brady teased me for my love of grits. Buttered, with pepper. He had moved from Wisconsin and couldn't believe some of the "weird crap" we ate in Titusburg.

Next message: "Lee's cool, Twigs. You should hear his song list." That was Brady's roommate. They'd just met yesterday, and so it seems they'd hit it off.

Message number four: "Did you buy your books? I just bought mine—they're heavy. You're going to need help, so ask some jock guy to carry them to your car. See how much I care? How was work and the Dinkster today?"

I'd have a story to tell Brady on this one.

No, I hadn't bought the books. I planned on doing that Monday after I got my class list, and hoped I could buy some cheaper, used ones, since money was tight. When wasn't it tight? I pretended to care, since Brady and everyone else I knew had left for college somewhere far away from this dump town. I'd be attending the grand institution of higher learning at Hinkney Community College, one town and about six traffic lights away. The sharp memory of college rejections flooded back again. Senior year had made me itchy for a lot of reasons and studying for college exams had been about as important to me as mowing. It wasn't that I didn't care in high school, but try as I might, I couldn't concentrate, especially on math. Dad had been my math-help-go-to parent. He even used to make a game of calculating shootout survival statistics when we watched old westerns together. My math survival suffered without Dad's help. I tried. Brady helped me study and I had hoped to get into the same school with him, but I needed a scholarship. They don't shell out money if you skip math questions on college exams. They don't shell out acceptance letters either.

Brady's last message made me forget all about school, about everything for a minute.

"About to go to this freshman orientation barbecue thing, Twigs. I'm sitting here thinking about that last swim in the lake." Brady paused. His steady breath flowed through the phone to my ear. I could almost smell the sweet mint from the ice cream we'd eaten before heading out to Eagle Lake. He had tasted perfect. Brady's message continued, "Very nice—so very nice." Another breathy pause, then, "Call me."

I felt a pang, a yanking need in my gut, all over, to lock my lips onto his. Did Brady know how much I needed him? It was more than that first love thing, though Mom harped on that all the time. Whatever. Didn't matter. Brady was the only one who got me besides Dad. I ignored the voice in my head reminding that Brady was gone now, too.

I pressed number one on my phone, and waited for the connection to click to Brady's cell. He had called me five times from two hundred miles away. What a boyfriend! I realized my call hadn't gone through and looked at the message on my phone. Out of range. Shit discount service. I had switched to a new plan, hoping to save money since Mom made the phone bill my responsibility when I turned eighteen. All of my friends were away at college, and I figured we'd e-mail each other. But Brady, I had to call. I needed to hear his voice. We didn't even have a landline in the house anymore, which I hated. If Dad wanted to call, he couldn't.

"He'll just have to show his face," Mom had said. Then she'd whispered to herself, but I heard her words loud and clear, "But I don't expect that anytime soon."

I decided to e-mail Brady and hoped he'd check his computer later. Our out-of-date computer lives in the dining room on an old desk from the deaf school where Mom works. On the top left corner of the desk, someone had carved "Signers Give Great Handjobs." I'd been in third grade when Mom brought the desk home. Before I'd even thought about asking what the carving meant, she had said, "Don't ask because I'm not telling you." Dad had laughed and laughed when she'd said that. It was one of the few times I remember them laughing together, sharing a secret joke.

The computer sits crammed in the corner, next to a sewing machine covered with floral fabric for curtains Mom started making but never got around to finishing. There's barely room to walk around the piles of magazines stacked against the walls—all of Dad's *Popular Mechanics*, which Matt claimed for his own—plus the table and four chairs.

I noticed a hot-pink Post-it note, which reminded me of Mrs. Raymond's killer nails, taped to the computer screen. It was from Marlee. "At Gretchen's for a sleepover." My sister never asked, she just announced, which Mom would never have let me do at her age. Since Matt left for Iraq, Mom had checked out on most of her parenting duties beyond paying rent. More so with me than with Marlee, as if she'd been zapped of any motherly Twigs feelings. I knew she worried about Matt, and I did, too. I figured it had to do with missing Dad more than she showed or maybe because I'd been so close to him. I'd been his movie buddy, even though he'd always invited the whole family to join us. Marlee and Matt didn't care a whit for cowboy movies, and Mom would flash one of her sexy smiles and say, "Dale, I'm not a westerns' gal, pardner. You knew that when we met." Dad would smile and say, "It's just us, Twigs." I liked it that way. No one disturbed us when we watched those movies and we both got caught up in the stories, even the ones we'd seen over and over, like *High Noon*. After THE END flickered across the screen, Dad would tuck his thumbs in his belt loops and say, "I'd love to live at that time, even for one day." It was easy to imagine him as a Wild West sheriff. I think Mom could see him that way, too. Sometimes she called him "Cowboy," which always made me smile.

Bottom line, with Dad and, now, Matt gone—Mom had gotten weird.

I dashed off a note to Brady: "Got your calls. Miss you SO much. Bizarre day at work—I'll tell you later. My phone service is crap, so you have to call me. Always, Twigs."

I hit the Send button and then wished I'd signed, "Love, Twigs." So I sent another one with just that. Then I worried that Brady might wonder why I hadn't put that in the first message. So, I wrote another message: "Sorry I forgot to write 'Love' in the first e-mail. It's been a strange day." I clicked a final Send and pushed the chair back from the computer.

I grabbed a yogurt from the fridge and poured a glass of orange juice. Looking out the window over the kitchen sink, I saw that Marlee's bird feeder had fallen from the pecan tree in our backyard. Two squirrels scurried over the millet. I could have shooed them away, but if the feeder was broken, I knew Mom wouldn't buy a new one. Might as well let the squirrels enjoy it. Matt or Dad could have fixed it. Fallen branches and rusted lawn furniture made the yard look like the lonely place it'd become. Maybe I'd get out and do some work, really weed the space, like Dad had always done on Saturdays.

Right now, though, I had to get out of this ugly smock and get my hair clean. I was about to turn on the shower, when I heard my phone ringing. I grabbed a towel and rushed down the hall to the kitchen where I'd left it on the counter.

"Brady," I answered, assuming he had gotten my collection of e-mails.

There wasn't a sound. Well no voice anyway, but I heard a dinging, like a bell. A small sound, like you hear when you walk into some quaint country store, a friendly way to let the owners know that you're there. Not like the obnoxious buzzer Dink used at the pharmacy.

"Brady?" Maybe he was at that barbecue and decided to call me. "Can you hear me?"

The bell jingled again. Then, ever so lightly, or maybe I imagined it, a cough, more like someone clearing their throat but barely loud enough to hear. I held my breath and pulled the towel tighter around my body. My heart tha-thumped and I stood up taller, tensing on my toes, anxious to confront the person I thought was there.

"Dad?" I asked. I hoped.

I took a big breath and tried again, going with my gut. "Thanks for the graduation card. They held the ceremony out on the football field. Everyone was melting. You know how steaming Titusburg gets in June." Why was I talking about the weather? I paused. "I miss you, Dad."

Another jingle interrupted the silence on the other end and the line went dead. Or he hung up on me. He? My hands began shaking as I held my phone closer, as if it might help me touch the person on the other end of the line. That card of a crisp white daisy from Dad was taped on the mirror in my room. "It's your time, Twigs. Love you." It had been signed in the tight scrawl that was uniquely his. I had spent that whole steaming ceremony scanning the bleachers and hoping he'd show up to see me get my diploma.

I let out a long breath but didn't let go of my phone.

Outside, squirrels and birds skittered around our overgrown yard, and I waited, hoping the phone would ring again. Had my father just called after more than two years of nothing but a daisy card?

Chapter 3

After chewing my lip raw and pacing the kitchen for nearly half an hour, I gave up hope—again. Thinking of Dad always pulled and pushed at my emotions. Just call me human taffy. I felt that ball in my chest, the tight, painful one, egging on my tears. I could almost hear Mom's voice, "Don't waste water on him. Bet he's not crying over us."

"No!" I shouted at my cell phone. At the kitchen. At Dad or the jerk-off who'd just called and made me think it was Dad. At the world. I almost smacked my phone against our old linoleum, wanting to watch it snap, crackle, and pop into a million pieces, but I stopped. If I broke it, then how could Brady call me? Or me him? Besides, I'd only had the phone a month and I didn't have enough cash for a new one.

So, I nudged—shoved—crammed—my anger and hope back inside, locked away in quarantine. I looked to see if Brady had tried to reach me while I'd been on the Freak-Out-Twigs call. The NO MESSAGES icon glared back at me—Brady hadn't called. I slapped the phone off and set it on top of the microwave.

A long shower of scalding hot water pricking my skin helped ease some of the anger I felt, but the disappointment remained. Crying never cured anything for me, so it seemed useless to waste the tears. Then I remembered Helen Raymond and her out-of-control sobs. There was something thrilling about her and how she'd felt everything as if her nerves were on fire—sad, mad, indignant, and, most of all, proud. How'd she do that? Let it all go and then strut out of the store like the world belonged to her?

The water began to run cold and gave me a chill. I'd pruned up my fingers and hadn't even washed my hair yet. Or maybe I had. I always lost track of time in the water, whether in the shower or at the lake, especially with Brady. He had a knack of keeping me warm, even in cool lake water. High hills surround Eagle Lake, keeping it virtually wind free. Dad loved going there, too. Our whole family did—we'd have stone-skipping contests. Dad and Marlee against me and Matt. Dad always brought beer to celebrate his wins or losses, while Mom lounged in a lawn chair reading magazines, circling recipes she planned to try. Those days were the happiest memories of my folks being together, as if the lake air and sunshine somehow erased all the silent tension that filled our home.

I grabbed the shampoo and speed-washed my hair in cold water, watching beige and orange streams of color slide down my arms and into the drain. The water was frigid now, but I shampooed twice more, squeezing my hair free of every ounce of fake color possible. I'd never dyed my hair, though I'd considered it when Mom once said, "Too bad Marlee's got all those golden highlights and your hair matches your name." She was right, but I didn't need to hear it.

I threw on Dad's old robe, which he rarely ever wore, but it still reminded me of him. I'd made the navy blue terry-cloth robe my own, shortening the sleeves and raising the hem, so it didn't drag on the floor. Marlee says it fits my "homeless chic" look, but her preference for flowers and pink will never be me.

My comb was missing from my dresser and I banged into my sister's girly, stuffed poodle–filled room to steal it back. We had a regular set of arguments; whose turn it was to take out the trash, mow the yard, and clean the toilets were a few on the long list. The question of comb ownership ranked near the top. We had other combs in the house, but we both preferred this wide-toothed one. The last time I'd grabbed it from Marlee, she'd yelled, "Bitch!"

"Ah, you're not perfect!"

"Don't tell Mom I cursed!" she had screamed and fled to her room.

Now, comb in hand, I grabbed my phone from the kitchen, checking for calls again. Nope, still no Brady. E-mail was another bust, but I sat at the computer anyway, gazing at the screen, and tugged at the tangles in my hair. Maybe concentrating on the e-mails would entice Brady to send me some sort of message.

Thinking about him, his chest, and that warm skin under my fingers made me breathe a little faster as my thoughts raced over Brady's body. Shifting my butt in the chair nearly tipped it over, but I managed to grab the edge of the desk and catch myself before I crashed. Way to kill the mood. Nothing like a wobbly dining-room chair to stop a sex memory—not that I have that many—and the best are all with Brady. Call me a girlfriend computer. I have every encounter with him etched, stored, and saved in my head and every other part of my body.

I fingered the mouse and scrolled through old e-mail. Most were for Marlee about cheerleading practice, student-council meetings, and what her friends were wearing for the first day of school. Mom had a few from guys I'd never heard of, usually with a "Let's meet for drinks" kind of message, which disgusted me. She had three e-mails full of "You know you're a redneck when. . ." jokes from someone named Lou. Way to romance my mom there, Lou!

Sure, single parents can date, but Mom had managed to forget that she still had a husband somewhere. I mumbled aloud one of my daily thoughts, "Come home, Dad," and the other thought echoed that one, "Stay safe, Matt."

Then there were the postcard-style e-mails from Matt. "Hey. Iraqified here. Freaking." or "Hey there. Ate a camel spider today. Won $50 in a bet. I'm so damn cool." I laughed at that one again. Mom and Marlee had been horrified, but it made me feel good knowing Matt was being Matt. Stupid at times, but always lovable, even in a place no American soldier wanted to be.

I stopped combing my hair and surfing e-mails—something wasn't right. Matt usually wrote today—Friday. It's when he had downtime from oiling the tanks or cleaning the Hummers, whatever it is that U.S. Army mechanics do. Where was his message? I quickly scrolled back and realized he hadn't written last week either. I'd been too busy spending every moment with Brady before he left to notice. Maybe Matt had written, but Mom or Marlee accidentally trashed the e-mail. I checked the trash, the spam, and the junk files and then rechecked them. Nothing. No new e-mail from the military address since the Friday before last.

My breath came fast again, harder too, but not because of Brady memories. All those gruesome television news images filled my head now. I never watched the news anymore. It stayed off in our house since Matt left for Iraq. Matt? Where the hell was he? I jerked up from the chair and banged into the dining-room table right behind me.

"Shit!"

I rubbed my side, cursing my lack of height and how I'd bumped the table in that same exact spot too many times to count. Maybe Mom had printed out Matt's latest message, which she sometimes did, if he wrote something mushy. He had the knack of making Mom cry with his letters, though it was always late at night when she didn't think I'd hear her. Entering her room, I walked past her unmade bed, covered with a pile of clean laundry in need of folding. The bedside-table drawer gaped open and I pulled it out to find a random supply of condoms—way to be safe, Mom—a bottle of Nyquil, and an old issue of *Redbook*. That was it. No tear-stained letter from Matt.

Next, I scanned the top of Mom's chest of drawers, which held a vanity tray of perfumes—she always had to buy the latest celebrity scent. Those overpriced, fancy bottles sold her every time. Tucked next to a purple diamond-shaped bottle was a tiny card, like you get with flowers. Someone had written on the card in A+ worthy print:

CAN'T HIDE HOW I FEEL.

YOU MAKE MY HANDS WARM. XOXO, LOU.

"Make my hands warm?" Gag. I didn't want to picture what that meant. And who the heck was Lou? The jokester e-mailer? I flipped the card over. A heart was drawn on the other side with "Be Mine" in the middle. Why would Mom keep a cheesy Valentine from one of her bed buddies?

I tugged out the top drawer, filled with more thongs than a Victoria's Secret store. A minuscule black-lace thong with the price tag still attached caught my eye. Sixteen bucks for a few inches of silk? Without any tinge of guilt, I shoved it in the pocket of my robe. I continued digging through Mom's underwear and discovered a piece of paper—tightly folded and creased like some sort of origami design. A letter, but not from Matt.

Eve,
I miss you. I know you're angry, but I'll always love you.
I had to go and you know why.

I stumbled backward and slumped down on the edge of Mom's bed, still holding the paper. Parkinson's hands—that's what I got just then—those uncontrollable shakes like Grandma had before she died. No date. No signature, either, but I knew the writing. Dad. Dad. Dad. His face engulfed my mind. He had written Mom since he left! He had contacted her and she'd never said boo about it. I looked at the words again, running my fingers over the blue ink. No mention of us—the kids. But Dad was reaching out, professing his love to Mom. Maybe he had written to us, too. I pulled open more drawers, searching, but not finding any other papers in the jumble of Mom's clothes. An ugly thought occurred to me. Maybe Dad had written to us, but Mom decided not to say anything.

A few tears fell on the paper before I could stop myself. "No!" It pissed me off to cry. I squeezed back the tears and wiped my cheeks. If Mom intentionally hid news about Dad or if he didn't care enough to write me, then screw them. Screw them both.

Bright twin beams from headlights moved along the wall, and I heard a car pulling into the driveway. Mom was home. Great. I fumbled—trying to fold the paper exactly as I'd found it and accidentally tore one edge. I heard the front door open as I shoved the letter from dear old Dad, tear-side-down, back where I'd found it. Maybe I'd bring up the subject of Dad over dinner. "Good pasta. So, have you heard from Dad lately?"

I swallowed my anger as I moved out of Mom's room. Matt's face smiled at me from his framed senior high school photo hanging in the hall. Ironic that Dad's been in contact and now Matt hasn't e-mailed. Too much real-life crap all at once. Oh, to be four again with no cares except whether I'd get ice cream for dessert.

I hurried down the hall toward the kitchen and stopped short when I heard Mom talking to someone.

"Excuse the mess," she said. "It was one of those rush-around mornings."

She wasn't kidding. Marlee had cheerleading practice at 6:00 A.M., which made no sense, but they had to practice when the football team did. She banged around so much that she woke me and I didn't have to go to work until 9:00. Mom had gotten up early to make Marlee pancakes and then must have fallen back asleep before leaving for her job. Breakfast dishes filled the sink and a plate with a half-eaten pancake floating in old syrup still sat on the counter next to the griddle.

"Come in, come in," Mom said. I heard some shuffling. "Put the bags on the table."

This came from the dining room and whoever was there with Mom—probably a guy—hadn't said a word. I pulled the belt on my robe tighter and tiptoed away from the kitchen. The last thing I wanted was for Mom's latest conquest to see me in a ratty old robe with limp, wet hair. Best to just hole up in my room and ignore them, which I'd done plenty of times when Mom brought home her "house guests."

"Twigs!" Mom called.

I froze but said nothing.

"Twigs, we bought Chinese! Spareribs, too." Mom waited for my answer, like I might jump for joy at the notion of greasy spareribs. "She's here, just being rude," I heard her report to the silent stranger.

Yep, I was rude. Why the hell not? These men weren't anything to me—nothing to Mom either. Why should I be nice? Usually I put on a stone-face act and hid in my room; that made life easier on everyone. Marlee could chat with a rock, which describes the personality of most of these guys, but that's not my way.

I almost made it into my room when Mom appeared, moving down the hall with that fake smile she plasters on for these "guests."

"Twigs? Didn't you hear me call you?"

"Yeah." I plunged ahead without a breath. "Mom, have you heard from Matt?"

Her smile faded and she touched her fingers to the side of her head, as if I'd given her a headache.

"I've been working, Twigs." She glanced at the wall and straightened a photo of Marlee's eighth-grade cheerleading team.

"Mom, he didn't e-mail today. And not last Friday either."

"Twigs, my friend is here and he was gracious enough to buy Chinese for us. We'll talk about this later."

"Later? We'll talk about Matt maybe being dead in Iraq later?"

"Stop it." She sucked in a big breath through her nose and released it, all yoga-calm, unlike me. "They might be on a communications blackout, or there's a problem with the army's computers." She sighed, "They've probably got Matt working a different shift and he hasn't had a chance to write."

"You don't care, do you?" I knew it was the wrong thing to say the moment it popped out.

Mom clenched her eyes shut, and her shoulders rose and fell as she took another big breath. She opened her eyes, staring me down. "I won't even answer that."

A shadow down the hall got my attention and a tall man appeared behind my mother. He waved at me. My efforts to hide had failed. And I'd learned nothing about Matt's whereabouts except that Mom didn't want to think about it. Zero for two. Great.

I stared past Mom at the waving guy. He seemed vaguely familiar. He looked brown-bland, about fifty, a little beefy around the middle, and wore a white business shirt with a loose red tie hanging at his neck. Another clone of Mom's men. At least this one had hair.

He knocked on the wall, getting Mom's attention, and she turned to face him. I now understood why he'd been so quiet because Mom began signing to him. I couldn't follow her speeding hands—too fast for my skill—but whatever she said, made him laugh. His barking laugh and the way he tilted his head up made me think—human seal. Okay, not nice, but that's how this guy sounded.

"Lou, this is my daughter Twigs," Mom signed and spoke aloud this time.

"Madeline," I said, beginning to sign out my name, but Mom spoke and signed right over my hands like she hadn't heard me.

"Twigs, this is Lou. He ran a leadership conference for the staff today. He can read lips." Mom grabbed the arm of my robe, giving me a nudge. My chance to escape had vanished.

I waved a little hello. "Hi, Lou." The name zinged in my head. Was this the "make my hands warm" guy? Deaf Lou reached out to pump my hand, nearly squeezing it in two. His hands were warm, hot even. Then he began signing faster than Mom or any of the people she worked with that I had ever seen. Fast-talkin' Deaf Lou.

"You can call me Madeline," I said, but Lou was signing to Mom and missed my lips.

"Oh, yes." Mom watched his hands. "I forgot about that." She turned to me. "Lou met you already, Twigs. He was at Matt's going-away party."

There had been a lot of people to see Matt off to Iraq. I remembered there had been a lot of deaf friends from Mom's work all signing with beers in hand, but I'd been too busy looking for Dad that day. I hoped he'd surprise us all. I didn't remember meeting Deaf Lou, who was now signing again.

"You are so right, Lou," Mom laughed, leading us into the dining room. "She is a tiny thing—our little Twigs."

I shook my head. "Mom, I told you to call me Madeline!" I signed the letters of my real name to Deaf Lou. He began signing something else, and I caught him signing the word for twigs. Mom laughed.

Ah, crap, I knew what was coming next—the story of my name.

"Let's get dinner on the table and I'll tell you all about it," Mom signed to Deaf Lou and then, without signing, spoke to me, "Get the plates, Twigs. First, some clothes on your back, please."

"Madeline," I said, giving her a look that I'm sure Deaf Lou noticed, but I didn't care.

"You're Twigs," Mom said, "regardless of your real name."

I pretended not to hear.

Walking away, I heard her say, "I don't know. Maybe she tried dying it and messed up."

I rushed into my room and looked in the mirror. A calico cat stared back at me—well, calico hair did anyway. The left side of my hair, mostly dried, had splotches of blonde and orange mixed with my drab brown. Nothing I could do now. Gee, thanks for the dye job, Helen Raymond.

I threw on some leggings and an oversize Titusburg High T-shirt that still smelled like Brady. Then I grabbed plates in the kitchen and carried them to the dining room. Deaf Lou and Mom were sitting so close I wondered how they kept from going cross-eyed reading lips that way.

I banged the plates on the table to get Mom's attention. "Sorry for taking so long." I could see Deaf Lou lip-reading. Mom had brought home deaf men before, but it was always weird watching a stranger, who I knew wanted to hump her later, be so focused on my lips.

We spooned Chinese food onto our plates and ate in silence. I liked that part about eating with a deaf person—very little talking while using utensils. Deaf Lou signed a bit with one hand, but mostly we were quiet. Besides three Almond Joy bars at work, I hadn't eaten since the coffee milkshake I'd made myself for breakfast, so each bite of the spareribs and spicy Kung Pao made me forget about Matt and Dad for a few minutes.

Then Mom set down her fork and began telling how I got my name. "Twigs was premature and absolutely the ugliest, tiniest, most alien-looking baby you could imagine."

I interrupted, clanging my fork on my plate, "Mom, if you have to tell this, just sign it, okay?"

Mom reached over and stroked my still-damp hair. She smiled in a way that made me feel five again and her touch felt nice, so good that I almost forgot Deaf Lou was there.

"How was work?" she asked, still smoothing down my hair.

"Weird." Usually I answered "fine" to that mundane question, but today had been different. I could have said more but chose to keep the Helen Raymond story to myself. The same way that Mom kept things to herself.

Mom drew her hand away and signed something to Deaf Lou, and he let out another seal-bark laugh. I ignored them and began clearing the table as Mom continued signing. I knew the story by heart anyway. I'd been so small at birth that the doctors had said my arms and legs were like little twigs. Dad and Mom brought Matt to the viewing room where they showed the preemies through the window. The nurses told him that I was just a baby twig now but would grow slowly and tall like a tree does. Matt, loveable even at four with a little lisp, had said, "Baby Twigs, gwo up, 'kay?" It stuck—with Mom, Dad, and the hospital staff—everyone. My real name, Madeline Annette Henry, was forgotten except on official paperwork. Filling out college forms had gotten me thinking it was time for a new me. The real me. Madeline made me feel bigger somehow. I had grown but still remained smaller than every other seventeen- or eighteen-year-old I knew and even some grade-school kids.

I stood in the kitchen loading the dishwasher and felt almost relieved to hear Mom giggling. "That tickles," she said. At least, she and Deaf Lou had moved on from talking about me.

"Twigs," Mom called, nice as pie. "Please bring me that bottle of red wine on the counter. And two glasses?"

Great. Now I had to be a bartender and fuel her romantic romp with cheap cabernet. It looked cheap anyway, this squat corked bottle with a bright purple label covered with a drawing of grapes. But it was wine, and that met Mom's rules. She'd accept a man who drank wine, even margaritas or daiquiris, but if he asked for beer, which reminded her of Dad, then the poor sucker lost his chance with my mom. I almost said, "Get your own wine," but it would cause a scene, and I didn't want that now. I wanted to check the computer again to see if Matt had e-mailed, so the sooner I got wine for Mom and about-to-get-lucky Deaf Lou, the sooner I could do that.

They had already settled in the front room on the couch. Deaf Lou had his tie off, the neck of his shirt open, and he sat with his feet in Mom's lap while she gave him a foot massage. I'd seen this signature move before. Mom would pause for a drink of wine and then her strong hands would bring *oohs* and *aahs* of pleasure as she progressed up the calves and legs of her victims . . . er, men. Then the whole party would move into what used to be Mom and Dad's bedroom. There, the *oohs* and *aahs* grew louder. Way to catch 'em, Mom.

Marlee somehow missed seeing most of these encounters and defended Mom when I'd once said she acted like a whore since Dad left. "Twigs, you have no heart. She's lonely." I wondered if Dad was that lonely, too.

Cheap wine. Corkscrew. Two glasses. Check. I set everything on the coffee table and murmured a quick good night. "Time for me to get my stuff together. College starts on Monday, remember?"

Mom murmured, "Night, Twigs," and just kept on massaging Deaf Lou's feet. He signed good night and waved one of those farewell-but-I'm-glad-you're-going waves. I quickly checked the computer again. Nothing. Not even the usual spam offering megavitamins unapproved by the FDA or Marlee's eBay alerts for stuffed-poodle auctions. I wondered if our e-mail was busted or something, but there was no bothering Mom to ask now.

I grabbed my cell phone from the kitchen and ignored the kissing sounds emanating from the living room. Deaf Lou may not talk, but he sure can smack those lips. Gag. I hustled down the hall and into my room, closing out the world behind me. Stacks of cheap school notebooks were piled on the floor near my sliding closet door where a photo of Brady's face hung at my eye level. I gave it a big, smacking kiss of my own. "Call me, Brade," I whispered to his image. "God, I miss you." Then I added, "And I miss Matt. You too, Dad—ass that you are for leaving us."

Plopping on my bed, I tucked my phone on the pillow next to my head. I needed to talk to Brady, no matter how late he called. I stared at the *High Noon* poster tacked on the back of my bedroom door—Gary Cooper has his arms wrapped around Grace Kelly and gazes at her like the goddess she is, or was. As usual, the love sparking between them in this image made me sigh, and, in no time, I fell asleep.

The doorbell rang and I sprang up, leaping off my bed with a stale taste of spareribs still in my mouth, making me wish I'd brushed my teeth. My alarm clock read 10:34, too late for anybody but Brady. Maybe he'd driven home from college to spend the weekend with me. Another Eagle Lake night would be pure heaven. I peeked through my curtains and saw a big car parked in the driveway—one of those shiny, black, official-for-something-or-someone kind of cars. I pressed my head against the glass, angling my eyes to see who stood on our doorstep. I could only catch a glimpse of a man there, but enough to see he wore a military uniform.

"Matt," I whispered. Terror twisted and flip-flopped my insides. "It's Matt."

Chapter 4

The doorbell rang again and I jumped away from the window, afraid the army guy or guys out there might have seen me. I didn't want to answer that door. Opening it would only bring bad news about Matt—horrible, life-changing news. My body began shaking, fear taking over. "Mom," I muttered. And then again louder, "Mom!" She might annoy me, but I wanted her next to me to face what came next.

Another ring along with loud knocking jolted me into action. I peeked out of my room and down the hall toward the living room. Mom's door was open and Deaf Lou stood there. He appeared surprised to see me. I had forgotten about him and almost yelled, "Hey, I live here. Not you!" But yelling at a deaf man was useless.

Deaf Lou wore an undershirt now with his business slacks, but they hung loose without a belt. Yep, he'd rushed to put them on. Anyone could read the guilty aura surrounding him—a sorry-I-just-slept-with-your-mom kind of thing. Points to Deaf Lou for showing some conscience, I guess. I'd seen enough men in this house to know the ones who didn't care if I knew what they did with my mother.

"Where's Mom?" I asked, but the dim hallway light must have kept Deaf Lou from reading my lips, because he shook his head.

I walked to Mom's bedroom door and Deaf Lou moved aside. Mom sat half-slouched on the side of the bed. A torn condom package lay near her feet on the floor. It seemed to scream, "Mom hooked up tonight!" That and the flimsy purple negligee she wore. This one must have been on a hanger in her closet, because I hadn't noticed it earlier in the thong drawer.

"Mom, someone's at the door." She reached out to me, but I was beyond her grasp.

"I can hear that, Twigs. Why don't you answer it?" It wasn't a command, more of a plea.

Her eyes had that glazed look that I'd seen often enough in Dad, but this time it wasn't wine or sex. No, she was afraid of answering that door, just like me. My back was to Deaf Lou, and I made sure he couldn't read my lips by cupping my mouth like a megaphone.

"I'm not answering it."

"What?" asked Mom.

One of the straps from her negligee fell, loose against her arm, and she let it slide. Deaf Lou cleared his throat, as if to let us all know that he could see her breast. Maybe Mom had been playing shy and he hadn't had the good luck to see them yet. I reached out and tugged the flimsy strap back up to Mom's collarbone and she put her hand on mine. It felt dry, papery even, but warm—and a sudden memory of holding her hand at a dentist appointment made me want to cry. She had protected me then, but what could we do now?

The doorbell rang again and Mom's eyes said it all. Terror. Anguish. Scared shitless over what would happen if we opened that door. I shook my head and drew my hand away from her, retreating like a whipped dog. Maybe I was eighteen, but I wanted to be the kid now—I needed to be. Mom would have to step up whether she wanted to or not.

I turned and made sure Deaf Lou had clear sight of my lips, "Lou, I've got to go. Can you get the door, please? Thanks."

I waved my hands, signing a huge thank-you, and brushed past before Deaf Lou could stop me. I felt a whoosh of air at my back as his questioning hands signed away madly, wondering, I'm sure, what the hell he'd gotten himself into with the Henry family.

I'm not a bad person and Deaf Lou seemed nice enough, but I knew what that doorbell meant. My brother had been blown to bits in some brown, unhappy, foreign place. The dusty scenes that Matt had described in his e-mails filled my head. I wondered if those army mechanic friends he always mentioned, José and Stevo, had died, too, in the same accident-bombing-assault-barrage-attack. Were their hometown doors being bombarded right now like ours?

I ran. Down the hall, past the empty wine bottle Mom and Deaf Lou had enjoyed, past the computer without a new Matt message, and most of all, away from the front door. Those army guys weren't leaving. I could hear them talking through our thin walls. A muffled sound followed by a familiar voice. The one and only Mr. Platton, our reliable neighborhood watchman.

"They're home but probably asleep by now," Mr. Platton yelled, loud enough to wake the street. "I saw Mrs. Henry bring home Chinese."

It didn't surprise me that Mr. Platton knew what we had for dinner. He could probably remember what every person on our street had for breakfast two weeks ago.

I didn't wait to hear more. I rushed through our kitchen into the garage, and grabbed my Rollerblades, where they'd been chucked under Dad's old workbench for as long as I could remember. An outdated hobby, maybe, but I always loved skating and Rollerblades made me feel tall—well, taller, anyway. Now it was all about speed. I wanted to move as fast as possible. I avoided leaving through the garage, because they—those bad-news guys—might see me. I hoisted my skates under one arm and tiptoed back through the kitchen to avoid Mom and Deaf Lou, and then through the sliding-glass door out to the backyard.

"Ow!" Bare feet on pecan shells hurts, something I hadn't thought of in my rush. Socks and shoes? In my bedroom. Cell phone? Probably still on my pillow. I considered dashing back inside on a sock–cell phone run, but when I slid the door open a bit, I heard Mom's voice, "No, this isn't Mr. Henry." I bet she loved explaining Deaf Lou to the army guys. I pictured Mom still wearing the purple flowing number or had she put on a robe? It didn't matter, really. What do you wear to hear about the death of your son?

I moved through the darkness of our yard toward the back fence, through the weeds, over pecans, and past the broken bird feeder, which made me think of Marlee. Maybe I'd be seen as a coward, leaving home so I didn't have to face certain bad news. No, I had a new story. I'd decided to become the dutiful daughter now, off to bring my little sister home in this time of family crisis. Although I could have just called Gretchen's house, except I didn't have my cell phone, and in matters as sensitive as these, shouldn't the horrible news be delivered face-to-face? Wasn't that the whole reason the army death-announcement squad had bombarded our house? They wanted a little face-to-face.

I threw my skates across the chain-link fence that bordered the home behind ours and then climbed over. Mr. Platton must be avoided. I knew he was sitting on his porch, watching every move of invasion on the Henry house. "Full report. At oh-nine-hundred," Mr. Platton could tell the neighbors. "Men entered, had their say, then left. News flash: Matt Henry has expired."

The thought of Mr. Platton telling the neighbors about Matt triggered the spout in my eyes and tears streamed down my face. I grabbed my skates and kept running through the back neighbor's yard, nearly falling over a frightened cat, and out to the street in front of their house. I sat on the curb and pulled the blades onto my sockless feet.

Yep, I cried, but not the gut-wrenching sobs that Mrs. Raymond had spewed out earlier. She'd known her husband had cheated, ruining their marriage. My quiet tears were those of anticipation, of the sadness to come. Then that cat I'd run past, a gray-striped tabby, moved into my peripheral vision and sat a few yards away.

"Merrow?" the cat spoke.

"I'm okay," I answered, because it had felt like a question. "Well, not really." What the hell was I doing? I clambered up to standing and found my balance, and the cat skittered away. There were spots of lights dotting the street from various garages and porches and a single streetlamp at the end of the road. I had to get to Marlee. She was at Gretchen's house, which was on a street somewhere on the far side of Titusburg High, about three miles away, so I began skating.

I'd only gone a few feet when someone shouted, "Twigs!" I gasped and nearly toppled over, but windmilled my arms to regain balance and kept moving.

It was an unknown voice calling from behind me—our backyard. The man's voice pushed me to rush forward to escape. It wasn't Mom or Mr. Platton calling, or even Deaf Lou. I'd been called, ordered it seemed, by some strange army guy to return.

"Twigs! Twigs Henry!" the deep voice seemed to echo around me.

Maybe Matt had to follow military orders in life and death, but not me.

And then there came a horrid screech from Mom, "Madeline!"

The shock of Mom's frightened voice screaming my real name sent me bolting. I reached the end of the street in no time, a regular Olympic speed skater, ignoring dogs barking and a couple making out in a car. Turning toward town, I quickly traveled three miles on the main road—moving forward, avoiding honking cars, cracked pavement, and potholes. The almost half-moon smiled at me, a gentle reminder of one of Matt's e-mails: "I won't say it's dangerous here in Iraq, but even the moon wears a bulletproof vest."

I licked salty tears as they continued to flow; a steady mental mantra of Matt-Matt-Matt matched my skating rhythm, as I pushed each foot forward. The school loomed ahead—the eighty-year-old main building jutting out toward the road, backed up by the "new" addition, built sometime when Dad and Mom had gone there, typical high-school sweethearts.

It felt weird, looking at the place where I'd just spent four years. Barely two months had passed, but graduation already seemed eons ago. I blinked back more tears remembering how Matt had actually called that day, surprising me, "Yo, Twigs. Titusburg High's most likely to be my sis and shortest grad." I wished I had a tape of that call since it might have been the last time we'd ever talk. Matt had even managed to make me forget about Dad not being there to see me get my diploma.

I zoomed off onto the side road, toward the football field, where I could cut through to Gretchen's street. Except for the few security lights mounted on the main building, it was scary dark back there and I had to slow down to maneuver over the old pitted asphalt. The football field and bleachers sat empty now, but they would be filled next week for the first game of the season, with Marlee cheering on the team.

I skated through the field gate and made my way onto the track that ran around it and cautiously skated forward. My eyes had adjusted to the darkness and I knew the track was fairly level so I kept moving. I focused on getting to the goal post at the far end of the field as I whisked past the metal bleachers on my right. Then I saw something move—two lumps or people, I guess, crouched on the far end of the bleachers. I wasn't afraid—after-hours bleacher humping was a well-known sport at Titusburg High. It annoyed me that I'd have to skate past a couple of twits trading body spit, but I had to get to Marlee.

A familiar voice whispered loud enough for me to hear, "Shhh. Someone's there."

"Huh?" asked someone else—a teen guy voice.

"Marlee!" I yelled and skated over to the fence that ran between the track and the bleachers. My sister sat about four rows up and even in the darkness, her white skin and white lace bra were shining like some sort of searchlight.

"What the—" It was the guy again.

"Twigs?" Marlee screeched. "What are you doing?"

My fourteen-year-old sister grabbed her shirt and held it across her breasts as she ran down the bleachers toward me.

"What am I doing? Why don't you answer that first?"

The unknown guy—this perpetrator intent on humping my fourteen-year-old sister—lumbered up next to her. I recognized him. Black skin and huge. Tower of Isaac. He was only a sophomore, maybe a year older than Marlee, but he'd been the biggest guy at Titusburg High when he started last year. Not much of a football or basketball player, but big enough to frighten any opponents playing on the field or court with him.

"Tower of Isaac, right?" I asked.

"Do I know you?" He squinted down at me across the fence.

"Isaac, this is my sister, Twigs. Twigs, Isaac." Marlee had suddenly become Miss Manners.

"Wigs?" Isaac leaned closer to get a look at me. If he fell over the fence, he'd crush me, but I was in no mood to care.

"I'm Madeline and I just graduated from here. What were you doing to my sister?"

"She's older than you?" Isaac ignored me, directing this to Marlee.

"Yeah, Twig is little," Marlee said, emphasizing my name, "but she's my big . . . er, older, and annoying sister."

"Yep, I'm older than both of you. Now listen while I annoy you some more." I'd had enough. "Marlee, you lied about being at Gretchen's and now I find you out here bleacher-humping?"

"Hey, we were just fooling around—no sex." Tower of Isaac put up a hand, as if swearing an oath.

"Thanks for clearing that up for me." I pointed at my sister. "Marlee, you know Mom wouldn't like this."

"Mom would understand." Marlee threw her bare arms around Isaac, and though she's half a foot taller than me, she still only came up to his chest. "Isaac told me he loves me."

If I hadn't been so anguished about Matt, I might have laughed. When Marlee made her announcement of love, she looked just like Mom in an old high-school photo with Dad before they got married.

"I do love you." Tower of Isaac could have been at his wedding, because his "I do" screamed truthfulness.

"Marlee, stop shitting around."

"Cursing's not godly," said Tower of Isaac.

Not really knowing Isaac Townsend, huge jock friend to all at Titusburg, I never expected a religious reprimand from a guy trying to do my sister.

"Um, so screwing on the bleachers is considered godly?"

"Twigs! We weren't doing anything!" Marlee screeched loud enough to remind me why I'd come looking for her.

"Yo, listen to your sister. She speaks true." Tower of Isaac pointed one of his giant fingers down at me. His hand was bigger than my whole head.

I decided it was best to ignore him. I reached across the fence, grabbing my sister's shoulders, and gave her a hard shake. "Listen!" I shouted. It felt weird touching Marlee—I probably hadn't held her since she was a baby. I grasped her hard now, to keep my balance.

"Ow!" Marlee winced.

Tower of Isaac didn't realize I had caused her to wince and, thinking he held her too tightly, he took a step back.

"Marlee," I shook her again, demanding attention. "It's Matt. Something's happened."

"What?" Marlee's eyes widened. "What happened?"

"I don't know for sure, but Mom needs you."

"Matt?" Tower of Isaac asked Marlee.

I answered, "Yes, Isaac. Not only does Marlee have a sister, but she also has a big brother in Iraq, too, who may be dead. Too busy hooking up to share family info, I guess."

Tower of Isaac ignored me and turned to console Marlee, who had begun sobbing, "Hey, it's okay. I have a cousin in Iraq, too."

Tower of Isaac smoothed away the tears streaming down my sister's face.

Seeing him touch her that way gave me a pang. I wished Brady were here. He'd help me handle this and I could use the TLC, too.

Tower of Isaac looked at me. "Twigs? That's your name, right?"

I nodded, not wanting to waste time over my name now.

"I don't drive yet, but my dad can drive us over to your house, okay?"

The way he held Marlee under one arm, like Gary Cooper and Grace Kelly on my *High Noon* poster, made me reconsider Tower of Isaac. He may have been about to give it to Marlee, but he wasn't exactly the jerk I'd imagined. I gave him another nod.

"He'll drive you, too." Tower of Isaac guided Marlee away from the bleachers, and began walking toward the woods and the houses beyond. He motioned for me to follow. "I live back here."

"It's okay. I'm going to skate back," I stammered. "I'll probably beat you there." I knew Marlee would be more helpful to Mom than me, and I didn't have the strength to face home and bad news yet.

As I turned to skate back to the road, I heard Tower of Isaac comforting my sister, "God's watching your brother, Marlee. I'm sure."

A vision of a white-bearded old man hovering in the sky popped in my head—a Santa-God smiling a wide, fake grin over an Iraqi desert. Skating fast, I tried to keep that smile in my mind so I wouldn't see Matt, lying there near some burned-out tank, with open, empty eyes.

Chapter 5

Skating past the high school, I heard the clock in the town square begin to chime. I counted along with each out-of-tune bong, until the sound stopped. Twelve o'clock. Midnight here, so that made it 7:00 A.M. in Iraq. Good morning, war. Coffee with that pita, please—or whatever they ate for breakfast in Baghdad. Was Matt still in Baghdad, or anywhere now? I braked at the main road, swirling around on my skates to stare at the building where Matt had reigned when he was a student.

Never a scholar in any subject except machine shop, Matt had Dad's kind of charm, the kind that both men and women liked. He'd rebuilt the vice principal's old farm truck, making it run like new, and he never failed to compliment every female in school, even Mrs. Darby, who had to be the world's-oldest-living-lunchroom-lady complete with extensive nose hairs and a few missing teeth. Not surprisingly, Matt always had a girlfriend, or three, so that made him one of the "it" guys with jocks, stoners, and geeks alike.

"Matt, you know how to love people," Mom had once said, and I agreed. She'd been crying and tossing Dad's clothes in a garbage bag for Goodwill a few weeks after he'd decided he needed to disappear for a while.

Matt helped her, while Marlee and I watched them clear the house of every sign of our father.

"Good thinking, Mom," he said. "Let's toss all of his stuff. Dad's been due for a new look. I'll take him to Sears when he comes back."

When Matt said that, Mom's tears stopped. She shook her head. "We loved each other too much."

I didn't get that. "How can you love someone too much?" Mom didn't answer; she just kept filling boxes with Dad's life.

We'd snatched our Dad souvenirs quickly that day, hiding everything from Mom. I managed to grab the ratty old robe plus a few photos, and Marlee snagged one of his stained work shirts. Matt found the real treasure that Dad had left on the center of the dining-room table—his wedding ring. I watched Matt tuck it deep in the pocket of his jeans before Mom saw it and flushed it down the toilet as she'd done with her matching gold band.

My legs slowed—tired from skating, tired from everything. A car whizzed past, honking, and I whipped around to get a glimpse of a long, baby-blue convertible—one of those old-fashioned movie-star show cars. I could only see the back of the driver's head, a woman maybe, her bright yellow hair blowing in the night wind. Could it be Helen Raymond, hair-dye bomber? No sure way to know since the car was now out of sight, so I began skating again in the same direction, toward home. Toward Mom and Marlee. Helen Raymond's day had been shitty, too, but she took action and felt better. It was time for me to do the same. Face the family, the future. Just like a real grownup.

I skated hard and made it to our street in about half an hour and streaked past the small houses to ours halfway down the block. A boring maroon car was parked on the road in front of our house. Not the black death-squad mobile that I'd seen before. I'd barely turned into the driveway when Mr. Platton's door opened and he stepped out onto his porch.

"Hey there, Twigs. Mighty late, huh?"

I nodded. What else was there to say to a lonely old man in striped pajamas? The Chesters' Saint Bernard began a series of deep woofs across the street.

I whispered, "Mr. Platton, we're waking the neighbors."

"Oh, they're not asleep." Mr. Platton's voice carried like an "Attention Shoppers" announcement at Kmart. "Tom Chester was just out here a bit ago chatting with Marlee and her nice, black—" Mr. Platton shook his head. "No, excuse me. I know better. Her African-American friend."

I glanced across the street and then at the maroon car. It must belong to Tower of Isaac's dad. Tom Chester was a retired Titusburg football coach who'd loved watching Matt play on the team. He'd talk the game to a blade of grass, but maybe they hadn't been talking football. Maybe everyone in the neighborhood had been at our house since the visit from the army guys. Did everyone but me know what had happened to Matt?

Mr. Platton, mind-reader extraordinaire, spoke, "They'll find him, Twigs. I'm sure."

My mouth fell open. I closed it and opened it a few times, gaping like a fish. I think I nodded, too, wanting to believe my neighbor.

"You'd better get in there." Mr. Platton turned to go into his house. "Your mom needs you."

My mom needs me? My head nearly exploded. What about me needing her, Mr. Platton? Did I scream out loud? I must not have. Mr. Platton's porch light went dark, and I listened to the Chesters' dog woof a few more times, as if answering me. "Too *woof* bad, Twigs. *Woof.* Suck it up to *woof* take care of your family. *Woof.*"

I skated up to our porch and sat on the crumbling steps. It wasn't the wide veranda that surrounded Mr. Platton's house, where he lived and thrived.

It took a few minutes to remove the skates from my sweaty feet. Blisters had popped out on my heels and big toes. Maybe my feet had grown some, even though the rest of me still seemed stuck in a fifth-grader's body.

Behind me, our front door opened and a tall man stood silhouetted against the lamplight from the living room. I could make out a dark face and a uniform and wondered if one of the army guys had stayed behind.

"Are you Twigs?" the man asked.

I shrugged and slung my skates in the grass next to the porch steps. I wanted to be mature Madeline to face reality, but instead I was blistered and feeling my short Twigs self again. I wiggled my toes, noticing how light my legs felt now my skates were off.

"Twigs?" Marlee peeked around the man in the door. "That's her, Mr. Townsend. Why isn't your phone on?"

"We were concerned," Mr. Townsend said. "Isaac and I were about to go looking for you."

"I'm here," I managed to say. Mr. Townsend moved aside and I stepped into the living room. No fancy foyers wasting space in our house.

Marlee hugged me like she hadn't seen me in years, which felt bizarre since it'd only been about thirty minutes. Her face was blotchy from crying.

I stared uncomfortably at Mr. Townsend. Easy to tell this man was Tower of Isaac's father since they were the same size—extra-huge. His head nearly reached the ceiling. Except for a bristly mustache, neatly trimmed across his top lip, he looked like his son. The uniform wasn't military, but the stick-straight way Mr. Townsend stood made him look as important as any general. An embroidered *Brinks Security* patch was stitched above his shirt's chest pocket.

"Glad you're safe, Twigs. Marlee and your mom need you here." Mr. Townsend shook my hand. His firm grasp controlled my whole arm.

There it was again. How my family needs me.

Mr. Townsend pulled back the crisp cuff on his shirt, checking his watch. "My shift has already started, so I've got to go." He took

Marlee's hands in his own. "Tell Isaac to stay here as long as you need him. He can walk home later."

Where was I? Was this my house? A strange man was telling my sister to keep his son here, the one who'd been groping her earlier.

Confused, I forced myself to snap to attention. "What's happened to Matt?" My voice was as shrill as I felt.

Mr. Townsend winced. "Goodbye, now," he said and was out the door before I could hurt his ears again.

"Twigs, we're all in the dining room," Marlee said. "Lou's made hot chocolate."

With that, she turned and flipped her hair in that "Get a life" way she'd developed since she'd outgrown me in more ways than height.

"Where's Matt?" I yelled after Marlee, but she had already left the room.

I stomped into the dining room where Mom sat, red-eyed and pale except for the makeup tear streaks down her cheeks. She was tucked into Deaf Lou's armpit like she'd been glued there. Deaf Lou held a mug of something—hot cocoa, I guess—to her lips. Maybe he couldn't speak, but his eyes sure did. "I'm still here. I didn't leave like you did."

A roll of partly unswirled toilet paper, along with crumpled pieces of tear-swiped tissue, littered the table. Tower of Isaac, seated next to Deaf Lou, was writing something on a piece of paper. Marlee had planted herself behind Mom and stood there rubbing her shoulders.

"Twigs." Mom pushed the hot chocolate away, splashing some on Deaf Lou's hand. A grimace of pain spread across his face.

"Where's Matt?" I asked, standing at one end of the table. There was no chair left for me even if I'd wanted to sit.

"Twigs," Mom repeated and then turned away, sobbing into Deaf Lou's shoulder.

Deaf Lou touched Marlee on the arm, signed something with one hand, and tilted his head at me.

"Twigs—" Marlee's voice cracked—"they don't know where Matt is. He—he disappeared from his unit sometime last week."

"Sometime last week? What do you mean? Mom?" I wedged myself closer. "Mom? Tell me what's going on!"

Mom couldn't stop crying. No one said anything, as if speaking would make the news true.

"The MPs believe he may be AWOL," Tower of Isaac spoke up, and both Marlee and Mom burst out crying.

"No, no, no." Mom shook her head. Deaf Lou caressed her shoulder as if he'd been doing it for years. What was he doing here, anyway? Mom gulped. "Matt's a good boy. He'd never do that. Go AWOL."

"AWOL?" I realized it was bad and searched my head for the meaning. AWOL. One of those words you don't use or hear much, especially living in Titusburg.

"We didn't know what it meant, either," Tower of Isaac said, looking at Marlee.

"Mr. Townsend told us, Twigs," Marlee said, "because Mom was too upset to explain. It's Absent Without Official Leave."

Mom reached over and tore off a strip of toilet paper, wiped at the mascara streaks on her face, and blew her nose. "You should have been here, Twigs. The officers explained everything."

I swallowed, trying to understand. Matt wasn't dead. Or maybe he was and the army just didn't know it yet.

"His friends saw him leave, Twigs," Marlee said. "They were working on a tank, and Matt had to take a whiz."

"A whiz?" I asked, and Marlee nodded.

I paced in the little bit of room I had on this side of the dining-room table. That didn't sound like Matt at all. Tower of Isaac looked down at the table, as if embarrassed at our pee talk. Leak.

"No, that's not Matt," I said. "Matt would say, 'take a leak.'" Everyone here, and the army, too, must be very wrong.

"I didn't believe them, either," Mom said, barely above a whisper, "but they recorded the whole thing." She turned in her chair and pointed at the computer. "It's right there."

I looked at the computer screen. It wasn't our home page but an official military site. Bold black letters—**UNITED STATES ARMY COMBAT OPS**—filled the top of the screen. Deaf Lou reached one of his long arms around Mom's back and moved the mouse to click on a long number highlighted in blue at the bottom of the screen.

"Listen, Twigs," Marlee said.

Matt's voice entered the room.

"So what are we? Eight kilometers or so?"

Somebody laughed, a tinny, far-away sound. "What's it matter, Henry? No ladies your type in Basra?"

"Oh, every type is my type."

That was all Matt. Marlee let out a half laugh.

"Ssshh," I hissed at her and moved closer to the computer.

Lots of clanging and metal-on-metal gongs filled the room, as though something was being pounded or hammered. I covered my ears to muffle the noise. So did Marlee and Tower of Isaac. Mom pressed her head against Deaf Lou's chest and he held her close, oblivious to the sound.

"Holy jihad, Henry." It was the same guy who been speaking before. "You busted it."

"Naw, I can fix anything," Matt said. More clanging. "Hey, you think we'll go to Basra when the convoy comes through?"

"Nope, I heard we're heading south." No speaking for a few minutes. "Hey, Henry, don't sweat that shit e-mail. Families freak sometimes, you know."

"I told you to shut up . . ." Matt's voice seemed angry. A loud grunt came from the other guy. Matt shouted, "Twist to the right!"

"Okay, okay! Sorry."

Mechanic sounds, no talking, but anyone listening could feel the tension in that tank. Matt was upset. Families freak? What did that mean? I barely breathed, waiting to hear my brother's voice again.

"Hey," Matt paused. I could hear his feet and his voice moving away from all of us. "I gotta go whiz."

Whiz. Then the recording stopped. Whiz.

"That's it?" I asked.

"That's it, Twigs." Mom lifted her head. "At least, that's all the MPs brought and downloaded for us. The black box recorded Matt's last words inside the tank. Two soldiers standing guard outside the tank watched him walk beyond a burned-out jeep to whiz." Mom said the word like she'd eaten something rotten. "Then he was gone."

"I wrote it all down." Tower of Isaac slid the scribbled paper toward me. "See."

"Gone?" I asked.

Mom lowered her head. Deaf Lou signed something and she nodded. He maneuvered the mouse and clicked back to our home page. Marlee had been whispering in Tower of Isaac's ear. She didn't hear the little trilling computerized bell, but Mom and I heard it as if it were a sign from that Santa-God above.

"E-mail!" I shouted, and raced around the table behind Mom and pushed Deaf Lou's hands out of the way.

"Matt!" Mom said. "Please, let it be Matt!"

We all crowded around the computer as Mom signed the info to Deaf Lou. I clicked on the NEW MESSAGE icon. I'd read the words five times before I was aware that Mom had begun screaming. In what felt like slow motion, I turned to see her faint into Deaf Lou's arms. Marlee sagged against Tower of Isaac, and he stroked her face, calming her. Everyone had someone to lean on except me.

Demanding my attention, the blue-white screen screeched words from someone I'd never even known to look at a computer. No doubt I'd had a bizarro day, but this had to be the topper.

Eve, Twigs, and Marlee,

I'm looking for Matt. He hasn't e-mailed in over a week. I'm very worried. Please e-mail me with any news. I check in at this address every few days. Dale

Not an e-mail from Matt. No, not Matt. Matt's AWOL. But Dale. Dale Henry. My AWOL Dad, Dad, Dad.

Chapter 6

Matt walked alone down a dusty road, just like in one of those westerns. Only he walked in Iraq and it wasn't some gang out to get Matt, but the U.S. Army anxious to lock him up for desertion. "You don't walk away from the army, Henry!" some evil soldier bellowed at Matt. This man was huge, even bigger than Tower of Isaac, but he looked just like our dad. His giant arms stretched for miles, trying to reach Matt and grab him back, but those long, cartoon-like fingers just couldn't quite touch my brother.

My cell phone's incessant ringing woke me from the nightmare—that and the fact that I really had to pee, or take a leak, I thought. That's what Matt would say and I knew it. I stumbled over to my desk and grabbed the phone, praying it was Matt or maybe Dad, ready to step up and rescue our family before we all disappeared.

When I heard Dink's voice, I cursed myself for not looking at the caller I.D. before answering.

"Twigs? Where are you?"

"On my way, Dink." I scrambled around grabbing clothes.

"On your way?" Dink sounded like a girl screeching over the latest pop idol. "It's eight-thirty. I have that thing in Hinkney. You were supposed to be here early, remember?"

I sucked in a breath to keep myself from telling Dink what I wished he'd do with his thing in Hinkney—whatever it was, because damned if I remembered or cared. "I'm on my way," I repeated, because what else was there to say.

"That's not good enough, Twigs. If you make me late . . ."

"Gotta hang up. Cop behind me." I slammed off the call and threw on the same clothes I'd worn the day before. "Damn," I muttered. I'd forgotten about the splotches of hair dye on my Uptown Pharmacy smock. I quickly turned it inside out and backward. Dink would spew if he saw the beige and orange stains, making it look like some kid had dumped a diaper on me.

A look in the bathroom mirror only confirmed the mess Helen Raymond had made of my hair, even more evident in the morning light. The mismatched streaks seemed appropriate somehow; chaotic hair color to go along with the chaos of my life. Despairing Mom and promiscuous sister bookended by my disappearing brother and e-mail from a long-gone Dad.

A glass of orange juice would have to do for breakfast. I rushed past Mom's and Marlee's closed bedroom doors into the kitchen and stopped short when I saw Deaf Lou standing at the counter making coffee. His back was to me, so he didn't know I was there. Great. I jabbed him on the shoulder to get his attention, and he turned, nearly dropping the coffee pot.

"Why are you still here?" I overenunciated each word, making sure Deaf Lou caught every move of my lips.

He held up his free hand and slowly signed letters to answer me. "E-v-e n-e-e-d-s m-e."

I blinked at him and so he raised his hand again, but I pushed it down, stilling his words.

"I got it. I got it." So he thought Mom needed him. I had to give her credit. She knew how to get men to do what she wanted. Most of them anyway—Dad had been a different story.

Deaf Lou was right, though. Mom needed someone right now and it took the pressure off me if he stayed here. I just wish she remembered I needed her, too.

Deaf Lou gave me a little smile and placed the coffee pot in its cradle. He grabbed the magnetic notepad off the fridge and scribbled something with the small attached pencil.

He watched me read his words. "I met your mom a long time ago, but she was with your dad. I've always had a crush on her." He tilted his head, giving me a shy smile.

"She's still with my dad." Even as I said it, it sounded like a lie.

Deaf Lou pointed at himself.

"If you think so," I said.

I couldn't take the look of pity that popped into Deaf Lou's eyes. He turned and opened the fridge and seemed more comfortable in our house after one night than I'd ever really felt. He took out a carton of eggs and held them toward me with a questioning look.

Deaf guy, Mom-screwer, and now egg-cooker—it was too much. I turned away without a word, even a signed one, and left the kitchen. I walked past a sleeping Tower of Isaac on our living room couch and out the front door. It had been a regular party at our house; I was the only one without a sleepover friend.

Mr. Platton sat on his porch reading the paper, but I jumped in my car before I could hear him say, "Morning, Twigs." Or ask, "Did I hear your dad e-mailed?" He would know. Somehow Mr. Platton would already know, and I didn't want his neighborly wisdom now.

Dad had been in touch with Matt. That e-mail made it obvious and the more I thought about it the more pissed I felt. Matt had never mentioned a word about Dad in any of his letters or e-mails. He'd been home for a two-day leave last Christmas. Had Matt been in touch with Dad then?

I puttered behind a slower-than-slow truck of junk, probably heading to the Hinkney weekend flea market but driving the speed of honey. Matt would have passed the truck, but my crap car didn't have the pickup of his Charger. Dad had brought that old, engineless Charger home from work one day, and he and Matt had worked on that car every spare moment.

I was already way late for work, but thinking of Matt's car gave me an idea and I decided to make a quick stop. Dink might fire me, but this was important. Maybe I could find something out about Matt and Dad. I maneuvered my way into Bell's small parking lot, full of cars in need of repairs, and left my engine idling, as I ran into the open garage.

"Hey there, Twigster!" Chad Bell grinned from where he sat working on a tire and waved a greasy wrench at me. "I'd say you've grown since the other day, but I'm on the ground so it's hard to tell for sure."

Chad had been in Matt's high-school class and famously stupid. He wasn't even a good mechanic. Matt used to say, "Lucky his dad owns a garage, or he'd never get a job."

"Chad, have you heard from Matt? Or my dad?" I didn't want to spend any more time talking to him than I had to.

"Your dad?" Chad ignored the first question. "You hear from your dad, tell him to get his sorry ass back here. He left a lot of work undone when he split."

Chad's father stepped into the garage. "Twigs, is that you?" I hadn't been at Bell's since I'd come by looking for Dad a few years ago, when he'd first left. I'd never even stopped by when Matt had worked here before he'd joined up. "You look more like your dad than ever."

I didn't know if that was a compliment or maybe a put-down to Dad considering the state of my hair.

"Hi, Mr. Bell. You haven't heard from my dad, have you? Or Matt?"

Mr. Bell's bushy eyebrows rose a bit. "Matt? He stopped by here when he was in town at Christmas. Is he okay?"

"Um, we're not sure." I nearly sobbed at the truth of it but held myself in check.

"My, my," Mr. Bell paused, clearly concerned. "Have you asked that girl?"

I had no clue what he was talking about and my face must have shown it.

"We were busy closing up for Christmas Eve when Matt stopped by, but he had a girl in the car, right, Chad?"

Chad spit on the ground. I guess that helped him think. "Mexican chick, I think. Or some kind of Latino. Not white, that's for sure."

"Who was she?" I asked, not an ounce surprised at Chad's racist memory.

"Don't remember. Matt said her name, but it wasn't American." Chad spit again and the slimy gob landed near my foot. He grinned. "Bet she's wild in the sack."

Mr. Bell shot Chad a look that shut him up. "Sorry Twigs, I don't know much. We were giving out Christmas checks and drinking eggnog, so things were a bit crazy here. I hope Matt's okay."

"Me, too," I said. "Nothing from my dad?"

Mr. Bell shook his head. "Not a word. Damn good carburetor man. I could still use him."

I could still use Dad, too, I thought. A father should be useful, right? I shook Mr. Bell's hand and scooted away before Chad could spit at me again.

But dumb Chad had actually helped a bit. As I raced to work, I thought about what he'd said. When Matt had his short holiday leave, he'd spent a few hours on Christmas Eve going to see friends. At least, that's what he'd said. Mom had told him to invite everyone over, but Matt had insisted on driving around. So he'd had some mysterious girl with him and she didn't sound anything like one of Matt's old girlfriends from Titusburg High. Maybe he'd gone to see Dad, too.

I pulled into the little parking lot next to Uptown Pharmacy and shut off my engine. Matt had never been one to keep secrets. That was more my style—keeping to myself to most, except Brady, who'd managed to get into my head, as well as other parts of me. Shit. Brady. Why hadn't he called? I reached for my phone, which I always kept in the empty ashtray when I drove. Double shit. In the rush to get out of the house, I'd left it on my desk.

Dink's fists pounded on my car window.

I jumped in my seat. "Holy crap!" I yelled through the glass.

Dink's few hairs were out of place and his mustache looked askew, as if he'd taped it on crooked that morning. I knew he was all bluster, but Dink looked like he'd consider murder if he didn't need me because of this "thing" in Hinkney.

"You're getting docked big-time." Dink pulled on my door handle and began yanking me out of the car before I'd unbuckled my seat belt.

"Ow! Wait, Dink!"

"You've made me very late, Twigs, and I'm unhappy. Do you see that?"

Anybody within two miles could see Dink was unhappy. He was ape-shit mad. So mad, it was funny, but since his anger was aimed at me, I couldn't laugh. Too bad, I needed a good laugh.

I tugged my arm out of his grasp and continued the lie I'd started. "When you called, the cops pulled me over. I was on the cell phone while driving. So, in a way, this is all your fault."

I think I noticed actual steam coming out of Dink's ears—a real-life cartoon. I continued, "Luckily, I talked my way out of the ticket. I told them my boss had called with a pharmacy emergency." This lie would do the trick, I knew, since Dink would never check with the Titusburg police, all four of them. He'd gone to school with one as a kid, a real bully, and Dink believed they were out to get him. Maybe they were; he owned the only car in town ever given parking tickets.

"Just get in there," Dink commanded. "Mr. Franks is swamped at the pharmacy and there's a line at the register." Dink pushed me toward the door of the store and turned to get into his car. "Remember that you're on until closing."

Funny, how I got yelled at for leaving the register yesterday, but now Dink eagerly walked out on his own store. No use mentioning that since he had already slammed backward out of his parking space. Dink rolled past with a scowl under his droopy mustache and shook an accusing finger at me before he squealed out of the lot.

I breathed a sigh of relief. Dink being gone might be the one bright spot to help me get through the day. Sure, I'd be busy, but that would keep my mind off Matt and Dad.

"Would you like a Twizzler?" I spun around and faced the cigarette thieves from yesterday. The tall jerk-off held a cigarette pack out at me. Bobblehead stood so close that I got a slam of smoke blown into my face.

"Hey." Bobblehead waved and then coughed.

It took me a minute to focus. What were these boys doing here? Shouldn't they be sleeping in, like I wished I were doing? Maybe they hadn't been in bed yet. I looked around. Titusburg seemed deserted, a regular ghost town.

"That some ugly-ass hair you got there," Jerkboy said.

I couldn't argue with that, so I turned to go inside.

"Bitch," Jerkboy spoke again. He said it with such pride that I might have been flattered, if the day hadn't gotten off to such a shitty start.

I decided it best to ignore these two.

"Good thing your doofus boss is gone. We can come in and take as we please."

They had been watching me with Dink? Shows how gosh darn interesting Titusburg is, if hanging out at the Uptown Pharmacy parking lot is the big event in your day. I turned to see Bobblehead nodding in agreement.

I had to laugh. "Go ahead, take. Why don't I just call the cops right now!"

Jerkboy lunged at me, throwing me off balance, and Bobblehead yanked my arm back.

"Ow! Let go." I pulled, but Bobblehead held fast.

Jerkboy stood so close that I could smell morning breath combined with a stale cigarette stench wafting from his mouth.

"Why don't you show me some respect right now?" he threatened. The way he said it made me think he was repeating something he'd heard before. Then he sneered, "Would you talk to your daddy like this?"

My daddy? What daddy? "Do you talk to your daddy like this?"

Jerkboy blinked and the shiny skin on his forehead pulsated in front of me. Seeing my chance, I grabbed it. I wrenched my arm away from Bobblehead and shoved my index finger right at Jerkboy's eyes and pushed hard. Then I ran, ignoring the screaming curses behind me.

Whipping around the corner and bursting into the store, I startled a group of customers standing at the register. All their eyes locked on me. An elderly man at the front of the line pushed the buzzer again, as if to emphasize how long he'd been waiting.

"Sorry, sir." I scrambled behind the counter and began ringing up his assortment of foot creams. I reached over the counter and grabbed a box of Snickers from the front display case and took out one of the candy bars. I offered it to the man. "A gift for waiting."

He appeared confused for a moment and then smiled, revealing huge, overly bright false teeth. “Why, thanks.”

Then I saw the boys standing at the window, smoking and staring in at me. Jerkboy clamped a burning cigarette in his teeth and thrust his hips against the large glass pane. Then he aimed his two middle fingers at me as smoke curled around his head. He mimicked shooting me, blew off his pointed fingers, and shoved them in his pockets.

I forced myself to ignore them and focused on the people waiting to check out.

“How rude,” someone remarked from the back of the line and a few others muttered in agreement.

My hands shook from fear and the adrenaline of the moment. Or maybe it was because I suddenly felt hungry, ravenous even. It had been a long time since that Chinese food last night.

“Free Snickers for everyone,” I announced, taking one for myself before passing the box down the line. I needed breakfast. Besides, wouldn’t this count as making the customers happy? What Dink didn’t know . . .

The next person in line stepped up and I took a quick bite of milk chocolate and caramel-covered peanuts. I glanced toward the window to see the boys turning away. Jerkboy glanced over his shoulder at me and if it’s possible for eyes to glint, his certainly did. I didn’t know whether to puke or run, but my stomach flipped when he ran his tongue across his thin upper lip, a regular big bad wolf out to eat little girls like me.

Chapter 7

The day was nonstop customers. Saturdays always were, but usually Dink was there, actually helping. Mr. Franks had a continuous line at the pharmacy but managed to shell out the drugs in record speed. "People get paid on Friday," he'd once said, "and buy their Prozac on Saturday." The way Mr. Franks smiled all the time—I figured he sampled his own products. I could use a few samples myself. The bag of Doritos and eight Snickers bars gave me enough energy to work, but they couldn't stop the thoughts of Matt.

A couple came in the store arguing and the woman said, "Matthew, shut up, would you?" Our Matt never argued with anyone, not even when Mom yelled at him for joining the army. Not even with Dad when he reached for his thousandth beer of the night. He'd just ask, "You sure you need that one, Dad?" And Dad's answer never changed, "I need 'em all, son."

Between customers, I used the store phone to call home for a news update.

Marlee answered and gave me a list: "Mom's asleep, Lou's e-mailing the army for more info on Matt, and Isaac's out getting pizza for everyone."

"Need me to bring anything home?" I asked.

"Um, some of that Wet n Wild Pumped Pink nail polish," Marlee said. Her concern for Matt was not enough to warrant drab toenails.

I hung up on my selfish sister. Her pumped-pink toes would have to wait.

Freedom came at 8:00 that night when I walked out the front door. Mr. Franks locked up behind me, his smile fading a little as he said, "Night, Twigs," and shuffled back to the pharmacy. Across the town square at Titusburg Bar and Grill AKA TBGs, a batch of Saturday-night smokers lingered outside the entrance nursing their beers and laughter rippled through the air. Most days after work, Matt had hung out at TBGs, charming the waitresses and playing pool. Unlike Dad, Matt never drank.

Marlee, twat that she was, would've have called me at work, if there had been any news about Matt, so I decided to go over to the bar and see if anyone there had heard anything. A huge car, a baby-blue vintage something, parked in front of the bar seemed to be the center of attention. People circled the old-fashioned movie-star car that Dad would've called a "classic."

I crossed the town green and noticed a woman sitting in the driver's seat, watching TBGs. Her profile seemed familiar. She must have felt me looking at her, because she turned and yelled at me through the open window.

"Hey, it's you!" Helen Raymond yelled, and a few drinkers turned to stare at me.

I stopped short, still crossing the street, and a car honked at me to get out of the way. I hopped out of the road and Helen reached a fake-nailed hand toward me, as if to stop me from crashing into her. A few patrons blew streams of cigarette smoke my way, seemingly annoyed that I'd interrupted their conversations.

"Are you okay, honey?"

Helen Raymond's yellow hair and long, hot-pink nails glistened in the outside bar lights, and then her plump hand circled my arm. Maybe it was eating too many Snickers, or worries over Matt, or seeing this woman again, but I felt faint. It would have been so easy to slide away out of sight, under the car, down the manhole cover, through all the pipes and dirt and molten lava, sucked into the center of the earth. I wanted to just disappear, but I didn't.

"Um, thanks," I said, and pulled my arm from her as gently as I could. I gave the car a quick once-over and smoothed down my calico hair, relieved to find Mrs. Raymond didn't have any throwing objects in grabbing range.

"Well, you helped me yesterday," Helen Raymond laughed. "Payback." She spit out the word and her breath smelled, not beery, but there was no doubt that she'd been drinking something other than water.

What more did I have to say to her? "Well, thanks, Mrs. Raymond."

"Helen." She smiled. "We've met twice. That makes us friends, right? Call me Helen."

"Okay, Helen." She smiled up at me—I was tall for the moment. "Well, bye."

"Oh, no, no, no," Helen cackled.

Helen Raymond sounded like some sort of deranged witch but a nice one. The outside bar folks stopped midconversation, midsmoke, and glared at her—at us.

"You've got to stay and watch this, girl." Helen Raymond did the "girl" thing again as she'd done at the pharmacy earlier, but she was right this time. I know I looked like a girl and now I felt like one, too. I choked out a sob, missing my big brother and needing my mom.

"My, my." Helen rubbed my arm with one hand and placed her other hand on her chest, almost covering that deep cleavage. "You've got a broken heart, too."

I bawled, a regular tear-fest right there for the smoking drunks to enjoy.

Helen took action and opened the car door, nearly knocking me over in the process. "Come on in here, girl. I mean it." She slid across the silver bench to the passenger side and patted the seat.

The fact that Helen really seemed to care and actually wanted to make me feel better meant something. Besides Brady, who cared even though it was definitely combined with lust, no one really gave me much attention. My body was tired, my head ached from crying or from lack of real food, and my legs felt wobbly, so I slumped down in the car, drew my legs inside, and closed the door.

Helen began digging in her giant pink bag and then thrust a tissue at me. "You need to blow, girl."

I took the tissue and wiped my nose. "Mrs. . . . er, Helen, my name is Twigs, remember?"

"What?" Helen's gaze bounced from me to the opening bar door. She straightened in her seat, at full attention, eyes focused on the exiting couple. A tall, thin man wrapped one arm around his date's waist and the petite blonde rested her head against him. They walked toward the main square and Helen slumped back against the seat.

"Not them," she said, clearly disappointed.

"Who?" I asked.

"Stuart and his whore." Helen's eyelids lowered along with her voice.

"Is that your husband?"

Helen's lips quivered; I was sure she would begin bawling, too. We were a real pair. Neither of us said anything for few minutes.

"How do you know he's in there?" I asked.

Helen let out another cackle. "I know because we're sitting in his car."

I jerked my head around, as if expecting her husband and his whore to jump out of the backseat and yell, "Surprise!" Then maybe we'd all laugh and go inside for champagne. But the look in Helen's eyes said it all.

"This car belongs to your husband?"

"Yes. Mine's at home, safe and sound." Helen patted the leather dashboard and smiled. "I cleaned out Stu's bank account yesterday.

Thanks for the tip about that free coffee. I've been following him and his whore all day, so I just waited. It's easier than driving back to Hinkney."

It was as if she were reciting from her daily planner. She'd omitted the "Freak out and trash Uptown Pharmacy" and "Throw hair dye at Twigs" entries.

"Uh, Helen. Why are you sitting in your—" Did I say husband or cheater spouse?—"um, Stu's car?"

Helen's eyes never left the bar door. "I'm going to run Stu and his whore over—back and forth several times, if necessary—until they're both pancake dead."

Quiet again, except for the short quick breaths from Helen. I'd almost started laughing, but this was no joke and it wasn't just hair dye this time.

"Helen . . . " I began, unsure what to say. I'd never met anyone this intense, and I couldn't help feeling a bit in awe of her and what she planned to do, even if it was insane.

Then Stuart Raymond, the cheater with two first names, appeared on the steps. I had never seen the man before, but Helen gasped, and a barely audible "Bastard" came from her lips. She reached over and pounded on the car horn. Yells erupted from every beer-drinking smoker outside the bar, but the loudest came from a tall, balding guy. "Helen, what the—what are you doing?" he screamed a few times, all the while cradling the elbow of a younger, bland blonde. He held her elbow as if stopping her from running away.

Chapter 8

Helen Raymond wanted to commit murder.

She didn't blink, just stared at Stuart Raymond and his whore. Mr. Raymond's face seemed to jump out, 3-D style, as he told us to get out of his car.

"Helen, be reasonable, please. And who is that little girl?" he asked, jabbing his finger in my direction.

Okay, I could barely see over the steering wheel of this huge car. Still, it pissed me off to be called a girl. Of course, that didn't mean Stuart Raymond should die. I looked from the cheater and his whore, since I only knew her as that, to Helen.

"You can't do that, Mrs. . . . Helen," I spoke softly, as if my voice might tip her over the edge. "You don't just run people over."

"I do." Helen reached across the seat and turned the key in the ignition. The car's engine started without even a single foot pump. I could almost hear my dad's voice, "Listen to her purr."

Without taking her eyes from Stuart Raymond and his whore, Helen said, "Get out, Twigs."

The town clock mounted above the old Titusburg Courthouse began to chime, as it did every quarter hour. People need to know the time, except this clock had been wrong for years. The large metal hands centered on the giant Roman numeral twelve; it was either noon or midnight. It was really 8:15 and here I sat next to Helen, who was itching for a showdown or a rundown of her own.

The Saturday-night drinkers and smokers gathered nearby were enjoying the show, and more patrons came out of the bar. "Run him down," yelled a loudmouth drunk from somewhere in the crowd. Laughter rippled from the group. "Give him what he deserves," shouted one woman. "You got that right," her girlfriends whooped and hollered in agreement. "Get the blonde bitch, too!" someone else yelled. It wasn't clear if they referred to Helen with her fake hair or the whore, whose dye job looked near perfect. Whoever—it riled everyone up and suddenly it turned into a regular frenzy. *Jerry Springer Show* appearing live in Titusburg!

The noisy crowd pushed closer to the car and Stuart Raymond stepped up on the front bumper with his arms out wide. "Helen, get out of my car!" All he needed was some hair and a cross to hang onto and he could star in an Easter pageant, his blonde whore gazing up at him like Mary Magdalene.

Time passed in slow motion, pouring over Helen and me like a honey-soaked reality. My life flashed a little before my eyes. Were we Thelma and Louise with a do-or-die decision to make? Something about Helen's determination, her spirit, tugged at my emptiness. No—pulled, yanked at me. As I stared at Stuart Raymond, his whore, and the crowd, I imagined the scenario, no longer in slow motion, but a careening mowing down, taking them all out, killing every bastard in this suck-ass town. I hated them all—except for Matt. I hated them all—except for Brady, except for Dad. But they didn't exist here anymore. Matt might not exist at all. I hated everyone here, especially me.

"Twigs?" Helen's voice snapped me from my inner rant. Tears ran down my face, nose stuff, too.

"Yes," I whispered. Looking at Helen, I realized that she was someone I didn't hate.

"Get out or gun it."

Helen's command forced my hands to lift, as if a puppet master had taken control, and I placed them driver-ed perfect at ten and two on the large steering wheel. Stuart, who continued to stand air-crucified and pleading to Helen, stopped midrant and gaped at me.

"You're not old enough . . ." Stuart began.

"Oh, yes she is!" Helen screeched. "Gun it, girl."

And I did. Leaning into the steering wheel and stretching my short legs as far as I could, I shoved my foot onto the paddle-size gas pedal. I gunned it. The engine roared and revved, the car ready to lurch out and flatten everyone. People scattered, cheap beer spilling on the sidewalk as the mass of bodies careened away from the baby-blue monster that was about to attack. But God, fate, or some unknown motoring deity stepped in.

The car was in park.

Stuart laughed hyena style, mounted there like a hood ornament. He yelled over the engine's motor, "Helen, come on. Enough. We were done already. Celia had nothing to do with me leaving."

He gestured to his whore, who had moved up on the sidewalk when I started revving.

"Celia," Helen whispered.

She lowered her head, breaking her death stare, and it seemed to break my resolve, too. I took my foot off the pedal.

"Helen?" I asked, not sure what to do now.

"That's the name we picked for our baby."

"Oh," I said, but I didn't get it. Not really. Helen and Stuart were going to name a baby Celia. Okay. Now he's sleeping with someone named Celia. Okay again. "Do you still want me to . . . ?" What was I asking? Or doing?

"Let's get out of here," I said. "Does that sound good?"

Helen's head was still bent and tears dripped on her lap, dotting her pink leopard-print pants. She didn't answer, but I sensed her desire to kill had been zapped by that name thing.

Stuart Raymond jumped down from his crucifixion and moved toward me. Sweat glistened off the top of his head, where hair must have once grown. I couldn't look in his eyes, but that shiny head seemed threatening, an alien about to attack. This time I put the car in drive. I slid down far enough to reach the pedal and I gunned it, lurching forward. The driver's side-view mirror slammed into Stuart's arm as I drove forward.

"Ahh!" he screamed, lurching away from the car.

Bottles shattered and curses flew from angry drinkers forced to move or get hit. Just like on TV, the show had turned ugly.

"Sorry," I yelled out the window. But I wasn't. For once, people had to pay attention. Twigs is on the move, folks! Take notice! "Woo hoo!"

The car roared, and Helen and I sailed away from TBGs. Away from Stuart, though I saw a glimpse of him in the rearview mirror. Celia stood near him, gently cradling his arm that had been slammed by the mirror.

"Stuart's not dead, Helen, but he's in pain." It was weird, but I felt a little proud about what I'd done. That feeling lasted one second, and then it disappeared. "Oh, shit. I think I broke your husband's arm. And we've taken his car. Shit."

Helen remained quiet as death, just staring into her lap.

I drove around the town square and pulled into the little side lot where my car was parked at the pharmacy. My piece-of-crap mobile just made this gorgeous hunk of machine look even better.

We sat there, the two of us. I fiddled with the wiper knob and found the lights, but I didn't get out. I had hurt someone. I felt lousy, even if he did deserve it.

"Take me home," Helen said, breaking her silence.

Her statement made more sense than anything I'd heard all day.

"Why not?" I replied. Somehow it seemed the thing to do. Why go home anyway? Home to the Matt Mess. If there'd been any news about Matt, surely Mom would have called me at work.

Even if Helen had tried to kill me with hair dye, ruined my hair, and somehow made me attack her husband with a car mirror—she needed me. That felt good.

I revved the engine again and we pulled out of the lot.

"Which way?" I asked when we reached the only traffic light in town. Go one way and you ended up in Hinkney. The opposite choice led to another nothing town. Either way got you out of Titusburg.

"Right," Helen said. "I'm behind HCC."

I knew where she meant. Hinkney Community College, the grand institution I'd be attending in just under forty-eight hours, unless the cops got me for car theft and assault first.

Chapter 9

Helen slumped next to me, her eyes shut to the world, leaning her head against the back of the car seat. Headrests hadn't even been thought of when this beauty had been built. A low-backed bench seat must have kept a starlet's beehive in place for all of those movie premieres. My multicolored hair whipped in my face, blown every which way and sure to be tangled later, but I didn't care. It felt amazing to drive a car like this—no wait—this was more than a car. I had to call this machine the name it deserved—an Automobile, with a capital *A*. Dad would love this car, except maybe I didn't care what Dad would love anymore, considering he'd been in touch with Matt and maybe everyone else but me. What the hell was going on with him and Matt? Yeah, what the hell?

Helen moaned and mumbled, "Celia." She didn't open her eyes, but I noticed tears running down her cheeks.

"Helen," I asked, "you need me to stop?"

She only lifted one hand, as if it were full of heavy sand, and waved me onward. Even with my lousy-barely-able-to-graduate grades, I had enough smarts to see that Celia meant a lot to Helen Raymond, even more than her cheating husband. I pressed the accelerator, and the beautiful blue Automobile complied. We sped along County Road 131, the only paved way in or out of Titusburg. Nothing but late-summer corn and a few passing semis filled the view. I had spent a night with Brady in one of those cornfields, and I smiled at the memory. "Let's make our own field of dreams," he'd said. Oh, so sappy, but what girl wouldn't like hearing that from her boyfriend?

What would Brady think of me driving with someone like Helen? Hopefully, she'd loan me her phone and I could call him later. It was the least she could do after I stole her husband's car for her and then assaulted him with it.

A-1's Porno-Gun Shop, with its permanent Christmas-light display, appeared ahead, marking the Hinkney city limits. Soon afterward, County Road 131 widened into two lanes. We passed through a few lights, then by a Walmart, a McDonald's, and the prison-gray Conder County Hospital, and approached Hinkney Community College. It topped the hospital in its ugly design, with the same depressing paint job and no windows. I'd been on a student tour already and the entire place smelled like mildew. I wondered if they piped in the smell to keep students awake during lectures.

Helen's eyes popped open as we sat at the red light in front of the college. "Turn right at the next corner," she said. She opened the glove box, which looked bigger than my entire car, grabbed a tissue from a box there, and dabbed at her cheeks.

"Okay." Nerves got to me. I'm not sure why, but I babbled on, feeling as though I needed to engage Helen and cheer her up if I could, "I'm going to school right there on Monday." I tilted my head toward the sad campus. "It'll be my first day of college."

"Oh, I'm sorry," Helen said. She knew as well as everyone that Hinkney was a college of last resort. You went to Hinkney if your college test grades sucked or you were broke—it was custom-made for me.

I laughed as I turned the corner heading along the side of the college. "Helen, thank you for being honest."

"I don't know how else to be," she answered. "Turn right again here."

"No, I just meant that my mom, sister, boyfriend—even my brother . . ." I paused, thinking of Matt. "Everyone else made it sound like going to Hinkney Community College is all I ever wanted and that it's a great stepping stone to whatever I choose to do in life."

"Stepping stone bullshit," Helen said. "Turn left at the corner."

"Exactly." I turned the car onto a road directly behind the campus. "Hinkney Campus Lane," I said aloud, reading the street sign.

"Fifth house on the right. Number ten," Helen instructed.

I'd have known her house, even if she hadn't given me the number. A pink flag with a bouquet of flowers printed on it jutted over the street from a pole stuck on top of a pink mailbox that was painted with flowers. I gaped at the floral motif, which included matching pink flowers in several hanging pots on the front porch. They looked too vibrant to be real. A bright pink Volkswagen Beetle sat in the driveway of the modest two-story home, thankfully painted white, with pale pink shutters.

"Park on the street," Helen said. "I don't want Stuart's car near mine."

I didn't quite understand that, since we'd taken her husband's car, but I did as I was told. It was clear that Helen had perked up, in the same way she had after charging a thousand dollars on Stuart's credit card.

"How'd you get to Titusburg without your car?"

"A coworker dropped me off. I told her I was meeting Stuart to talk. Some talk, huh?"

I concentrated on pulling Stuart's Automobile as close to the curb as possible, and Helen ran one long fingernail across the leather dashboard.

"In we go." She grabbed her bag and jumped out before I'd even put the car in park.

I ran along the driveway after Helen and caught up, just as she unlocked the pale pink front door, sporting a brass knocker in the shape of a daisy.

An annoying "arrf, arrf!" assaulted us.

"Sly!" Helen cooed. "Mama's home!"

The yips continued as Helen pushed the door open, and the runt terrier I imagined wasn't there. Instead, a motley, mangy-looking mutt, about knee high to Helen, bared its fangs at me, poised to attack.

"Sly, she's a friend," Helen said to the dog, while flipping on an overhead light. "Now hush."

"Good dog," I said, holding out my hand for the dog to sniff or eat, depending on its mood. Sly gave me a good whiff and then slobbered across my outstretched fingers.

"He likes you."

"Dogs usually do. They seem to think I'm part of their pack."

Helen had moved to a small table in what I guessed was a foyer and pressed a button on an answering machine. The room made me dizzy because the pink walls had stripes of floral wallpaper every six or so inches. As interesting as Helen seemed to be, I wondered if Stuart had really left her because he was sick of living a pink life.

I knelt and rubbed Sly behind his ear, or what must have been an ear at one time. The dog had some serious ugly issues, with chunks of fur missing in spots and one yuck-me-out milky eye. Looks aside, Sly leaned into my fingers, enjoying the ear rub.

"Helen!" a speaker voice barked, making me jump, and it wasn't Sly's fault this time.

"Helen, pick up the goddamn phone!"

Helen stared at the answering machine with a smile on her face. Confusing, but I guess she liked hearing how upset her cheating husband sounded.

"I'm here at the hospital waiting for X-rays. Celia brought me . . ."

There was a pause on the tape as if Stuart had flinched at saying Celia's name the same way Helen's smiling mouth had now become clenched and hard.

He continued, "I think you broke my arm, Helen."

"She didn't break it. I did." I wanted full credit for busting Stuart's arm.

"Sssshh!" Helen quieted me and replayed Stuart's message.

"I think you broke my arm, Helen," he repeated. "As soon as they set it, I'm coming over there to get my car." Stuart's voice dropped to a tense whisper, "I don't want to see you. I don't want any trouble. Just put the keys in the ashtray."

If time can stop, it did in that moment after Stuart slammed down the receiver of the phone at the hospital. I could see him there with Celia by his side. Helen must have been imagining the same thing, because neither of us moved or spoke. The silence in that foyer was thick pink, if that's possible. About as possible as time stopping, I guess. Sly broke the spell with an arf.

The answering machine came hurtling through the air and I threw myself against the floor. Helen wasn't aiming at me but at a large pink-floral frame with a wedding photo of her and Stuart grinning blissfully. From what I could see before I hit the rug with my face, Stuart had had hair when they were married and hers looked naturally golden, not the fake mustard it was now. I lay on the floor panting from shock. Sly stepped on my back and licked my ear.

"Sorry," Helen sounded crazy calm. "I didn't mean to scare you, but I can't look at him anymore. Here, get up." Helen offered her hand and pulled me to standing. "Just take it down, okay?"

I knew she meant the picture, so I took it off the wall. The silhouette was still there, a rectangle where they'd hung together for who knows how long. I turned it around and set it on the floor, facing the wall.

Helen was on the move again to the back of the house somewhere. Sly trotted toward her but then returned and sat next to me. The dog didn't seem to know what was going on anymore than I did.

I heard Helen stomping around and slamming things, so I took a quick moment to call Marlee. I grabbed Helen's cordless from the small table and dialed.

"Hello?" A voice answered that I didn't recognize.

"Uh, is this the Henry house?" I asked.

"Yes, who's this?" the man's voice asked.

My heart skipped, literally, or stopped. Was Dad back? Would I have forgotten his voice? I could barely breathe but managed to speak, "Uh, this is Twigs."

"Twigs, hey, it's Isaac. Where are you?"

I gulped, angry with myself for hoping Dad had come home. Tower of Isaac was there, of course, eager to bang my sister in the middle of a family crisis.

"Twigs?" Tower of Isaac repeated. I heard a door slam somewhere in the back of Helen's house and Sly began arfing again.

"Yeah, I'm here. Any word from Matt?"

"No word. Your mom is a mess. Lou is with her. Marlee's not so good either."

I'm not that great myself, I thought. Sly's arfing intensified, and the dog began scratching at the front door. I didn't know what to do.

"Is that a dog, Twigs?" Tower of Isaac asked. "Where are you? Marlee thought you got off work a while ago."

"I did." I cradled the phone at my ear and went to the door, trying to pull Sly back. The mutt had a lot of power for an old dog. I dropped the phone and it clattered on the floor near Helen's wedding photo. I grabbed it, but the connection had been cut off. Sly was annoying me now, and he obviously needed to go outside.

"Helen!" I called. "Can I let Sly out?"

I waited and called again. "Helen?" Sly let out a round of arfs, shrill enough to make me hold my ears. Even so, I heard the crash in the front of the house. I yanked open the door and there Helen stood, on top of the hood of the Automobile, holding a sledgehammer. I noticed that all the side windows were gone, and Helen was working on taking out the entire car.

"Helen!" I screamed, but it only egged her on. She gave me one of those just-try-and-stop-me grins.

"Whee!" Helen yelled. Her hair frizzed wildly around her head and appeared to glow in the streetlights.

Like Zeus, or one of those Greek gods throwing thunderbolts at Earth, Helen heaved that long hammer with a force I'd never seen before. The windshield cracked and sent shards of glass airborne. This wasn't one of those up-to-date safety windshields, but thick plate glass, probably installed by hand back in the day.

"Die, car! Die!" Helen screamed.

Sly's arfs had ceased. He stood next to me in the driveway, along with a group of curious neighbors, gathered for the best show in town. Together, we watched Helen murder Stuart's car.

Chapter 10

The neighbors' muffled talk didn't stop Helen. Her sledgehammer smashed everything: the headlights, the side-view mirror that had hit Stuart's arm, even the big round steering wheel. This rant had to play out. Helen kept shouting while hammering the Automobile, "Come and get your car, Stu!" Sly leaned against my leg, and I could feel him trembling. He'd probably witnessed plenty of fights between Helen and Stuart, but this vision of his mama killing a car was a shocker.

One of the neighbors offered me a hand to shake, followed by another on-looker. They introduced themselves as Chris and Pat. "We're the nosy neighbors and friends of the Raymonds."

"Damn shame," Chris said.

They seemed nice enough, but I had a tough time telling them apart in the dark yard. Even worse, I couldn't tell which one was the woman. They both wore sweats and oversize T-shirts, and with names like Chris and Pat, I hadn't a clue.

Chris and Pat both tried to coax Helen down off the car, but she just kept on slamming metal and ignored them, me, and everyone else. I found her neighbors easy to talk to, or maybe I was just hyped up from all the excitement. Out of character, I chattered and babbled on, telling them what had happened in Titusburg, including how I first met Helen during her hair-dye attack.

"It's been coming," Pat said. I think it was Pat.

"Stu asked for it, if you ask me," Chris said.

"Don't get me started," Pat replied.

It was obviously a discussion they'd had before. I took a chance and asked the question that had been nagging me all night. "Uh, who's Celia?"

Two or three of the neighbors looked down at the ground and I did the same, wondering if that would reveal the answer.

"You'd best not ask," replied someone.

"Why not?" Pat asked. I knew then that she was a woman. Something in the way she brushed her short hair away from her ears before answering my question, "Celia's a baby, or at least the thought of one."

Chris leaned in close after checking that the car-wrecker couldn't hear the following, "Helen got pregnant a little late for safety, and she went through the whole thing."

"Still one of the best parties this street has seen," another neighbor threw in.

Pat gave him a look, "Yep, but maybe it was bad luck to have a big barbecue like that."

Chris touched her arm. "Now don't start on that again." He turned to me. "Twigs, we had a big block party for Stu and Helen. They'd been trying to have a baby for years. Damn near everyone in Hinkney showed up and there were more baby gifts than Walmart could hold."

I got it then. Helen had lost a baby. Helen finished killing the car at the moment of my realization. She flung the sledgehammer into the yard, barely missing her pink flower mailbox. She marched up to us and tossed the keys to Chris.

"Chris, I need a favor." Helen wiped her hair out of her face. Other than a bit of sweat on her upper lip, she looked like she might have just come back from taking Sly for a walk.

"Anything, Helen," Chris said.

"Drive that thing." Helen pointed at the smashed car, never again to be a perfect Automobile. "Please—drive that thing to the hospital, and give my whore-screwing husband his keys."

Chris's mouth hung open. Pat nudged his arm and answered for him, "Helen, I doubt if that car is drivable now."

"I didn't touch his precious engine!" Helen screamed. "Did I, Twigs? Did you see me touch his engine?"

"Uh, no." I quickly shook my head, stroking Sly for comfort.

"Sly, come to Mama." Helen knelt and reached out for her mutt. He trotted to her, though caution seemed to slow the dog's gait. "If you don't take that thing out of here, I'm going to take it myself." Helen stood, her face close to Chris's, and added, "Right now, I don't trust what I might do to the bastard."

I knew. Everyone standing there knew what Helen might do to the bastard.

If Chris didn't help her, then we might all be accomplices to a heinous crime. After seeing what Helen did to Stu's car, I shuddered to think what she might do to him.

"Okay, Helen. Okay," Chris said. "I'm just going to grab a tarp to spread across the seat, so I don't have to sit on all that glass."

Helen smiled and nodded, happy to have his agreement. Chris stepped into his garage next door and quickly reappeared with a large canvas paint tarp, which he and Pat spread across the bench seat I'd been sitting on just a short time before.

Helen began walking to her front door, with Sly trotting close behind. I stood there, unsure of what to do. Like she'd done in the car, Helen seemed to read my thoughts.

"Come on in, Twigs," Helen called out. "You don't want to be alone any more than I do."

Even with Brady, I saw myself as alone. Not a loner, per se, since people were usually around—at home, work, and school. My aloneness was more like those old westerns when the hero stands in the middle of a dusty road and knows the worst is coming—and it's fight or die. Maybe both. I haven't figured out how to fight or die yet. See how wacked I am? Fearing the worst. Is Matt facing the worst now—Iraqi torturers, and dying in some dirty, forgotten place? Probably so, and there isn't a damn thing I can do, but be here, right now, with Helen. I walked up her driveway, joining her.

"We need piña coladas," Helen announced, as she walked into the house. I'd had a piña colada–flavored smoothie last summer at the Hinkney water park with Brady and it made me puke. But the way Helen said it, I imagined an island beach, isolated and beautiful.

Before I entered Helen's house, I heard the crunch behind me as Chris turned the car away from the curb and drove through crushed glass. He looked over and gave me a thumbs-up. I returned the same, feeling weird making a gesture I'd never used before.

"Take care of her, Twigs," Pat shouted from next door. She sat in a small, nondescript Nissan or something, with the window down. "I'll be back with Chris as soon as we deliver Stu's heap to him. He's going to shit. Excuse my French. If you need anything, Helen's got us on speed dial." She gave me a wave before driving off.

One wicked piña colada later, sitting at Helen's kitchen table, I'd told her my entire dismal life story. Then I understood why it's called "demon" rum, because one strong coconut drink got me talking more to Helen than to anyone else I'd ever known. Or maybe the fake pink flowers everywhere made me feel as if I'd stepped into a fairy book and required me to tell my tale.

"My Twigs, my Twigs," Helen kept laughing after her fourth blended colada. "Sweet thing, you really needed to talk, didn't you?"

I babbled something about her listening even better than Brady.

"Men never listen, dear. They hear when they want something. Don't forget that lesson. It'll serve you well."

I nodded and suddenly felt the Snickers bars I'd munched on hours before gurgling in my stomach. Chocolate-caramel peanuts arose to meet me again, mixed with coconut-flavored rum. I spewed puke all over Helen's kitchen floor, an amazingly nice, beige-not-pink, tile.

"Sly, stop that!" Helen yelped, as the dog began licking up the mess.

The sight of that made me retch even more. "I'm sorry, I'm sorry," I repeated, freaking out at the mess I'd created in Helen's pristine kitchen.

"For a little thing, you sure can hurl." Helen grabbed paper towels from her kitchen counter.

"One of my many talents," I laughed.

It got Helen laughing, too, and we couldn't stop, even while holding our noses to clean up my barf. We laughed while climbing her stairs and she showed me a room with a pink twin bed, adorned with a small heart pillow embroidered with *Celia*. We laughed when Helen called Sly into her room and while saying good night.

I lay there staring up at the pale pink dotted-swiss wallpaper. It spun slowly, or seemed to, but not enough to make me sick again. I thought of what Helen had said about my amazing hurling talent and it sent me into another round of giggles. I giggled at where I was, in this house in Hinkney, with a woman who had given me more attention in the last few hours than Mom had in years. Somehow that pathetic thought made me giggle even more. So what if my dad was gone, my brother had disappeared, and Brady had forgotten about me? It was all just so damn funny. Laughter filled me and filled that empty-little-girl pink room. It stopped only when I slept.

Chapter 11

A foul odor woke me. It took only a minute to realize the smell came from my open mouth. I'd never brushed my teeth after my piña-colada pukefest. The thought of it combined with the smell of my own breath nearly made me retch again. I swallowed and felt parched of spit, my throat and mouth as dry as all of Conder County on Sundays. Water was needed ASAP.

I stumbled out of the pink bedroom and into a hallway bathroom with floor-to-ceiling pink tiles that were probably "the thing" when this house was built. Bending my head under the faucet, I drank like a camel after crossing a desert, long pulls of water sloshing into my mouth and on my hair. I took a little Aim toothpaste from the medicine cabinet and finger-brushed my teeth. Finally, I splashed my face and looked in the mirror over the sink. Alive, yes, but cotton-headed and numb with a piña-colada fog filling my eyes. "Twigs, never drink, okay?" Dad had half-asked, half-told me once. Sage advice from a man nursing his eighth or eighteenth beer of the night.

"Good advice, Dad," I mumbled to my reflection. "Asshole."

This was the first time I'd thought of my dad that way, though Mom had uttered the word about him more than once since he'd left. It took Matt's disappearance for the asshole to surface. Maybe if they found Matt dead, shot by some Iraqi sniper, my father might show his face for the military funeral.

"Happy thoughts for a Sunday morning there, Twigs."

I ran my fingers through the mess on my head, trying to erase my evil thoughts. The pinkness of the room did little for my pasty complexion, though the image of my multicolored hair made me smile. Either I was getting used to it, or the splotchy colors made me look taller, cooler . . . something. Unless I found time and motivation to dye my hair today, this would be my going-to-college hairstyle. Maybe this look is just what I needed for my grand entrance to Hinkney Community College tomorrow.

Leaving the bathroom, I saw that Helen's door was shut to the world, but I heard a soft whimpering and could see a paw reaching from under the doorframe. Sly needed out. I slowly turned Helen's doorknob so as not to wake her, and Sly ran past me and down the stairs before I'd given him a good-morning pat. I followed, finding the mutt scratching at the front door.

"Hey, Sly, where's your leash?" I looked around the foyer. No leash that I could see. The cordless phone and recording machine lay on the floor, abandoned from the night before. I bundled the heap on the small table and put the phone in its cradle. Sly barked, impatient to do his thing outside.

"Okay, okay." He'd been fine the night before during the car murder, not running off, so I opened the door and he ran straight toward Chris and Pat's house. Sly straddled the driveway, edging the grass, and, with expert precision, left a mound right next to the driver's door of Pat's car.

"Sly!" I shouted, as if that might make the dog clean up his mess. He was already trotting toward me, tail wagging—proud of his morning accomplishment.

Pat must have been watching because the door of her house opened. "Thanks a lot, Sly," she shouted across her yard. "Don't worry, Twigs. Sly and our cat, Boxer, fight over that spot. It's the most pooped-on place in Hinkney. If Stu were here, he'd clean it up, but I doubt we'll be seeing him anytime soon."

I wandered over, so I didn't have to yell back, and shielded my eyes from the bright morning sun. Sure to be a scorcher in Hinkney, and it would be another ten degrees hotter in Titusburg. A personal steamy hell for every citizen. The glint of the sun off Helen's pink car got my head thudding, and I wobbled a little.

"You okay?" Pat asked. She wore the same gigantic T-shirt and gray sweats she'd had on the night before. The dark shadow on her upper lip made Pat appear even more masculine in the daylight.

"Just a little tired." I bent to pet Sly, who stuck next to me like a shadow. Maybe when Pat yelled Stu's name, it got the dog nervous that there'd be more crazy car killing. "So, what happened with the car?" Just like one of those annoying people who slow down to watch a traffic accident, suddenly I wanted to see the gore.

"Well, when Chris parked Stu's now-heap in the hospital lot, he got a lot of looks from those security guards. One even said, 'You shouldn't be driving if you've had an accident,' thinking Chris was a patient going to the ER. Stu and Celia were still in the waiting room. He looked like Sly's poop there, excuse my language, and in a lot of pain."

I had to bite my lip not to grin, partly because of Pat's cursing style and partly because Helen would be happy to hear this. "Wow, that's too bad." It was, but Stu deserved a little pain for what he'd done to his wife.

"It got worse." Pat sat on her top step and motioned for me to join her.

"Sly? Twigs!" Helen called.

Helen emerged from her front door, a regular soap-opera diva, in a flowing pink-satin gown with a matching robe that tied right under her massive chest. The effect made her look even bigger chested, if that was possible.

"Wow!" I exclaimed.

"Yep," Pat chuckled. "Helen sure dresses for bed, doesn't she?"

"How'd you sleep?" Helen walked over and enveloped Sly in her billowiness. The mutt disappeared in the pink fabric.

"Hard," I answered. Helen looked up from Sly to me. I realized that she had asked her dog the question, not me.

"Well, how's the bastard?" Helen stared at Pat, ready to hear the news. She appeared calm, though she patted Sly a bit fast. I hoped that Helen wouldn't throw her own dog if she got upset again.

"His arm is broken, from where your car hit him."

I grabbed my own knobby bone, envisioning the moment last night when I'd slammed into Stu's arm with the side mirror. Helen lowered Sly to the ground and placed her hands on her hips, in a Superman stance, making her pink diva robe flutter.

"But that didn't hurt him as much as seeing his car." Pat paused and looked at Helen before she continued, "When we told him what you had done, Stu ran out of the emergency room to find his car in the lot. He screamed so much, the doctors thought he might give himself a heart attack. I'm surprised you couldn't hear him over here—he sure was loud enough."

"Ha," Helen replied. No maniacal laugh.

She cocked her head toward her house, as though she'd heard something and then walked back without a word, with Sly right on her heels.

Pat nudged me to follow her. "Keep her distracted. And hide the knives."

"Knives?" Broken bones were one thing, but sharp weapons and blood? Matt might be facing sharp weapons or worse in Iraq, I thought.

"Just kidding," Pat said. "Just keep her mind off Stu, if you can."

A woman I'd met the night before was telling me to keep another woman I'd met two days before from harming herself or her cheating husband. Still, I liked the challenge and that someone needed my help.

"Okay," I agreed. "I'll try."

"Thanks, Twigs. Chris and I have this family thing today. We'll be back about four and get Helen over for dinner then."

Pat went inside and I'd just started walking back to Helen's house when she came running out in a low-cut floral blouse and bright pink capris.

"Sly, stay!" Helen pulled her front door shut. "Mama loves you and will be back soon!"

"Hop in, Twigs!"

Helen was already opening the door of her pink VW. Something in her tone, or maybe the odd look in her eyes, made me nervous. "Helen, where are we going?"

"We've got to find Stu."

"Really?" I asked. "Helen, do we really need to find Stu?" I immediately regretted asking because of the grimace on her face. Hadn't Stu been bad enough and now I'd betrayed her, too?

Sly's barking from the house filled the silence between us, and then a car swerved onto Helen's street, heading in our direction. Someone was calling my name. I saw Marlee's face first, in the back, sitting next to Tower of Isaac.

"Twigs!" Their arms waved from the car window. "There she is!"

Then, as if in slow motion, I watched them tapping on the shoulder of the driver. Deaf Lou had his hands tight on the wheel and I realized it was his car, the one he'd parked in front of our house on Friday night, pre–Chinese food, bonking my mom, and Matt's disappearance. Mom sat next to him, her head leaning out of the passenger-side window and her face tight with anger and fatigue. "Twigs! Twigs! How dare you!"

How dare me what? Had something new happened to my family? It felt like months since I'd last seen them.

"What in the world?" Helen asked, as if God would answer. I wondered the same myself. Hey, God, how'd Mom and Marlee and their man candy find me here?

Mom leaped out of the car before Deaf Lou had even braked next to Helen's driveway. She somehow defied gravity and appeared in my face, screaming over Sly's protective yelps.

"I've lost Matt. Your dad left. I can't have you leaving, too!"

Marlee whined much the same, "Why are you here, Twigs? You're so selfish! How could you leave like that with Matt missing?"

"What were you thinking, Twigs?" Mom asked.

Not much of anything, truth be known. Weird, but I hadn't been thinking of my family at all since I woke up. A little brain break, though I wish Matt had been found.

"Uh, sorry." What else could I say?

By this time, Deaf Lou and Tower of Isaac had joined the women, like twin support beams. Helen hadn't spoken and I wished she'd throw some hair dye or something. Then came the biggest sentence from Mom—the one that sucked the breath right out of me and even stopped Sly's barking.

"Well, Twigs, is that all you have to say for yourself?"

Matt's disappearance and/or Dad's e-mail must have uncorked something, because I couldn't remember the last time I'd seen Mom this emotional. I opened my mouth, closed it, and tried again. My eyes wandered up, away from everyone, and I noticed a huge cloud in the late summer sky. It might appear as a train to some on first look, but to me, it was three smiling faces—Dad, Matt, and Brady. The special men in my life who had somehow left me—they were watching all this happen. Their cloud smiles got me giggling, even more than the drinks last night.

Then I felt a thump on my arm and Deaf Lou glared at me, demanding my attention. He signed, his fingers inches from my face, slow and deliberate, so I would understand. "Speak." He spelled out every letter. "Answer your mom."

The clouds, the street, everyone, and my heart ceased moving, or so it seemed.

Helen came to my rescue and finally broke the silence. Though Pat had asked me to distract Helen, it had shifted to her doing that for me.

"Care to join us at IHOP?" she shouted, thinking Deaf Lou could hear her that way. "Doesn't pancakes sound good?"

Chapter 12

When your Funny Face pancake arrives with a whipped-cream frown instead of a smile, you know you're in for a bad day. As if I didn't know it already. First, there'd been the hangover, then Mom and Marlee yelling while Deaf Lou flipped his shouting fingers in my face, and finally, the IHOP waitress had given me a kid's menu. I couldn't imagine things any weirder, but bizarreness had become the norm in my life these days.

Helen headed the table we surrounded in the back room at IHOP, where we joined the usual Sunday morning Hinkney eaters. Families gathered, complete with screaming toddlers and drooling grandpas, and a group of Goths filled the corner—still decked out in Saturday night black cloaks and ebony nail polish, their drowsy faces topped off with smudged raccoon-style eyeliner.

"Eve, would you pass the strawberry syrup, please?" Helen asked my mom, who sat at the other end of the table.

It made perfect sense that Helen would eat pink syrup. Mom blatantly ignored Helen and dumped more sugar into her coffee. She was obviously still angry with me, but clearly peeved at Helen, too. Tower of Isaac reached for the syrup container and even offered to pour for Helen. The perfect gentleman while ogling Helen's deep cleavage. Then he splashed a hefty amount of pink goop on top of his own stack. He had already begun on his third stack of All-You-Can-Eat pancakes, and Marlee cheered him on like this equaled a winning touchdown. "Look at him eat, Twigs!" she'd exclaimed with sickening glee, proud of her man.

I watched Tower of Isaac's huge, dark hands grasp a fork laden with a massive bite of fried dough. Pink syrup dripped down his wrist and the thought of him mauling Marlee popped in my head, making me twitch. Not because I thought it was weird or gross, but I realized that I'd probably enjoy those hands on my breasts, too.

I had to talk to Brady. My heart and head knew it, and my body had begun to go through withdrawal. Two days since we'd even talked, much less kissed. Yeah, I could use some mauling of my own right now. Besides, Brady would say the right words to keep my mind off my sister's boyfriend. And they'd be soothing ones, too, about Matt's disappearance, Dad's e-mails, and Mom's anger.

"You're my normal," I'd told Brady once when we'd first admitted we felt more than lust for each other. "Your what?" he'd asked. "You're the only part of my life that seems right, Brade. Not some freakazoid reality show, with me as the one everyone conspires against and wants to vote off." That's how I thought of Brady—my normal, my right brain, in my half-brained world.

"Your daughter's been a huge help to me," Helen announced to my mom, the table, and the room. Mom looked at Helen this time. Her face remained completely impassive, the over-the-top emotions she'd revealed in Helen's front yard all tamped down.

Mom hadn't said much since we'd been seated at the table, except to order breakfast crepes; after that she and Deaf Lou had signed to each other, ignoring the rest of us. They kept their hand movements small, trying to hide the words. I could only make out a few specific ones: "Matt," "Call the army," I think, and "punish," which must have had something to do with me having been gone all night.

"I said that your daughter's been a huge help to me." Helen's voice carried enough to silence the screaming toddler two tables over.

"If only she'd do the same at home," Mom replied but not to Helen. This barb hit its mark.

"How did you find me?" I blurted.

"Isaac did it," Marlee cooed, wrapping one arm around him and hugging him close. "He knows people."

Her prideful smirk soured the whipped cream in my mouth. "People?"

"It's nothing," Tower of Isaac replied. "My oldest brother is a highway patrolman and he helped locate where you'd called from last night."

"Mom was so worried," Marlee said.

"You were, too," Tower of Isaac replied, his arm moving under the table, clearly rubbing Marlee's leg. I gagged on the lie. The only thing Marlee ever worried about was if her hair frizzed.

Helen had stopped eating and just stared at my mom. She and Deaf Lou paused from their sign-language huddle and returned the stare.

"I thought you might like to know what a huge help your daughter has been to me while I've been going through a difficult situation." Helen took a swallow of tomato juice. The red mustache on her skin above the pink lipstick made my stomach flip. "If I had a daughter who'd helped a stranger like Twigs did, I'd be damn proud."

I pushed back my chair, unable to breathe or swallow. Too much noise about me and now Helen had brought her dead daughter into the conversation. She didn't say Celia's name, but I felt it hanging there, just above my head. My pancake stuck somewhere between my mouth and my throat. I jumped up from the table and my chair fell backward, hitting the handle of a wheelchair.

"Hey!" exclaimed the family behind us, as if I'd flung a chair at them.

"Sorry," I muttered, picking up my chair. I patted the handle of the wheelchair to apologize. An old man with watery eyes gave me a resentful sneer.

"Twigs," Mom said, "take a seat."

I backed away and signed *bathroom*, waving my arms and fingers, more like guiding an airplane in for a landing than sign language. Everyone in IHOP watched me. I know they did. How could they not notice as a pint-size, wheelchair-hitting twit about to puke from family overload raced past?

I'd barely made it into the stall, when my Funny Face returned on me. Piña coladas last night and now pancakes. Mental note: No food or beverages that begin with the letter *P*. Standing there, wiping my face with strips of toilet paper, I realized stress ruled my stomach today. I admired Helen, but I'd had enough of her for now. We Henrys had a real family crisis. It wasn't that Helen's problems didn't matter, but did I want to be like Dad and desert my family? I had to deal with Mom and Marlee, possibly Dad, and Matt—especially Matt. I had to find out if he was still alive.

I exited the stall to find a woman changing her daughter's diaper on one of those disgusting fold-down plastic trays some doofus named "Baby-Changing Station," a pit stop for infants. I washed my face and hands and heard the babbling sounds that only babies can make.

"She's talking to you," the woman said.

"Oh?" I turned to get a paper towel from the dispenser. Babies always liked me, probably because I'm kid-size. The infant, now fresh and changed in her mother's arms, reached out for me. It was impossible not to smile at her, face flushed and round, a perfect circle topped with soft blonde wisps.

"I like your hair," the woman said.

"Oh?" I asked again.

"How'd you do that?"

I glanced in the mirror at the trio of colors from Helen's surprise dye job.

"It wasn't hard." That sounded lame.

"Excuse me." The woman carried a loaded diaper to the trash bin behind where I stood.

The smell curdled the air around us, but the baby's smile erased the stench for me. She held out her little arms, beckoning me to take her, offering pure love. At least, that's how I saw it. A hug from this baby might be magical somehow and fix my world. Brady would materialize to hold and kiss me. Dad and Matt would come home to stay, sober and safe, making our family whole and happy again.

"Ow!" The girl's fingers had locked on my hair.

"Matty!" Her mother gently pried the baby's fingers from a hunk of my hair. "Sorry about that."

"It's okay." I rubbed my head. "Matty?" Mom still called Matt that whenever she spoke to him on the phone, her pet name from when he was little.

"Yes," the woman replied. "It's short for Matilda, a family name."

"Oh. Well, bye, Matty." I waved at the girl, her arms out, still offering love or hair pulls and smiling as sweetly as our own Matty.

Marlee nearly pulled me from the bathroom, where she stood right outside the door. "Twigs, come on. Can you take any longer in there? We're leaving."

Helen and Deaf Lou stood at the register, flanking my mom, each with their money out.

"I'm buying. This was my idea," Helen said.

Deaf Lou signed, his fingers filling the air in Helen's face with purpose.

"He insists," Mom translated, but Helen just grinned.

"No!" Helen shouted right at Deaf Lou, still expecting him to hear. "I'm buying. Or my husband is." With that, she thrust the same credit card at the cashier that she'd given me two days ago at work.

Stuart Raymond's Visa. "Put a hundred-dollar tip on that," Helen instructed.

"Wow!" Tower of Isaac said.

Mom's and Marlee's eyes were as big as pancakes, too, impressed by Helen's extravagance. The cashier seemed uneasy and I could relate.

"Helen, I think there's been enough . . ." I began.

"Enough what, Twigs?" Helen's eyes glinted. "Pain? Stuart's pain will end when mine does."

I wondered if pain like Helen's, or Stuart's, or mine, ever really ended.

Deaf Lou thrust his cash at the cashier once more. Mom put her hand on his arm, pulling him back, and signed him the news. Helen's tip would trump that offer every time.

Helen hugged me as we stood in the IHOP parking lot. "Twigs, I'll see you again. Don't worry." I hadn't been worried about seeing her but felt tears in my eyes when she said it. Her strawberry-syrup breath was warm on my ear. "You've got something, little girl, don't let them tell you different."

"You do, too," I said, actually liking the way she'd called me "little girl" this time. It felt like one of those tearjerker-movie goodbyes, and now I wondered if I'd ever see Helen again.

"Oh Twigs, you don't have to tell me I've got something," Helen said. "I've got . . ." She hesitated, searching for the answer. "I've got . . . Sly." She pulled back from me and laughed, giving us all a wave as she unlocked her pink car. "I've got to get home and take my sweet baby for a long Sunday walk. We both need the exercise."

With that she was gone, and the air around IHOP seemed thick without Helen's energy zapping us all to life. I climbed into Deaf Lou's car, crammed against the window in the backseat next to Marlee and Tower of Isaac whose knees nearly reached the ceiling. Deaf Lou turned on the engine and lowered the electric windows, giving the air conditioner time to rev up against the oppressive late August heat.

A car pulled into the space next to ours, and Deaf Lou waited for them to get out before he backed up. A boy jumped out of the back door. The driver, a heavy man, leaped out of the car, yelling. He yanked the kid by his shoulders and began shaking him harder than the law allowed, I'm sure. The boy's head moved in the air with a snapping force.

The boy pleaded, "Dad, Dad! Stop! Please. I didn't mean it."

A woman had gotten out of the passenger side of the car. She had a bruised cheek and held the hand of a scared girl.

"Let Brian go. Please," she said to the man, her voice quivering. "You're scaring Dina and people are watching."

Yes. We were. We were all watching.

"Let's go," Mom said, signing to Deaf Lou to leave.

"That's one mean white man," Tower of Isaac spoke a quiet truth, and no one disagreed.

"Come on, now. Let's go eat." The woman's voice managed to cut through the man's public anger. He released his grip on the boy called Brian. My eyes locked onto the boy's as he rubbed his neck, and I'm sure he saw me gasp.

"Jerkboy." His bad-boy attitude had annoyed and even frightened me yesterday, when he and Bobblehead had threatened me at the pharmacy.

"What?" Marlee asked.

I didn't answer. Jerkboy saw me—maybe even heard me. He squeezed his eyes shut and then opened them, as if I might disappear. As Deaf Lou pulled away, I realized Jerkboy's day might suck worse than mine.

Chapter 13

A virus, or stress, or something, gripped my insides all day, keeping me on the verge of puking most of the time. Piña coladas and pancakes aside, it was a crappy Sunday. I left Brady a number of annoying e-mail messages, reminding him that he'd have to call me because of my cheap cell service. I was pitiful, pleading in each one.

Need you, want you—call me.

Can't call you, Brade. So, it's up to you. A lot of shit here.

Brady, my love, my sweet, are you there? Twigs needs to hear your voice.

And the sappiest of all—

I heart you.

I kept checking my phone, sure to find a message waiting that I'd somehow missed.

"Brady's dissed her," Marlee told Tower of Isaac, after she saw me do my hundredth phone check.

"Shut it, Marlee." It was enough that I felt dissed, whether or not it was true. I didn't need to hear it.

"You shouldn't talk that way to your sister," Tower of Isaac said. "Family is all you got."

Something else I didn't need to hear. My family had begun to vanish, leaving no forwarding address.

Marlee and Tower of Isaac sat at the dining-room table along with Mom and Deaf Lou. Mom had a map of Iraq spread in front of her and was marking little *x*s and dots and dashes on it with a neon pink highlighter, as if it would help her figure out where in that big tan blob her son might have decided to go. A regular treasure map with Matt as the booty.

"I'm taking Marlee to my church," Tower of Isaac said.

Church-of-his-pants I figured, from the way he eyed my little sister.

"We're going to pray for Matt," Marlee added, her eyes appropriately brimming with tears.

"Well, it couldn't hurt," Mom said. "That's nice of you, Isaac."

This from a woman who hadn't stepped inside a church since Grandma's funeral on my thirteenth birthday. Lucky thirteen! I think the trouble between Mom and Dad had begun that day. Dad had pulled the funeral procession over, stopping the hearse and a long line of mourners, to buy a beer to drink on the way to the cemetery.

"Can't blame a man for needing a drink when his mom dies, Eve," he had explained.

Mom had been pissed and embarrassed. I can't say that I blamed her, but I was too young to get it. She stood apart from Dad at the cemetery, grasping the arm of a deaf coworker, while checking to make sure her beer-drinking husband noticed. He did but didn't seem to care. Dad had barely talked to any of us that day, and I knew he was upset over Grandma, but it hurt just the same. He knew how much I'd loved her, too.

The image of Marlee at church actually helped soothe my dancing stomach, but I sure didn't want to hang with Mom and Deaf Lou. Why this guy, a stranger except for bonking my mom a few times, had made our house his home was beyond me. He tapped me on the shoulder a few times and signed, "You okay?" I shrugged. How could I be okay? And what business was it of his? But at least he asked. I had to give Deaf Lou points for that. He and Mom spent the day surfing the Internet and leaving countless phone messages in some anonymous military voice-mail box. They'd gotten the number from the card the army guys had left behind with instructions to call if Matt tried to reach us, but that didn't stop Mom.

"This is Eve Henry, Matthew Henry's Mom, Army Division 125, Alpha Company, Khartoum. You said you'd call. Has there been any news? Please, I'm asking for someone to call me back." Then she sobbed into the phone before Deaf Lou took it from her, replacing it in its cradle.

"Mom, they're not going to call you unless they know something." Maybe not, but her call made sense to me.

"We were told to call if we had questions. I have one."

"What's that?"

"Where is my son?"

Deaf Lou could read Mom's lips loud and clear and wrapped an arm around her, allowing her to sob on his shoulder. I had to give Deaf Lou another point. A man in the house equaled Mom too busy to bug me.

I wallowed in my room. It's a talent I excel at when I allow myself. There've been a number of "Where's Dad?" wallow-fests. I gave in to this one since the picture of Matt taped to my mirror made it so easy to be pathetic. It had been taken the night before he left for the army. His mass of friends had thrown him a huge party, and most of Titusburg had been there. Dad would have loved it—a real multikegger bash. In the photo, Matt stood in front of the banner they'd made him: MATT HENRY ROCKS IRAQ. Matt rocked—everyplace and everyone.

"See you when I see you, Twigs," he'd said the next day, with a brush of his lips against my cheek. Then he'd climbed onto the bus, grinned, and waved goodbye.

I whispered to his photo, "Hey, bro, how about now? I want to see you now, Matt." I'd had this same conversation begging the universe to bring Dad home, too, and it hadn't worked yet. But I knew Dad was alive. His recent e-mail proved it; with Matt, I wasn't so sure.

"Please, please don't be dead. Okay, Matt?" I stared at the photo lost in wallow-time and waited for a sign of hope from the universe—Matt's mouth in the picture to start talking to me, or aliens to arrive, or a unicorn prancing by with my brother in tow. Something phenomenal had to occur to prove that MATT HENRY STILL ROCKS! But the photo kept absolutely still. No magic sign. No movement. Nothing.

Boredom set in and I gave up wallowing and sorted through my old high school notebooks, ripping out used pages, so I could reuse, recycle, restore, and save a few bucks. I doubted I had enough saved to buy all the books I'd need for college, much less paper for taking notes.

"You can afford gas or books," Brady had joked about the cost of school, though he'd gotten a full scholarship. He only had to buy gas and not even much of that since he lived on campus.

I kept my phone in my jeans pocket, listening for the ringer, and nudged one iPod ear bud into my ear to hear the mix Brady had made me. He'd given it to me at the lake our last night together. "Listen to it when you miss me. Third one, Twigs. It's all you."

The New Wave wind-chime effect turned me off at first, but when the voice rose above the melody, it brought tears to my eyes. Didn't take much today. Some weird language floated into my head—Swedish maybe—but the woman's voice sounded both lyrical and haunting. Brady had wild taste in music, but he'd nailed this one. It felt like me. I imagined a breeze moving through me and I closed my eyes and lay on the floor, listening.

"Tweeeeeeeeeegggggsaaaa." The singer repeated this in every chorus along with other Nordic-sounding words, as though she'd caught her tongue on my name. It was funky, weird, and exactly why I heart Brady. Heart, legs, breasts, and all the rest—I body the guy.

* * *

A ringing phone cut through the strange music filtering in from my ear bud and I awoke in the same clothes I'd been wearing and puking in since yesterday. I yanked the bud from my ear. The ringing persisted as I jumped up from the floor and flung notebooks around, frantically searching for my cell. Then I realized it rang from my hip and pulled it out of my pocket. Checking the display, I saw Brady's name and the time: 12:04 A.M. I'd been sleeping for hours.

"Hey, how's my college girl? First-day jitters?"

"Brady," I paused, rubbing drool off my face, as if he could see me. I ran my fingers through my tangled calico hair, willing myself awake.

"Twigs, my roomie, Lee, is great. You're going to completely get him. He likes old movies, too, but it's all Bogie stuff. You know, *Casablanca*. Lee's got an older brother here, a junior, so he's been showing us the best places to hang."

Brady seemed strange, rambling on like this, caffeinated or something. I didn't care about his new roommate.

"I miss you." The words bounced back at me, lame and boring, and I wondered why I couldn't express the true longing I felt.

"Yeah, me too," Brady said. "There's a place here called Reeb's. Get it? Beer spelled backward. It's just a block off campus."

Brady hesitated, as if he expected me to respond to the news about this beer place.

"Reeb's?" I asked, not sure what else to say.

"I know, I know. Beer's not my thing, but it's a good spot. Right near the college and they don't check IDs for beer. You'll love it."

"Okay." I sat on the edge of my bed, bracing myself to tell Brady the important stuff. "Um, it's been tough here."

"Really? Your mom again?" Brady had heard more than a few of my mom complaints.

"Well, sort of, but it's more about Matt this time."

Brady had never met Matt; he'd left for Iraq a month before Brady moved here. Then silence filled my phone.

"Brady?" I asked. "Brady?" Still, there was no answer. "Shit! No!" I screamed at the lost connection.

"Whoa! Twigs! What's wrong?" Brady's voice filtered through my instant rage.

"Oh, you're there?" I took a few deep breaths. "I thought I'd lost you."

"I'm here, just distracted. Sorry." Brady laughed and I heard muffled voices on his end of the line. "Lee's here with some of our floor mates."

"Floor mates?" It sounded like some product you'd use to clean grimy kitchen stains.

"You know, other people who live on this wing. We already have study groups set up and poker nights." More laughter floated through the phone. A shrill girl's giggle nailed itself into my skull. "HCC will have the same sort of thing for you, I bet, even if people don't live on campus."

"Did you hear me? About Matt?"

"Just give me a minute," Brady said.

"A minute for what?" When Brady didn't answer right away, I realized I'd lost him again, though I could hear him in the background.

"Half pepperoni, half cheese," Brady said. "Tell them to burn the crust."

More giggles erupted and I plopped down on my bed, staring up at the stained ceiling, where it leaked whenever it rained. "Cheaper to move your bed and use buckets than repair the roof," Mom had said. Home improvements ranked lower than mowing the lawn in this house.

"Sorry, Twigs. Really," Brady said. "We're getting pizza. Campus food sucks. What about Matt?"

"Oh, so you need to go?"

"No, no. Lee's getting it. There's a place right behind the dorms."

"Oh." Brady had never lied to me, as far as I knew. But he was leaving something out here. Or someone. More folks than Lee might be sharing that pizza. I wanted to talk about Matt, but I also wondered who owned the giggle. "So your floor mates are nice?"

"Yeah, yeah. Everyone's great. We're psyched to be here, but I'm worried about some of the classes. I hear the econ prof is crazy tough. It's my first class tomorrow, nine o'clock."

Schoolwork chitchat had never been my thing. I'd been too busy trying not to flunk out at Titusburg High, barely getting through senior math.

"You'll be fine," I said, not really knowing what else to say. Economics was not a subject I pretended to know anything about.

Brady's voice dropped, "I'll be fine when I see you next week."

Starlight and full-moon memories popped into my mind. Right now that night at Eagle Lake seemed part of someone else's life, not mine. Brady had made me promise to drive up to see him over Labor Day. Two hundred miles hadn't seemed so far then, but now I wasn't so sure.

"You still want me to come?" Brady seemed worlds away from my life now.

"Twigs, how can you ask that? Of course I do." Brady laughed. "Lee's already sick of hearing me talk about you."

"You've been talking about me?" I hated my neediness, but it felt damn good to know Brady still wanted me and not giggle-girl.

"Talking, thinking, needing," Brady answered. My guy. Still my guy.

"Yeah, me too." Though I hadn't really been talking to anyone but Helen Raymond the last few days. Thinking and needing, though? Yeah, in every way.

"When can you get here?"

"Um, I think I can leave after work on Friday. If Dink won't give me Saturday off, then I'll have to call in sick."

"Okay, hope this week at HCC is all you want it to be and more." Brady laughed at that. He knew I didn't want to be at HCC, or anywhere else except with him. "Hey, I hear Lee calling. Let's talk tomorrow night. I want to hear about your first day, okay?"

I heard a yell, "Midnight pizza's here!" and Brady's voice in my ear.

"Want you so much, Twigs," he said. "Bye now."

"Bye, Brade. Want you, too," I answered as he clicked off.

I looked at my phone. 12:30. Midnight-and-a-half pizza. I could use some pizza almost as much as I could use Brady, but both would have to wait.

I shrugged off my clothes and got right into bed. Night quiet filled my room and I might have been alone in the whole house. Turning on my side to sleep, the people I wanted to see most were there, as always, looking at me from old photos on my dresser. Brady. Dad. Matt. They each stared back, willing me to keep loving them. "Damn," I said to the air. I forgot to tell Brady about Matt. Nice, Twigs, nice. Selfish ass that I am, too busy imagining Brady's mouth on the giggler instead of acting like a grownup. I wanted to dream about Brady, naked, of course, with his mouth on me, but Matt filled my heart and head, too. How could I dream of anything else?

Chapter 14

Sleep never came after Brady's call, due to that long floor nap and my brain's nonstop chatter. I kept thinking about Matt, Dad, starting college—everything. After hours of tossing and more tossing, I got up at 4:00, farmer time. I showered and spent longer getting ready than usual, even putting a bit of Marlee's gel goop in my hair to calm the flyaways. I smoothed all of my hair over one shoulder, keeping the calico pattern in front. I wanted to own this look, if possible, for my first day of college.

In our dark house, I sat at the dining-room table filled with Iraqi maps and computer printouts. Most of it was information on where military action had occurred in the past week. Mom had done her research, though I doubted it would do any good. I checked the e-mails to see if there was anything at all from Matt, Dad, or the army. Nothing.

I wolfed down three bowls of Corn Puffs and would've eaten more if I hadn't finished the box. Marlee would yell at me later, but I had school today and she still had a week before ninth grade began. She'd have to make do with toast before "Rah-rah-rahing!" at cheerleading practice.

Gathering my things, I headed out the front door, glad to have college to keep me busy while we waited for any news from or about Matt. The driveway was empty—my car gone.

"Holy shit!" I yelled.

"Morning, Twigs."

I jumped at my neighbor's greeting. Did the guy sleep on his porch? "Mr. Platton! You surprised me!"

"Sorry about that." He sat casually in his chair in the predawn light. The newspaper hadn't even been delivered yet. "Just listening to the morning."

"Oh."

"Car trouble?" Mr. Platton already figured out I was looking for my car. He'd make sure the entire street knew this info before breakfast.

"Huh?"

"Well, since your car wasn't here all day yesterday, I figured you had it in the shop."

When Dad and Matt were around, no one on our street ever put their car in the shop, since we had two mechanics living here. They even repaired a minivan on Christmas once for relatives visiting Mr. Platton.

"My car's not in the shop. It's at work." I could picture it, dusty and forgotten in the Uptown Pharmacy parking lot. "I'll have to wake Mom up to drive me over there."

"She's not home."

I then realized that Mom's car wasn't in the driveway either.

"She went with Lou," Mr. Platton said. "He's nicer than most of those guys she dates, isn't he?"

No way would I discuss my mom's sexual partners at dawn, or anytime, with Mr. Platton. "When did they leave?"

"About midnight, I think."

That meant exactly midnight, because Mr. Platton could account for every second of every day on our street. It must have been right before Brady called me. I wondered why Mom didn't wake me to let me know she was going somewhere or leave a message, at least.

"Do you know where they went?"

"Lou wanted to drive, but your mom insisted on two cars." Mr. Platton paused. "I'm pretty sure they went to see someone about Matt."

I'd been standing in the driveway, my book bag at my feet, but when Mr. Platton mentioned Matt, I ran to his porch. From the angle he was sitting, I could see a long nose hair jutting from one nostril and the golden morning sun glinted off his wire-frame glasses.

"What about Matt?" My voice pierced the early-morning quiet.

"Now, calm down, Twigs. Your mom wanted you to go on to school. There's nothing you can do. They haven't found him yet."

I wanted to throw a rock at Mr. Platton's head and knock him off his chair, but I took a breath instead. "Who did my mother go see, Mr. Platton?"

"Eve didn't tell me, but I think I heard her talking to Marlee before she drove off with that big black boy. I think your dad called, Twigs, and had some news. Eve went to see him."

"Dad?" I could barely get it out.

"Well, I'm not sure. But yes, I think that's what I heard. You're supposed to go to school, okay, now?" Mr. Platton stood up and leaned over the rail of his porch as if he had special wisdom to impart. "College is important."

I looked at him, unsure how to respond, so I didn't. Instead, I sunk to my knees, soaking my jeans in the morning dew. Mom was somewhere, right now, seeing Dad. Maybe she'd been seeing him all along and it was one more thing I hadn't been told. My fingers clung to the grass and I began pulling it out, blade after blade, clumps tossed in the air.

"Hey there, Twigs. It's okay, just calm down." Mr. Platton was off his porch now, an event that didn't happen very often. "Mrs. Platton will have your hide and mine, too, if you mess up her precious yard."

"Why? Why doesn't she love me?" I screeched at Mr. Platton and the world. Dogs began barking around the neighborhood. I don't know how or why that came out—the rage at my mom when Dad was the one who had left, but it's what I felt.

Mr. Platton pulled me up from the ground and I let him lead me to his garage, the one he had built next to his house years before I was born. Everyone who lived on our street knew his story. He claimed to have captured an alien who'd landed nearby and kept it in a bunker buried beneath his garage. Folks were never sure if Mr. Platton was joking or not, but Halloween pranksters always came looking for the bunker. I'd looked once or twice myself. If it existed, it was well hidden.

Mr. Platton guided me to his Buick, which seemed brand-new, no scratches, not even a smudge of dirt anywhere. He gently pulled the strap out and buckled me in the passenger seat. Tears fell from my face and Mr. Platton pressed a white cloth handkerchief into my hands.

"I'm driving you to get your car and you're going to school now, okay, Twigs?" Mr. Platton asked as if he wanted an answer, but I knew it didn't matter what I said. "That's all you have to do today."

He pulled out of his driveway and into ours and reached out of his car door to pick up my book bag, full of old pens and half-used high school notebooks labeled Titusburg Titans.

Mr. Platton turned on the local big-band station and Frank Sinatra's voice filled the car. "The best is yet to come, and, Babe, won't that be fine?" Mr. Platton sang along with Frank, and I hoped they were right. Whatever Mom was doing with Dad didn't much matter, as long as Matt came home safe and alive. I sniffled and Mr. Platton took that as a signal that I wanted to talk.

"You're going to love Hinkney College. Mrs. Platton is on the garden committee there. They do the flowers around the main entrance sign."

I clutched my book bag to my chest and closed my eyes. Frank's voice swelled, promising better times for everyone who listened to his song, or at least for the woman he was singing to.

Mr. Platton pulled into the Uptown Pharmacy parking lot, empty except for my little lime green Geo. Someone had written in the dust on the back window, "You suck."

"That's rude and not true," Mr. Platton said, stopping behind my car.

I stared at the window and pictured Jerkboy running his finger along the glass. No proof, except the feeling in my gut.

"Thanks for the ride." I got out of Mr. Platton's car, fumbling for the keys in my pocket and opened my car door.

"You're welcome. Hey, Twigs," Mr. Platton called. "She does love you."

I choked back the lump of rage I wanted to spew at Mr. Platton. "You don't know shit!" I wanted to say, but I made nice and gave him a maybe-you're-right grimace instead. After a quick nod, I jumped in my car willing him to leave, but Mr. Platton waited until I started the engine before he finally pulled out of the lot.

Tears kept rolling down my face. I looked in my rearview mirror and saw the bit of makeup I'd put on earlier, now all smeared. What a great impression I'd make on my fellow Hinkney Community College losers. I considered driving straight to Duncan University, climbing into Brady's slim dorm bed, and wrapping myself around him, and staying there until I died or Matt returned, whichever came first.

Except I didn't know exactly how to get to DU; I didn't even know where Brady lived on campus. Even if I did find his dorm, with my luck, I'd probably discover one of his giggling floor mates bringing him breakfast and breasts in bed.

"Wipe the slate, Twigs," I said aloud.

Dad used to say that after a fight with Mom. "Wipe the slate, Eve. We're starting clean."

After I tried wiping the slate of my mind and the mascara off my face, I got out of the car and wiped "You suck" off the back window using an old napkin I dug out of my glove compartment. "Yep, I suck. Thanks for reminding me," I said to the world and to Jerkboy, wherever he might be. Even though he was a jerk, I hoped he was sleeping peacefully and not being hit by his dad.

Half an hour later, I reached the grand entrance of Hinkney Community College and took note of the wilting day lilies and purple irises that surrounded the sign. “Nice job, Mrs. Platton.” I pulled up to the guard gate where a guy sat munching a bagel. He wore jeans and a T-shirt and looked even shorter than me, but it was his nose that demanded attention. It was nearly as big as me, but the guy held his head high, nose proud.

“Morning!” Nose guy said, leaning in and checking out my car and me as if I might have drugs or guns sitting on the backseat of my Geo.

I tried not to look at the bagel stuck in his front teeth. “Hi. I’m starting today.”

“You’re old enough for college?”

I wanted to start off right here at Hinkney, so I nodded and only imagined ramming my fist into his nose instead of following through on the impulse.

“Yeah, okay. First day. Where’s your sticker?” He tapped the upper corner of my windshield, empty except for grime.

“Uh, I don’t have one yet. That’s why I came so early, to get it before classes start.”

“Oh, that’s too bad.” He frowned. “Twenty bucks.”

“What?”

“New campus rule. You have to pay a twenty-dollar fine that will be returned after you get your parking sticker.”

I looked over my steering wheel and for a split second considered slamming through the wooden security gate that blocked my way to the student parking lot. But the damage to my Geo would cost a lot more than twenty bucks. I had a bank debit card, plus every cent from my money jar, stuffed into my purse, ready to buy books. I needed this money.

“Look.” I smiled and tipped my head the way I’d seen Marlee do since the day she was born. It was that tip—among other things—that got boys to do whatever she asked. "I'm green—a newbie, and silly scared about starting college. I swear," I put one hand over my heart, "my first stop, even before buying books, is to buy a parking pass." I smiled and tipped some more and swished my hair around too, hoping it would catch his eye. It did.

"You couldn't decide?" the guy asked.

"Huh?"

"You couldn't decide, so you dyed your hair a lot of colors, right?"

I swallowed a few curse words and reached for my purse and a twenty. No way would I get out of this without paying. "I'll get this back, right? After I get my sticker?"

"Yep." The guard took the money from my hand before the reply left his lips.

A car pulled in behind me and honked, making me jump.

The guard's attention was diverted from me, and I forgot all about the money because Saturday night's murdered car filled my rearview mirror along with its driver. That baby-blue smashed classic, completely windowless, towered over the back of my Geo, as if it were about to eat it. Its engine idled, full of painful pings and complaining clanks.

"Christ! What happened, Professor Raymond?" Guard guy asked.

Professor? Helen lived a block behind where I sat right now. Convenient commute for a professor to get to work. He could walk, if he hadn't left his wife for a whore.

Guard guy had gotten out of the little booth and walked behind me, looking at the car.

"Rough weekend," Professor "Screwing Whores" Raymond said. "What are you doing, Coop?"

"Campus security needed some early help, that's all."

I slid down in my seat as far as possible. "Hey," I called out, keeping my head low.

"Just a minute," Guard guy said again.

Sweat popped out of my pores, although I felt frozen in place. I had to get away from Stuart Raymond and his car.

"Cut the crap, Coop, or I'll call security. What are you doing here?" Professor Raymond asked.

"Relax, Professor," Coop said. "I'm just here to meet the newly hatched." He made a *bawk-bawk* chicken sound and laughed. "I'm the first college guy some of these chicklets meet." He laughed at himself some more. "What happened to your arm?"

"Long story," Professor Raymond said. "Wait. Coop, you're not pulling that sticker scam again, are you?" Then I heard him open the door of his car and raise his voice. "You didn't give this guy money, did you?"

I pretended not to hear. If Stuart Raymond recognized me, he might have me arrested for auto theft and assault. He might think I helped Helen destroy his car. I heard his footsteps coming closer. Nerves made my legs shake and sweat ran down my face.

"Hey, you! You there!" Stuart Raymond couldn't let me alone, could he? His broken arm came into view at my side window, wrapped and slung across his chest. I leaned away from him, covering my face with my hand, as if that would disguise me somehow. "Did Coop here take money from you?"

"Just a joke, Professor," Coop said. He was back at my window now, edging in front of the professor, and he tossed a crumpled twenty in my lap.

"Asshole," I said.

"Freak," he replied quietly. Then loudly, "Welcome to Hinkney! Home of babe magnets like me."

"Cooper, cut it," Professor Raymond said. "You've got to watch out for scammers like this one." He leaned down and looked in at me.

I swooshed my hair over my face and grabbed my book bag. Then I buried my face inside it as if finding a secret chamber to hide the twenty.

"Thanks for the advice," I murmured.

Coop spoke up now, "Hey, I gave her a college memory, something to tell her grandkids someday." Then he pressed the magic button in the booth, the one that raised the wooden arm. Finally, I had my shot at freedom from Stuart Raymond.

I grabbed the gearshift and shoved my car into drive.

Stuart Raymond's good hand, the one not in a sling, still held on to my car door. "Listen, not all the guys here are like Coop, I promise you. If you need anything . . ." He stopped midsentence as recognition spread across his face. The friendly smile disappeared and horrified shock took over.

"What the—? You're . . . you're the one who—!" he blubbered and then began shouting, "My arm! My car!" He grabbed his chest with his free hand.

"An accident, I promise," I said. "Well, the arm part anyway. Sorry." I inched my car forward, praying I didn't run over his foot this time.

"You? You and Helen?" Stuart Raymond stuttered, panted, and staggered into Coop.

I gunned my Geo as much as it would gun. "Bye!"

For some reason, I felt the need to announce my departure. I didn't want to run into or over Stuart Raymond ever again, so I sped away, leaving him in my dust.

Chapter 15

Fugitive style, I kept looking over my shoulder to see if Stuart Raymond or Campus Security was after me. Certain dread told me that a posse of armed police would appear at any moment to handcuff me and send me down the river. Or string me up, old west style, on some hanging tree or shoot me down in the middle of the road. Nerves made my stomach lurch along with my driving.

Student parking lot A, the one nearest the main quad of Hinkney Community College, was still empty, but I kept driving, past lots B and C, and veered into lot M. What had happened to lot D and the rest wasn't clear, but M sat farthest from the guard gate, behind the Dumpsters on the ugly side of an ugly building. I parked next to those Dumpsters, hoping my car would blend in somehow, in case the one-armed man or the cops came searching for me. I wished I had Brady here to help protect me, or Helen's number so I could find out Stuart's teaching schedule and keep out of his way.

Locating my classes turned out to be nearly as difficult as finding Matt in Iraq. The school map must have been drawn for a different campus; none of the classroom numbers matched where I actually needed to go. After standing in an endless line for a parking pass, I ran, hair and spit flying, up and down corridors, into and out of elevators, and through numerous halls to find Comp 101. I skidded into the classroom just in time to hear the monotone instructions of a gray-haired professor.

"I do not tolerate tardiness. Arrive on time or don't bother to come. If you're sick, you'd still better be here if you want your notes. All notes must be handwritten. No laptops allowed during class unless otherwise instructed." Murmurs went around the room at that one. Not a problem for me; I didn't have one. The professor droned on, "No note-sharing is allowed. I will spot-check your notebooks. If note-copying is detected, you will be dismissed from this course."

I slumped in the first seat I could find and the professor stared at me, making sure I got every word. I was so happy to have actually found the room that I gave her a tiny smile.

"Name?" she asked.

I looked around to make sure this question was meant for me. The room was packed with the kind of students who looked like they'd rather be anywhere but here. We were all part of the Hinkney Community College losers.

"Name?" she repeated.

I cleared my throat. "Madeline Henry." I'd practiced writing my real name but hadn't spoken it much and it felt weird on my lips.

Professor Gray Hair pulled a thick computer printout off her desk, scanned it, and glanced back at me. "We already have a Madeline," she said, looking at the list. "I don't like duplicate student names. Let's use your middle name instead."

I looked around wondering who this Madeline was who'd gotten to class first. I smoothed out the crumpled campus map I still held in my hand. No way did I want to go by my middle name in college.

"No," I said to Professor Gray Hair. "I'm Madeline."

The way her lips disappeared into a tight line made people shuffle in their seats around me. She crossed her arms. My first college class and I'd messed up just by saying my name. I needed to get on the good side with this professor and made a quick decision.

I sighed, "Call me Twigs."

Nervous laughter erupted all over the room and Professor Gray Hair shot a harsh look at everyone.

She glared at me. "I have no Twigs in this class, no trees either, as far as I can see."

Someone stifled a giggle in the back of the room, probably the first Madeline.

Teachers at Titusburg High had known my nickname for years. Everyone knew me as "Twigs, Matt Henry's little sister."

"It's a nickname."

"Another thing I abhor is nicknames." Professor Gray Hair tapped her computer printout with her pen. She said this to the entire room of students, but it was pointed at me, no doubt about that. "This is college. You are adults, young adults, but adults, nevertheless."

And maybe it was lack of sleep, or the fact that Stuart Raymond lurked somewhere on this campus looking for me, but I had to say something.

"Ah, Mrs. . . . ? Professor?" I shuffled through my class schedule to see if I could find this lady's name.

Her head whipped toward me then, along with the hushed, surprised silence of every person in the lecture room.

"You're right. I am an adult. And I choose to be called Ms. Henry, so please mark that on your paper. Thanks."

I quickly looked away, shocked at myself. I grabbed my book bag and pulled out a notebook and opened it. My hands were shaking. The adrenaline of speaking out like that rushed through me, and reminded me of how I felt after Helen had killed Stuart's car. Freaked, but weirdly, a little happy, too.

Professor Gray Hair turned to her desk, grabbed a book, and slammed it on the podium. "The syllabus is now posted on the department website. It is your responsibility to print it, read it, do it. Unlike high school, you will not be coddled and stroked with reminders. As Madel . . . Tw . . ." She paused and shot me a bitch-in-command look. "As Ms. Henry stated, you are adults, so act as such."

My standoff ended in a whimper. The professor, whose name I still didn't know, kept holding up book after thick book, claiming we'd need all of these in order to pass her class. The high I'd felt withered as we filtered out of the classroom, now assigned a hundred pages of reading due in two days.

"Napoleonic complex?" I heard someone behind me say as we exited. I didn't know squat about Napoleon except that he'd been short and in charge of some French battle.

I turned to see a couple of girls and a guy talking, obviously about me. "Is there something you want to say to me?" I surprised myself. In high school, I would have just run and hid in the girls' bathroom until school let out or searched for Brady, whichever came first.

"Nah," said the guy, tugging at his sports jersey.

"Well." One of the girls pushed up a pair of ultraslim glasses and peered down at me. "I'm going to be a psychologist." The way she announced that, with such sureness, I had no doubt that she'd do exactly that. "I was saying," she continued, "that you might have a Napoleonic complex, the way you stood up to authority like that, considering your short stature. No offense."

I appreciated the truth from this girl, even if I didn't like what she was saying.

"None taken. And no, it's not some French mental thing. I'm as tall as I need to be." With that I walked away, like I knew where I was going.

"That's cool," I heard the guy say.

I'd have to get a book about this Napoleon guy, if I could ever find the college library.

"Bitchin' hair," the other girl said, loud enough for me to hear.

"Thanks." I shot a little wave at them, without looking back.

Napoleon and bitchin', that's me today. Better than the Twigs I had been this morning, afraid of everything. If Matt could walk off into the blur of Iraqi nothingness, what did I have to fear about Hinkney Community College?

That's when I rounded one of the several corners on my way to finding the food court/cafeteria before my next class. The Student Center appeared to be carnival central—banners flying, tables of hawkers begging you to join their particular campus club, counselor services "Always here if you feel down," and a massive line stretching out of the bookstore. A bunch of old tables, bolted-down chairs, and motley couches that had seen a lot of butt action over the years haphazardly filled the space, along with a gallery of vending machines featuring everything from soups to macaroni to double espressos. I could throw a few dollars into a machine and get preserved, packaged food, or stand in the line curling around the busy hall to get fried crap or pizza offered by HCC fast-food central.

I went with the packaged food, choosing a pack of Oreos, a box of Lipton just-add-scalding-water Soup, and a barely brown banana from another vending machine. Getting fruit from a machine, even bad fruit, was something I'd never done in Titusburg, so I'd moved up in the world.

Everyone at Hinkney must take lunch at the same time, or call it first-day madness, but I couldn't find an open seat anywhere in the entire place. Groups chatted, laughed, and munched on fried grease, reminding me of the high school lunchroom that Brady and I usually avoided by eating outside on nice days.

Book bag and soup in tow, I found a corner between the Mountaineers Club and Jews for Jesus tables, two groups hoping for new members. They basically ignored me as I walked by. Both groups took a quick glance at my hair before looking away, yelling for joiners with less colorful locks. I settled on the floor and leaned against a wall, slurping my instant soup.

I enjoyed people watching and imagined Brady doing the same at Duncan University, maybe eyeing the girls. I guess I couldn't blame him. I checked out the guys and the girls here, too. Each and every Hinkney co-ed I saw matched up with what I'd expected. We all looked like we should be operating a cash register for a loser named Dink. Guess my career was on the right track.

"Ow!" I screamed, as the wall behind me began moving, and pressing into me. I hadn't realized it was a door and it pushed hard against my entire backside. Hot mininoodles splashed on my arm. "Ow!" The Mountaineers and Jews for Jesus turned.

"Hey, you're blocking that door. You'd better move," one mountaineering dude advised. He jangled when he spoke with about a thousand of those rock-climbing clips all over his belt.

"Wait! Hold it!" I shouted at the door pushing me forward.

"What the fuck?" A voice came from behind the door, which I'd thought was a wall. "Stop blocking our door!"

"It looks like a wall!" I was up on my feet now and noticed a small latch instead of a knob on the door. Even the latch was beige, making the whole thing blend in with the walls. It had fully opened now, revealing a short hallway.

Suddenly, Coop appeared there, standing next to the guy yelling at me about blocking the door.

"Hey, watch out. She might drive over you." Coop grinned at me. His nose looked even bigger than it had in the early-morning light.

"You know this little girl?" the door guy said.

"I'm eighteen!" My voice was shrill then, and the noise level behind me dropped as everyone paused to look at me.

"She's the one who whacked Prof Raymond," Coop said.

I bent to pick up my stuff and run from the scene—something that had become a habit lately.

"Okay, " Coop was saying. "No harm, no chick. Get it? No foul. Fowl?"

I gave him one of my eat-crap looks.

"That won't work on me. I get those looks all the time."

The other guy had moved somewhere down the hall behind the hidden entrance and returned with a poster, which he began taping to the outside of the open door.

I read the hand-drawn poster to myself. WHNK RADIONEERS CLUB. BECOME THE VOICES OF TOMORROW TODAY! Drawings of phallic-shaped microphones filled each corner of the sign.

Coop watched me reading. “You want?”

“Want?”

“To join. WHNK.” He pronounced it like *wink* and gave me a big wink just to make sure I got it.

“No,” I said with a half-laugh. “Radioneers? How lame is that?”

“Not as lame as the mountaineers, musketeers, or Mouseketeers, but you’re about the size of a mouse, so maybe you’d prefer that club.”

“Whoa, Coop. You’re asking for it,” the other guy laughed.

“I’m taller than you, or close to it,” I said. “And he’s right, you’re asking for it.” Why I responded to this jerk, I couldn’t say, but life had been full of surprises lately.

Coop grinned at me and then shouted, getting his share of desired attention from the crowd, “Baby, if you look like me, you have to ask for it, because no one’s going to offer!”

One of the Jews for Jesus said, “Christ, Coop. Shut your fucking hole.”

I began laughing at that—at Coop, at everything—the same way I’d laughed at Helen’s that night after I puked. I’d have to tell her all about this. She’d love it. I backed away from Coop and the radio club door.

“Going so soon?” Coop asked.

“Got a class to find.”

“I suggest Jesus and a mountain guide to help your search,” Coop called out.

That made me laugh again. Such silly, stupid stuff this guy kept saying, but I needed to giggle. It felt good after a weekend of bad.

I flipped my hair over my shoulder, super girly all of a sudden, and pranced away. Coop had to have the last word, though. “Don’t join the TV club. Your color hair is custom-made for radio.”

Chapter 16

At the end of the day, I lugged a mountain of books that outweighed me back to my car by the Dumpster. My plan to buy only used books had been killed by those professors who listed new and improved books on their syllabi. *Must Reads*, they all had written on the lists in the bookstore. I kept twenty bucks to get me through the week and wrote a check to pay the balance of the books; it would bounce if they cashed it before I got paid on Friday. I'd fudged the date on the check and luckily the bookstore clerk hadn't noticed.

A folded crisp white piece of paper fluttered under my Geo's wiper blade. "Uh oh," I said to the world, assuming I'd gotten a ticket for lack of a parking sticker, which I now had. But instead, this was a note in a scrawl tough to decipher, but the name at the bottom jumped out at me: *S. Raymond*.

I scanned the parking lot, expecting to see Stuart Raymond perched somewhere, one arm in a sling and the other holding a gun trained on my head. The note was simple:

> **I don't know who you are. I could have you jailed for assault, but I won't. Obviously you know my wife, though I've never seen you before. Please let us handle our marriage dispute privately or I will notify the police.**

Pissed off, sure, and threatening, but Stuart Raymond was letting me off. Somehow that seemed even more disturbing.

It had been dark on Saturday night, but it wasn't hard to find Helen's house on the road behind the college. When I drove up, she stood in her front yard, watering the pink flowers surrounding the pink mailbox. Sly began his maniacal barking as I slowed down in front of the house. Helen didn't recognize my car and her gaze passed over my Geo, until she saw me.

"Twigs!" she shouted and threw down the hose, holding out her arms as if she expected me to run right into them.

That greeting made me smile. No one, not even Brady, ever seemed that happy to see me. When I parked and got out, Helen gave me a big hug, like a long-lost relative.

"That car is a bad color for you," Helen said. "It doesn't match your skin tone."

Unless I were a Martian, the Geo wouldn't match any skin tone.

"I didn't choose it for the color. It had been wrecked and Matt—my brother—rebuilt it with used parts. So, it came cheap."

"I like a good deal, too, but that car needs a dye job." Helen's reference to hair dye made us both laugh. Sly wagged his tail and leaned against my leg, in on the joke, too.

"You kept popping into my head all day," Helen said. "You're such a wild thing! You made me brave Saturday night."

Somehow I remembered it the other way around—that she made me do illegal things, like break a stranger's arm and take his car. Maybe I'd just been a repressed "wild thing" all these years and never realized it until I met Helen.

"Hey, you seem like you're doing okay today."

"You can't listen to Bob Marley all day and stay in a bad mood." Helen leaned in with a sly smile. "If only we could smoke some you-know-what like Marley. That would make those seniors forget their aches and pains. Not that I've ever partaken."

Seniors? Marley. Smoking? "Helen, what are you talking about?"

"Oh, sorry, I forgot that we just met, Twigs. I'm the entertainment coordinator at the Hinkney Senior Center. It was Jamaican Day today—all my idea, and they loved it. Except for that spicy Jerk chicken. Not good for elderly digestion."

Helen entertaining a bunch of old people was easy to imagine. She wore a tight pink-and-purple tie-dyed T-shirt. The neck had been cut low enough to parade her cleavage. I bet the men at the senior center loved that—kept their old hearts pumping.

I wanted to talk to Helen about my own heart-pumping day. "I started college today," I blurted out. "Right over there." I pointed toward the Hinkney campus. You could see the back of the prison-gray main building through the trees and yards across from Helen's house.

Helen turned away from me then, motioning Sly to come over, and she bent down to nuzzle her dog. "I'm not talking or thinking about that man today, Twigs." Though Helen looked at Sly, I heard every word. "Marley and Jamaica made me happy today, and I want to stay happy while I can."

I swallowed, not sure what to say. Instead, I pulled out the note, no longer crisp, from my pocket and gave it to Helen. She slowly unfolded the paper and read it before turning to me. The redness of her face popped against the pink-and-purple shirt, and I thought she might explode with a scream, but the color faded and she suddenly grinned.

"He's afraid of us," Helen said. "We've got Stu just where we want him."

I didn't want Stu anywhere, and truth be known, I felt more than a little afraid of him.

"I nearly lost it when I saw him this morning. Why didn't you tell me he worked there?" I rushed on, tired of keeping it all in. "I mean, I nearly hit him again. What do I do if I see him?"

"That's easy," Helen whispered, her lips barely moving. "You ask him if that whore will still want him after my divorce lawyer is done and he's left with zip."

Helen's Marley-happy high had turned vengeful, but at least she talked divorce now and not murder.

"Helen." I didn't want to make her mad, but I had to be clear on this. "We took his car. We . . . you destroyed it."

Helen picked up the hose and held it out to give Sly a drink. "That vintage Caddy is in my name, too, Twigs. I ruined my half of the car, the outside." Helen's grin spread wider than before. "The inside is still perfect. That's his half."

My cell began its nonstop beep and I pulled it out of my pocket. I had hoped to hear from Mom or Marlee all day, but there'd been no calls whenever I checked. A number I didn't recognize appeared and I expected a telemarketer selling discount chimney cleaning, or something else I doubted I would ever need in a million lifetimes.

"Excuse me, Helen."

She walked behind the bushes in front of her house and turned off the faucet and began rolling up the hose. Sly sniffed the grass around my feet, probably smelling Hinkney Community College. I hoped he didn't decide to use me as a pee spot.

"Hello," I said into my cell.

Pat came out of her house next door and waved at me. "Hey, Twigs." Another nice greeting. At the same time, someone on the phone said, "Twigs" in my ear.

I'd raised my hand, in the start of a wave to Pat, when I heard his voice.

My mouth opened and shut a few times, fish-style, trying to form the word, the question.

I finally croaked it out, "Dad?"

"Twigs," he said.

The man on the phone still hadn't confirmed that it was who I thought it was. It could have been Tower of Isaac or even Deaf Lou, miraculously speaking after a life of muteness. Dad had been mute for over two years and although I thought I remembered his voice, the brain forgets fast, even those you love.

"Dad? Is that you?"

"It's Matt." Confusion clouded my mind. "Matt? Matt! Where are you?" Sly, upset at my shouting, began to bark.

"No, Twigs, listen now," the caller, Dad, spoke again. "They've found Matt."

Helen's shirt filled my view, pink-and-purple psychedelic tie-dye swirling before me. It's the last thing I remember seeing before I fell on the wet grass, losing it just as I'd done early that morning at Mr. Platton's.

Chapter 17

I wanted to drown and end it all—why go on? Cold water filled my nose, my mouth, my eyes and ears, and Matt's face floated near mine. I reached out in the darkness and pulled him closer. Maggots crawled out of his mouth that had always smiled so easily. I began screaming at the bloated, festering holes where his bright eyes had been.

"Twigs! Twigs!" Helen and Pat called my name and my eyes fluttered open.

"Stop the hose, Pat!" Helen yelled. "She's coming to."

Helen's face was inches away from mine. "Can you hear me?"

"Yes," I said, wiping away water and shaking my head like a wet dog. Then I remembered what had caused me to black out and I bawled, "Matt. Matt. They found Matt." I thrashed and writhed in the grass, a worm eager to be squashed and forgotten.

"Honey, calm down. Matt's her brother, Pat." Helen had heard the story over piña coladas and breakfast at IHOP. "The one in Iraq?"

I shook my head yes and tears fell, covering my wet face.

"Now, just because they found him doesn't mean it's the news you think it is." Pat was rubbing my shoulder. "Chris's cousin's boyfriend's daughter got separated from her unit on a transport changeover and after hiding a few scary hours in a deserted tank, she was rescued. She was a little dehydrated, but fine."

"See, Twigs," Helen said. "Pat's right. What exactly did your dad say?"

I shook a little, taking in what Pat had just said. "I-I'm not sure." I paused, going over the phone call in my head. Mom and Deaf Lou had gone to see Dad. Mr. Platton had told me that. Had he really called me? "Where's my phone?"

I jumped up from the ground, frantically searching the grass. Then I saw Sly, crouched by the mailbox, chewing on something shiny.

"Sly!" I stumbled, still wobbly, and fell. I half-crawled over to him, with Helen and Pat behind me. "Sly! Give me that!" I grabbed my dented, slobbered-on phone from the dog's mouth.

"Bad dog!" Helen said.

"Does it still work?" Pat asked.

I jabbed at my phone and water poured from the hole where the charger wire connected. "Ahhh! No! No! No!" I stamped my feet, in full tantrum but scared more than mad. "My brother's dead—or not dead. Matt's dead or something, and they found him. I have to know what's going on!"

If flailing is ever added to the Olympics as a new sport, I'd win gold for the show I put on in Helen's yard. Neighbors coming home from work got quite an eyeful from the hysterical short girl in front of the Raymond house.

During my tantrum extravaganza, Helen had grabbed her phone from the house.

"What's your home number, Twigs?" she asked. She and Pat both had to ask a few times before I heard them. Pat lived up to her name and patted my back now, as if burping a baby, but it helped me focus on what they were asking.

I took a deep breath and reached for Helen's pink phone and called Mom.

After four rings, her voice asked me to leave a message. "Fucking voice-mail!" I screeched.

Helen and Pat's eyes widened, but they didn't say anything. If ever there was a time to curse, my life called for it now.

After Mom's interminable "Leave me your vitals" message stopped, I spoke, "Mom. It's me. Dad, or I guess it was Dad, called and said they found Matt. My cell is busted. I'm on my way home now. Please, please be there or come home and let me know what's going on."

I tossed Helen her phone and was in my Geo in seconds.

"I'm coming with you," Helen called out. "You're in no state to drive."

"She's right," Pat agreed.

Sly let out a whimper as if adding his opinion to the mix.

I grabbed the steering wheel and spun a U-turn in the road in front of Helen's house before her hand reached the door handle.

"Twigs!" Helen yelled in surprise as I pulled away and Sly began barking.

"Let her go," Pat shouted at Helen.

I heard all of this through my open window, but I couldn't wait, not even to apologize for running away like that. Getting home for news of Matt was too important, and it was something I had to do on my own.

Pressing the gas pedal as hard as I could, I pushed the Geo until it shook, like lime Jell-O on wheels. Wind whipped through the windows and my hair kept flapping enough to soak the tears that wouldn't stop coming. More than a few angry locals yelled and honked as I ignored the No Passing sign and raced ahead on the county road back to Titusburg.

Cars filled our street, parked everywhere, as I inched my way up the block. There was Mr. Bell's truck, Matt's former boss, and a big SUV that I recognized as Coach Mason's from high school. Matt had been his favorite athlete, excelling in almost anything the coach made him try.

There was no place to park, and I realized I had arrived late to this bad-news party. Mr. Platton's driveway was full, too, and people spilled out of our house onto our yard and into his. I stopped in the middle of the road, jumped out of my car, engine still running, and ran up to a group of people standing on the lawn.

I screamed at them, "Matt? What's happened to Matt?"

One of the women in the group looked at me and then at the others and began signing. Of all the people filling our yard, I'd chosen deaf ones to get my news flash. These had to be teachers from the school where Mom worked, friends of hers and probably of Deaf Lou.

The woman opened her mouth and began speaking slowly, trying to enunciate every sound, "Fund Mut."

I'm sure I offended her with my "What the hell did you say?" look, but "Fund Mut" wouldn't cut it for me.

Marlee and Tower of Isaac came out of the front door and I rushed at them. "What's happened? Marlee, tell me what's happened."

"They found Matt." A red I've-been-crying look dulled her bright blue eyes.

The deaf group signed at me, and the woman repeated, "Fund Mut."

Mr. Platton came out of my house then, and it confused me to see him there instead of in his chair on his own porch.

"Hey, Twigs!" He sounded chipper, which is the perfect word for Mr. Platton. "How was the first day of college life?"

"What?" I asked, more confusion setting in.

"Did you see your dad?" Mr. Platton continued. "He was out here before."

"He looked good, didn't he?" Marlee said. "I remembered him being taller, but he looked short next to Isaac."

"Somebody, please!" I shouted. "Somebody tell me what the fuck is going on?"

My screech got everyone's attention. A few more people I recognized as Matt's football buddies came out of the house and stared at me. I could see Mom sitting in the chair in the living room with Deaf Lou beside her, and they both looked out at me as if I'd ruined the party. The deaf group even stopped signing for a moment, obviously aware of the way I threw my arms in the air demanding answers.

"Lord forgive her," Tower of Isaac said, looking up to the sky where the Lord lived for him.

"Amen," Marlee said, like someone had pulled a string on her back and that's what this doll could say.

"Twigs." Mr. Platton said, "it's okay."

I think he'd said that to me once before today, or Helen had, but whoever had said it had lied. Nothing was okay today and nothing had been okay in my life since Dad left. I almost spit that fact into Mr. Platton's face, but he finally told me the truth.

"Twigs, Matt's in a military hospital in Khartoum." Mr. Platton was at my side now, with his hand firmly warming my shoulder. "He's alive but injured."

"Didn't Dad tell you?" Marlee asked. "He said he was going to call you."

If there's a physical way to feel your heart in your throat, then that's what happened to me. I was still confused, but I knew the one thing I really needed to know. Matt lived. He breathed. My brother still existed somewhere on this planet.

Mr. Platton or someone led me to the porch steps, and I sat there with Marlee and Tower of Isaac beside me. I felt mute, like most of the deaf group, and my ears had closed up to every sound, except the humming I heard in my head. Matt's humming. Whenever he worked on a car, you could hear his concentration through his humming. Always something patriotic like "America the Beautiful" or "This Land Is Your Land." Matt had rebuilt my Geo humming the national anthem over and over. "Stop humming that damn song!" Mom had yelled at him more than once.

"Dad looked great, didn't he?" Marlee's voice cut through the humming that filled my head.

"He did look fit," Mr. Platton said, standing nearby. It was strange to see him standing. Briefly, I wondered if his body missed his familiar chair.

"You saw Dad? Wait—" I veered backward in my thoughts. "What happened to Matt? What's his injury?"

"Twigs," I heard my name. We all looked out to the road, where my car still puttered in park, blocking the road and wasting gas.

"Who's that?" Mr. Platton asked.

"Hey there, Mrs. Raymond." Tower of Isaac and Marlee were up off the porch and running out to the pink VW idling in the road behind my car.

"Oh good, I found you!" Helen said. "That snippy boss of yours gave me your address."

"Dink?" I asked, though I knew who she meant. Helen at my house only added to the chaos of my day. Dad was here, but I couldn't seem to move my legs to go inside and see him.

"Follow me!" Mr. Platton said to Helen. "Twigs," he called back, "I'm going to move your car."

Everyone and everything moved and pulsed around and inside me. The deaf signers, the grass and trees blowing in the late summer breeze, and my brain. I watched Mr. Platton and Helen park the cars on his perfect grass, beside his full driveway. They stood beside her pink car talking like old friends even though they'd just met. They were the kind of people who could do that.

Marlee and Tower of Isaac held hands and stood close to each other talking about the Lord or cheerleading or who knows what and slowly made their way back to me.

I gulped in a breath of courage. "I can't believe he's here."

"No, Twigs." Marlee pushed her bare feet with shimmering blue toenails into the grass. "Matt's still in Iraq in a hospital."

Annoyed, my older-sister-than-you-and-you're-stupid attitude kicked in. "I know that, Marlee. I meant Dad. I can't believe Dad is here."

Marlee kicked some grass at me. “He’s not. He had to go.”

“What?” My voice peaked again, shrill enough to get Mr. Platton and Helen to look over. “After two years of jacking us over, he’s gone again?”

Marlee and Tower of Isaac exchanged glances and I could tell she was keeping something from me.

“What, Marlee?” I jumped up and jabbed a finger into my younger, but taller, sister’s face, threatening her. “What aren’t you saying?” Tower of Isaac backed off a little, probably afraid I’d climb up into his face if he didn’t stay out of this.

“Twigs, leave her alone.” Mom stood in the doorway. She somehow managed to look relieved and beautiful, even with circles of mascara filling the bags under her eyes.

“Mom, why did Dad leave?” I did as instructed, leaving Marlee, and ran up onto the porch next to her.

“He had to go, Twigs. There’s a lot you need to know, but it’s up to him to tell you.”

“What do you mean, he had to go?”

“Before you got here,” Mom said, making sure I got the point. “The whole thing about Matt was tough for him; he couldn’t handle you today.”

“Handle me?” I was shaking my head, trying to make sense of any of this.

“Handle seeing you.” Mom reached for my hand, but I pulled away. A memory popped into mind of her doing the same to me once when I’d been about five and had jelly on my fingers.

“I know you don’t understand, Twigs.” Mom let out a long sigh. “He doesn’t want to see you.”

Chapter 18

I felt too spent to scream, too drained to think, and too empty to react, so I did nothing. Avoiding everyone in my face, yard, and house, I retreated to my room and cowered there in self-loathing. If my own father didn't want to see me, why would anyone else? I even avoided Helen. I could hear her clearly, as though her voice knew the way down the hall and under my closed door. She had everyone laughing—Mr. Platton, Mom, Coach Mason—the deaf group included, with stories about the Senior Center.

"It's more like a harem center, in dire need of a Viagra injection," Helen said. "Some of those old men—bless their hearts—don't even realize that they've got a gaggle of widows after them."

Helen came into my room a few times. "Twigs check," she'd announce, but I ignored her and pretended to be asleep under a mound of bedding and pillows. She hesitated each time, smart enough to know I was faking.

"Oh, Gary Cooper," Helen remarked about my *High Noon* poster. "He's one of those dead movie stars you forget about, don't you?"

She waited for me to perk up and answer, but I let out an equally fake snore, hoping she would leave. She did.

During the final Twigs check of the night, Helen came in and said, "It's been a tough few days, huh? Parents can be as bad as cheating husbands. From what I know of yours, even worse sometimes . . ." She paused and let out a big sigh.

I did the same from under my comforter.

"I'll see you soon, Twigs." Helen gave my legs a pat through the covers before leaving me to my agony.

No matter how hard I tried to focus on thinking about nothing or Matt, or Brady—anything—my mind couldn't let go of the way

I'd been dissed by my father. He'd been e-mailing Matt in Iraq, had appeared at our house, and had talked to Marlee and everyone else in the world, it seemed, except me. It kept my mind busy all night.

* * *

I missed school the next day. Not hard to do when you wake up at 11:00 for an 8:00 class.

"Twigs!" Marlee pounded on my door and screeched at me. "Mr. Platton said Dink called his house looking for you. Said you didn't answer your cell."

I remembered my phone in Helen's yard and would bet it had become Sly's favorite chew toy by now.

"Crap." I'd managed to miss my first poli sci class and be late to work. Good way to start the day.

On my way out I passed Marlee, lounging on the couch and reading a book titled *Tanned Love* that I'm sure wasn't on the school summer-reading list. "Any more news on Matt?"

"I would've told you if there was," Marlee said, without looking at me.

"Yeah, everyone has been great about keeping me in the loop on family news."

Marlee ignored my comment and I rushed out for a grand day of minimum-wage work. If stocking tampons or ringing up Ex-Lax and appetite suppressants for the anorexics and overweight of Titusburg was considered a talent, then I'm the local expert.

Dink hounded me nonstop about being late. "We discussed this when you were hired." His greasy mustache wiggled whenever he scolded me, which happened a lot. "Twigs," he said, "this job could be a career starter for you, if you decide to open your own business someday."

Career starter? This is one of those statements that I'd save up to laugh over with Brady when I saw him.

"Dink—" I lowered my head in an appropriate guilt-ridden style—"you know how crazy things were yesterday, with Matt and all. And it's the first week of school. I still have to get used to the drive back and forth to Hinkney."

Dink didn't need to know I'd come straight from bed. He'd set up my Tuesday and Thursday schedule based on one morning class; the rest of my classes were on Mondays, Wednesdays, and Fridays. I hoped to pick up another job, maybe on campus or at a diner on Sundays, if possible. The way things looked, my prime study time would be while the rest of the world slept.

Dink smoothed his mustache and glanced up at the flashing red clock above the store's entrance. He cleared his throat. "Matt's a survivor."

He had graduated from Titusburg High a year ahead of Matt. While Matt had been everybody's darling there, Dink had been Nerd Supreme and still held that title.

Dink's eyes shifted, pausing for a moment on the orange stripe of hair draped over my shoulder. "Did they let you know how bad he's hurt?"

I shook my head. Dink wouldn't dare say an unkind word about Matt to my face, but it wasn't hard to miss his jealousy.

"Back to work, now, Twigs. Just be on time from here on out."

"Um, Dink?" It wasn't the perfect moment to ask, but I needed a day off to see Brady. "Remember, I told you about a month ago that I'd need this coming Saturday off?"

Dink raised his head a bit, so he had to look down his nose at me even more than usual. "We'll have to talk about that later in the week, Twigs. With people off for Labor Day weekend, the store may be busier than usual."

I had already worked on July 4th, and it had been quite clear that Uptown Pharmacy was not the place people spent their free time on a national holiday.

"Okay, it's just that I told you about this a while ago."

My voice faltered because Dink had already strutted off toward the back of the store. I'd have to be a nag about this, but seeing Brady was important, long trip or not. It might be our only chance until Thanksgiving break and I needed some TLC and a few days away from my so-called family.

I crouched down and shoved giant boxes of Stay Fresh Maxi Pads in the small space at the bottom of the shelf, an easy task and one that allowed my mind to wander. I realized that Brady had never called me last night. Or if he had, the message had been slobbered by Sly. With the crowd in the house, I'd never checked e-mail, so I hoped to find a ton of messages waiting at home.

"Boo!" Voices from behind, right in my ear, startled me.

I fell backward and sprawled on the floor, bumping over the 3-D cardboard cutout of a perky model jumping with glee while holding a box of pads.

"Gotcha!" they laughed.

I looked up at Jerkboy and Bobblehead. Jerkboy AKA Brian from IHOP spit on the floor just missing my leg. Bobblehead tried to do the same, but missed and dripped slobber on his own sleeve.

"Thanks for these," Jerkboy said. He held out a pack of Winston cigarettes, as if offering me one, and then tucked the pack into his back pocket.

"Hey! Security!" I yelled, hoping Dink would lope into view.

The boys ran and I stumbled over the cardboard lady, bending her head, and rushed after the escaping thieves. We all rushed past Dink, who should have been at the register, but was standing in Aisle 4 with an open can of Pringles and crumbs filling his mustache.

"Dink! Grab 'em!"

"What the—?" Dink said but remained stuck in place, except for his hand grasping another chip.

A woman was entering the store and I watched her move aside to let the boys zoom by.

"Stop them!" I yelled.

"But, but—" she stammered and I recognized her as I ran past.

"Twigs?" Mrs. Platton asked, as if expecting an explanation, but I had already sped out of the store.

I raced one direction, only to turn back, realizing the boys hadn't run this way. I turned around and bumped into a young woman with a baby stroller.

"Ow! Watch it!" the woman yelled and her baby began screaming in that I'd-just-gone-to-sleep-and-now-you've-woken-me way.

"Oh, sorry."

I scanned the area, looking around the town square, which, besides the two-room courthouse and police station combo, held only the bank and the Titusburg Bar and Grill. Beyond the usual elderly planted on benches on the town green and a few dog walkers, there weren't any kids around. Jerkboy and Bobblehead had disappeared.

Dink's mustache wiggled in high gear as I re-entered the store. Mrs. Platton gave me a little wave. She had changed somehow; I realized it was the short, stylish cut and the blond dye job covering her usual white curls. Where Helen's dye job made her look clownish, this honey blond worked for Mrs. Platton. She appeared twenty years younger.

"Why aren't those boys in school?" she asked.

I shrugged. "Not sure. Still on summer break, I guess." I turned to Dink. "Those are the same boys who were in here on Friday. We need to tell the police."

Dink's shoulders jiggled up and down with tension. He wasn't a favorite of the Titusburg police. One of the officers had been hanging out reading magazines one day and Dink all but accused him of loitering, "Not much crime today, huh?" Word must have gotten around because every Titusburg cop—all four of them—would repeat the phrase whenever they saw Dink.

"They'll come if Mr. Franks calls," I said.

"Speaking of Mr. Franks . . . my prescription." Mrs. Platton gave a little laugh and headed toward the pharmacy.

Dink held the Pringles can again, as if he'd pulled it out of the air. He chewed and said, "I can handle these kids. No need to involve the law."

The law? "Uh, Dink, I should've told you this, but the taller one, he's serious. I don't trust him. He flipped off the customers on Saturday when you were gone and kind of threatened me."

Dink polished off the Pringles and crushed the empty can as flat as he could before plunking it in the trash bin behind the register. He smiled. "Boys do that sort of dumb stuff. Your brother was a bit of a hellion, too, as I remember."

I blinked a few times, anger rising in my throat at Dink's comment. My hellion brother was lying in an army medical tent somewhere with who knew what kind of injury. Dink turned and walked toward the back of the store. I tugged at my smock ties, planning to fling it and my job away.

The crackling of the loud speaker filled the store and my head, along with Mr. Franks's voice, "Dink, Twigs. I'm at lunch."

I looked at the clock. 12:00.

Mrs. Platton appeared at the register, ready to pay for her prescription. My fingers still grasped at the tangled, thin ties on the back of my smock.

"Is everything all right, Twigs?" She seemed truly concerned. I had always liked her. She never nosed into your business like her husband.

I let my fingers drop and smoothed down my smock. "Uh, yeah." My anger at Dink wasn't worth losing this job, until I'd found another one first.

I took the white paper bag from her and rang up the amount on her medicine.

"So, how's your mom doing?"

"Uh, okay I guess since they found Matt. We'll all be better when we know how bad he's hurt."

Mrs. Platton's eyes widened. "Matt's hurt?"

This confused me. Mr. Platton knew everything and surely he would've told his wife, along with the entire neighborhood, everything about Matt. Then I remembered. "Oh, sorry, Mrs. Platton, I forgot. You've been away antiquing, right?"

Mrs. Platton's mouth dropped open and she didn't say anything. Her previous healthy, tanned face had drained of color.

"Mrs. Platton, are you okay?"

"Mrs. Platton?" she repeated. "Twigs, I haven't been Mrs. Platton for over a year now."

"What?" Somehow it all clicked in my head—Mr. Platton sitting on his porch morning to night and always alone. But I asked anyway. "You weren't away with your sister at an antique fair?"

"No, Twigs." Mrs. Platton swallowed and her hands flew up to her face. "Is that what Bob has been saying?"

I'd never known Mr. Platton's first name, but it made sense that he'd be a Bob. I nodded.

Mrs. Platton, or whoever she was now, pulled at the collar on her shirt. "We're still friends, but I left over a year ago and went back to my maiden name. I just had to do that." Mrs. Platton pulled a business card out of her purse and handed it to me.

I read the tiny print, surrounded with curlicues and ink flowers. Margaret Newlan. Ace Gardening Co-op, along with a phone number and address in Hinkney.

"I'm running a gardening center with my daughter-in-law and some friends. It's a lot of work but I love it," Mrs. Platton-now-Newlan said. "You might not understand this, but I had lost interest in life and needed . . . well, I needed something else." She held my gaze, willing me not to say anything about her life choice.

If it's possible to shrink like Alice in Wonderland, I felt myself getting smaller. At least, that's what I wanted—to shrink and disappear. It was impossible to separate the neighbor who constantly invaded my life from his porch and this Bob person whose wife of umpteen years had dumped him. But a lot of impossibles had been filling my life the past few days.

"Well," Mrs. Platton-now-Newlan said, "I've got to be getting back. I had to renew a prescription. My doctor's still here in Titusburg." She gave her bag a playful shake, making the pills rattle.

"Oh." I tried to smile, and then remembered Mr. Platton mentioning his wife's gardening. Margaret Platton-now-Newlan replaced her new-name credit card in her wallet. "Um, did you plant the flowers around the Hinkney College entrance?"

She grinned. "Yes, I did. Well, our co-op did, but I chose the flowers we planted."

I almost told her how pitiful they looked, but she was obviously proud of that wilting bunch of weeds. Instead, I said, "They spruce up the sign."

"Why, thank you! Well, I've got to run. I hope Matt's okay. Good to see you and tell your mom hi for me."

"Okay."

Margaret Platton-now-Newlan headed out of the store and I watched her walk down the sidewalk. She had that happy bounce in her step—the one always mentioned in TV ads for drugs fighting depression.

I chewed my lip, thinking about Mr. Platton, something I usually avoided like the plague. Maybe he spent so much time on his porch and in everyone's business because his house felt empty without his wife. Did he dream of her returning home the way I always imagined Dad doing?

Chapter 19

At midnight on Wednesday, after my second full day at Hinkney Community College for Losers and a lousy evening toiling for Dink, I practically hugged our computer when I got online with Brady for a late night catch-up chat. We'd both been shocked by the amount of homework thrown at us the first few days of Higher Ed, and we each tried to top the other.

Brady wrote first: *I miss you, but I've got to read 3,000 pages by tomorrow.*

I replied: *Must write eighteen essays and translate a book of Mandarin.*

Twigs, Lee speaks ten languages, at least. He can help when you visit on Friday.

I'm using my real name at HCC, Madeline. It's the grownup me. You like?

Madeline??? Maybe for HCC, but you'll always be my Twigs.

Way to make me melt, Brady. How am I going to study now?

Wait until you see me this weekend.

I want to come, Brade. You know I do. Much depends on Matt's situation. Army hasn't spilled about his condition yet.

I get it, but what about my condition without you?

I bet all those college hotties are already chasing you.

I'm too busy studying to notice anyone else.

We e-mailed back and forth until Mom came in, leaving Deaf Lou snoring in her bedroom. It's amazing how loud a deaf man can be when sleeping.

When I got home after work earlier, Deaf Lou had been sitting on our couch, reading the paper. He'd given me a wave and signed, "How's it hangin'?"

I had no clue how to respond to that in words, much less in sign language, so I just waved. A couple of pizza boxes littered the dining-room table. I'd been surprised to find a few cold slices of black olive, with a sticky note on one box—*For Twigs*—in what I guessed was Deaf Lou's handwriting.

I'd starting typing what I planned to do to Brade when I saw him next when Mom swooped in, bumping my chair.

"I'm on the computer, Mom."

"I can see that, Twigs. I need to check my e-mail. It's morning there."

There meant wherever Matt existed. Good morning, Iraq.

"Just a sec." I'd been hoping for some late-night hot e-mail chatter with Brade, but I wanted to know about Matt, too. I typed a quick farewell.

Mom's here. Must go. Miss you. All of you. Love, me.

My mother hovered close, waiting for me to finish. She rested one of her hands on my shoulder. It surprised me—the weight and warmth of this hand—one that hadn't given me a hug in longer than I could remember.

"Ah, that's sweet," Mom said, reading my e-mail to Brady before I clicked SEND. "Save a little of that love, Twigs, or a man will take it all. I speak from experience."

Mom squeezed my shoulder and she didn't seem sarcastic, but I couldn't be sure. I decided to let it go. Moving aside so Mom could sit at the computer, I couldn't help but smell Deaf Lou on her. The guy seemed okay, but I swear, his cologne could kill flies. I swallowed back a gag and grabbed my pile of books from the dining-room table.

"You can stay," Mom said. "I'm not going to be long."

I hesitated, and then dumped my heavy stack back on the table and sat down to read, or rather scan, a few of the two hundred pages of English Lit that Professor Hard-Ass had assigned. Mom muttered as she typed e-mails to the army, demanding news. It was difficult to concentrate, much less study, since being alone with her was a rarity.

"Just kill all our boys," she said, while reading the army's daily casualty list. "Damn stupid war."

It's one thing we agreed about. "Yeah."

Mom's head jerked toward me. I'd interrupted her military misery trip. She blinked a few times and then looked back at the computer screen.

"How's the studying?"

Was she actually concerned about my schoolwork? I tapped my fingers on the pages in my book. "Isn't the hospital supposed to contact you?"

Mom didn't turn to me but said, "They have hundreds of patients and busy doctors. I'm trying to find my needle in the dirt stack over there."

I let out a little laugh at her half joke. "Isn't it weird that they haven't called us yet or e-mailed?"

"Weird?" Mom kept scrolling through the injured list, searching for Matt's name.

"I mean, maybe Matt told them not to call. He walked off his post for a reason, right? Maybe he's avoiding us."

A pencil flew past my ear, and in the time it took me to realize she'd thrown it at me, my mother was up from the computer and towering over me at the table. I backed away, as much as possible, hunching down in the chair.

Mom's eyes had become hard and black, in that way she'd get when she was mad at Dad for being drunk. I flinched when her hands clenched the sides of my chair and trapped me in place. Did she want to hit me?

"You don't know anything about this, Twigs." Her stale night breath mixed with Deaf Lou's cologne made me wince. "You just don't know."

"You're right, Mom," I mouthed off, afraid and angry with her for so many things. "You and Dad hide a lot, don't you?"

Mom let out a weird laugh. "Dad?" She pushed away and my chair wobbled, but I caught myself before crashing over. "That's funny, Twigs, considering he's the one who left."

I jumped up, ranting now, only half-aware of Marlee with her sleepy face entering the room. Deaf Lou must have felt the vibrations of my screams or woke up to find Mom gone because he appeared in his baggy boxers, signing something like, "What's wrong?"

Words tumbled out of my mouth—ugly and loud—deafening us all. Such rage erupted at this woman, my father, the world. Even Deaf Lou could see my hate.

"Why, Mom? Why did he leave? I found that note in your panty drawer, tucked in your thong collection." Marlee let out a nervous half giggle and I continued, "Dad loved you, but something happened for him to leave like he did. It must have. Did you buy the wrong beer? Scorch one of his work shirts? Fuck too many men that day? What?" I gulped in a breath to finish off my rant. "What, Mom? What made Dad walk out on us?"

I stopped for a breath, pulled back my shoulders, and geared up to continue my outburst. Adrenaline spurred on my megarage-volcano, and if I hadn't been so mad, it might have felt good. Mom signed something fast to Deaf Lou, which I couldn't decipher.

Confused, Marlee ran to our mother, pulling at her robe. "What's she talking about, Mom?"

My little sister stood tousled and gorgeous in her oversize Titusburg football jersey, sporting Tower of Isaac's number. Maybe Mr. High

School Football Star had taken her virginity. Marlee appeared in that clichéd sort of way—like a woman in love.

"Marlee, did you know Mom had talked to Dad?" I demanded.

Marlee's eyes darted around the room, as if hoping to escape. "Uh, when he was here the other night, we talked about it." Marlee glanced at Mom, as if making sure she'd said the right thing. "And he wrote me a few e-mails."

"He wrote you?" I stammered.

Mom was reaching for me. "He wrote all of us at first, Twigs, to check in, but I blocked the e-mails," Mom said, "I didn't want you hurt. He didn't want to hurt you either."

I yanked away from her. "Well, that worked, didn't it?"

Deaf Lou wrapped one arm around my shoulders, steering me away from Marlee and Mom. He patted me, as if that would soothe away the angry Twigs I'd become. I elbowed him, forcing him back against the wall. My height insured that my elbow jab got Deaf Lou right where it hurts any man. He doubled over in agony.

"Twigs!" Mom rushed over to Deaf Lou, rubbing his back.

I tried to remember how to sign "sorry," but I think I signed, "I wash you" instead. Deaf Lou remained caved over in pain and didn't notice my effort. "Tell him I'm sorry, Mom, but this is between us."

Marlee let out a perturbed sigh. "Well, you're the one who woke us up, Twigs."

"No, Twigs." Mom knelt next to Deaf Lou, stroking him like the cat we'd once owned. It had run off about the same time as Dad. She began signing and speaking, "Lou's been here for me. He's here for us. You have to get used to it. He's staying." She leaned over and planted soft smooches all over Deaf Lou's head.

I pounded my fists on the table, toddler style, demanding her attention. "Why isn't Dad here, Mom? He loves you."

"Twigs, you're freaked." Marlee had plopped down in the chair at the computer table.

"Shut it, Marlee," I spat at her. "Mom, answer me."

Everyone shut me out, as usual.

Marlee turned away and began scrolling on the computer. The Cheerleaders R Us site that she was hooked on popped up on the screen.

Mom helped Deaf Lou stand and they began walking toward her bedroom.

I ran and jumped in front of both of them, blocking their way to the hall. Like some choreographed dance, Mom and Deaf Lou lifted their arms over my head and walked past me.

I wanted answers and wasn't giving up. "No, no!" I rushed them from behind and scooted past them again.

"Twigs, enough! Stop this!" Mom shouted.

Ignoring Mom, I ran into her room, and yanked open the drawer where I'd found the note from Dad. I jumped on her rumpled bed, towering over them both, and read aloud, very slowly so Deaf Lou could read my lips.

Eve,
I miss you. I know you're angry, but I'll always love you.
I had to go and you know why.

Mom stood in the bedroom doorway, with Deaf Lou behind her, his arms wrapped around her. She signed something to him like "Get me an ax," or maybe it was "aspirin." Whichever it was, Deaf Lou got the hint and left us alone.

She moved Deaf Lou's suit pants from the seat of her bedroom chair and draped them neatly across the back before sitting down to face me. "Okay, Twigs." Her eyes tilted up to where I stood on her pillows.

I felt amazing to be taller than Mom. "I'm listening."

"Dale Henry isn't my husband anymore." She paused, allowing that to sink in.

The note in my hand began shaking—or my body was shaking. I couldn't be sure. I wanted to ask Mom to repeat what she'd said but couldn't. No sound came out of my mouth, only gasps for breath. I slumped down on her pillows, note in hand.

"He left us. You know that, and how his drinking had gotten worse. He tried to hide it . . . We both know he didn't." She blinked a few times and swallowed. "But Dale left for another reason, too."

I wrapped Mom's floral sheet around my hands just to keep them still, though I trembled beneath the worn cotton print. "Why?" I croaked.

Mom arose from the chair and joined me on the bed. She gently rubbed my legs and if I hadn't been on an emotional seesaw, I might have enjoyed this little mother-daughter moment. Next her fingers touched my cheeks and turned the lock on my tears, and they came gushing out.

"You," Mom said.

I must have looked as freaked as I felt, so she made it clear for me.

"Dale wanted to tell you, Twigs. It's all part of his AA thing, making amends."

"Tell me what?" I blubbered, certain this wouldn't be good, but I had to know.

Mom left out a long, sad sigh. Everything about her drooped. "I know I have amends to make, too. I thought I'd protect you from the truth." Tears spilled down her face and dripped onto my jeans.

"What truth?" The air seemed to snap between us and my tears went on hold.

"I'm so, so sorry, Twigs. But your dad—I mean, that man, Dale—he's not your father."

Chapter 20

Running away when you're eighteen isn't as dramatic as when you're eight, but fleeing the only home I'd ever known was pure soap opera, perfect for a Lifetime movie. Mom followed me as I tore like a hurricane out of her room and rampaged through our house. I wanted to maim, kill, destroy her and my dad—or the man I'd always believed was my dad. Instead, I ripped Gary Cooper off my door and tore him into a million pieces. *High Noon* confetti littered my already sloppy room. I stormed through the dining room, past Deaf Lou and an equally mute Marlee. I grabbed every one of those expensive college books and flung them into my Geo.

They all followed me outside, and Mr. Platton, as if by cue, appeared on his porch in the middle of the night to see what he could see.

"Twigs," Mom said, stepping across the yard. "Come back inside. Please."

"Mom, where's she going?" Marlee asked. She and Deaf Lou stood on the porch.

I leaned against my car, panting from my marathon run through our house of lies.

"What about her?" I pointed at Marlee.

"What?" Mom asked.

"What about Marlee? And Matt?" I stepped as close to my mother as I could stand and poked my finger up into her face. "Is Dad their father?"

"Of course, he is," Marlee answered. "It's no big deal, Twigs. So we're half-sisters. It's nothing to get so wacked about."

So Marlee knew the truth. "Just me?" I asked Mom, ignoring my sister.

Mom nodded meekly.

Another nuclear blast up my ass. Matt and Marlee were my half-siblings?

"Twigs? Eve? Everything all right there?" Mr. Platton stood on his porch, a neighborhood watchman, checking the crazy inmates in the Henry prison yard. I'm sure he was alarmed to see me standing that close to Mom. Physical proximity had never been our thing, and now I understood why she avoided hugging me as she did Matt and Marlee. God knows whose loser DNA had created me.

"Go back to bed, Mr. Platton," I yelled, without taking my eyes off my mother. I couldn't fake nice right now.

"There's one more thing I want to know before I never see you again," I said. I grabbed her arm, making sure she knew I meant every word. "Tell me who my real dad is."

Then Deaf Lou bounded into the picture, once again, holding on to Mom's shoulders. I guess it was just as well because she looked as if she might pass out any second.

"Tell me," I repeated.

Mom put on her sad face and shook her head.

"Bitch!" Anger and tears seemed to pull my arm back, as if it wasn't part of me. I became an archer with an arrow and let loose, slapping my mother's face.

Deaf Lou tugged Mom out of my reach, and she sank into him as if shot by a bullet. I might have hit her again if Marlee hadn't run over and begun kicking me.

"Don't hit Mom!" she screeched.

Muffled cries of "Sorry" and "Stop" were coming from somewhere, maybe me.

"Whoa there, girls." Mr. Platton's voice cut through the moment. "No need to fight."

I ran from Marlee and jumped into my Geo. She followed and began beating on my car, easily denting it with her super-cheerleader strength.

I rolled down the window. "Get off, Marlee!"

Mr. Platton appeared again, his usual helpful self, and managed to pry Marlee from the hood. She raised a hand and with cheerleader flair, flipped me off. I ignored her and turned the key in the ignition.

"Twigs," Mr. Platton said, "you shouldn't have hit your mother."

"Thanks for the advice, Mr. P." I didn't like myself much then so I went right ahead and said, "Margaret Newlan says hello."

Mr. Platton's face aged about twenty years as my words hit. It was pretty clear by the pain on his face that he still loved his ex-wife.

"Okay, Twigs," he said, in a quiet voice. "We've both lost people, haven't we?"

The urge to leap out of my car and hug Mr. Platton filled me, but I choked it down. He didn't hate me, even for outing his lie. Everyone in my life had been lying to me for years, but Mr. Platton's lie I could forgive.

"Who's Marge Newlan?" asked Marlee.

"Margaret," Mr. Platton and I said together.

"She's an old friend of mine," he added.

I wondered if he'd tell the neighbors this part when he related the story of Twigs's Big Departure.

"I'm going," I shouted at my mother. "I need that name."

Mom moved away from Deaf Lou, head down as if ashamed, and started walking toward the front door of our house.

"You've been lying to me forever!" I shouted at her back. "At least give me my real father's name!"

Mom stopped and turned to face me. "I can't, Twigs," she said, "because I'm not sure myself."

Chapter 21

Through a shower of tears, I drove away from my house and from everyone there: a lying mother, one half-sister, Deaf Lou, and the one and lonely Mr. Platton. I headed toward Hinkney. No choice but to go on, family or not. I hadn't felt a real part of my family for such a long time, so why did the truth hurt as much as it did? Loss, maybe? No home, no Dad. My real father, I realized, had come from a parade of losers that Mom must have bedded with Matt toddling around.

"I'm a total massive mistake," I said to the air. "One Mom never wanted."

This must have been before she kept a bedside drawer full of condoms. Cue the ad with Mom frowning at baby Twigs and holding a box of Trojans—*Mistake Baby Prompts Safe Sex!*

I pressed my foot down on the gas pedal, making the Geo shake, or maybe it was me still shaking with rage. If Marlee knew we had different fathers, then Matt had to know, too.

"Half-sister! Half-brother! Half, half, half!" I shouted again and again.

Through my open car windows, the looming cornfields rustled in agreement as I drove past, sending flocks of sleeping crows skyward.

Did my grandparents know about me before they died? Had it been on my school and medical records all these years? Did Dad go on a drinking binge because of me? Did he leave when he learned the truth? I couldn't answer any of those questions with certainty, but I believed the answer to the last one was most definitely yes.

"We're not related, but I'm running just like you did, Mr. Not-My-Dad-Henry."

I tried to shake away the thoughts and questions and drove faster along the dark county road leading to Hinkney, like I'd done with

Helen just a few days before. Only then, she'd been the one upset and lost. Now it was my turn. It didn't matter anymore.

My name flashed in my head. Madeline Annette Henry? Dale and Eve Henry chose that name when I was born. That wasn't me either. I was Twigs. The last name of Henry no longer fit. Just Twigs.

I swallowed and shouted loud enough for everyone back in Titusburg to hear, "Fuck 'em all!"

Passing Hinkney National Bank, the bright sign blinked 2:34 and *Have a Hinkney Day!* I pulled into an all-night gas station/junk-food place about a block away from campus and fumbled around for change in the ashtray. The guy behind the counter in the empty store was on his cell phone. He didn't notice me waiting to pay for a hypercaffeinated drink.

The clerk whispered something into his phone that I couldn't make out. Then he began rubbing his hand on the zipper of his jeans. His hard-on was impossible to miss and after a few weird moans, he whispered, *"Te amo, te amo."* Spanish cell-phone sex right before my very eyes.

"Hey, *te amo* to you, too." I rapped my soda can on the glass counter.

The clerk's eyes met mine. He began laughing and spoke speed-Spanish into the phone. The same hand he'd been using to rub his crotch rang up my order and I tossed a batch of quarters down and grabbed my soda, leaving him to his cell-phone love. Perverted, yes, but something about this ridiculous scene muffled my anger at the world. Maybe I'd try a bit of Spanish on Brady.

"*Te amo*, Brade," I said, trying it out for size. *"Olé."* It beat thinking about my lying family.

Chugging down half of the Red Bull Ultra I'd bought, I decided to hole up in the college library. It remained open 24/7 and was the one bright spot illuminating the dark Hinkney campus. I thought about Coop as I drove past the sleepy guard at the entrance. Without a word, he raised the gate after a glance at my student-parking sticker. Coop had been one of the only people I'd talked to so far at HCC, and he seemed to know everything about the place. Maybe he'd know someone in need of a roommate with little income, like me.

Three A.M. during the first week of school made for a mostly empty library. A yawning student slumped reading in a chair behind the main desk and an Asian guy pounded away on one of the computers filling the center of the space. Neither one gave me a second look. I made my way to the World History section in the back; it was filled with thick, moldy-smelling books. I dumped my pile in the farthest corner on an old desk. I planned to dive into the English Comp reading assignment and forget the world and my life, if possible. Red Bull Ultra buzzed through me, making me twitch. Images of my mom drama zipped in and out of my mind.

The emotional roller coaster I'd been on all night slammed to a sudden stop, with me in the front car. I sat teetering at the top of the highest point in the ride, without a safety belt, and about to fall over the edge for the quadruple loop-the-loop. My heart began pounding. It was a Red Bull high or maybe a panic attack, but either way, I couldn't stop the shakes that made me fall, writhing, on the floor of the library. I wanted to cry out, send a verbal 911, but nothing came out of my gaping mouth. The blackness hit me and I welcomed it.

* * *

"Hey, hey, you're okay," said someone. I felt fingers poking me. "Hey, open your eyes."

"We'd better call security," said another someone with an annoyingly shrill voice.

"I am security," said the first voice. "I know this girl."

The someone shook my shoulders and I opened my eyes to see Coop's big nose and face inches from mine.

"Ahh!" I flung myself backward on the floor and bumped my head into the desk legs. "Ow! What the—?" I looked around, as if the desk might attack again.

"That's gotta hurt," Coop said.

"Yeah, it does." I rubbed my skull and asked the obvious, "I'm on the floor?"

"Maybe I'd better call 911," the shrill-someone said. A woman. I noticed her nametag: M. Deegan, Asst. Lib.

"She's okay. See!" Coop patted my arms and smiled at M. Deegan, Asst. Lib.

The way he announced it made me wonder if I really was okay.

He knelt next to me. "You're okay. We've all had bad nights, right?" Then Coop winked or had something in his eye. Hard to be sure. His face moved in front of mine, blocking M. Deegan, Asst. Lib., from my view. "You don't want an ambulance to cart you out, do you?"

He smiled, and in spite of Coop's big nose, I couldn't help noticing his brilliant baby blues, the color of Professor Raymond's dead Cadillac.

The blush I felt might have been because of his amazing blue eyes or the embarrassing realization that I'd been snoozing on the library floor. Coop held out a hand to help me up. My English Comp book lay sprawled under my hip, and tingles of pain shot through my neck and back as I stood. Coop spoke true, though. I didn't need and/or couldn't afford an ambulance, unless it could rescue me from the giant crater of lies my family had created.

"Shit," I muttered.

"See," Coop said, turning to M. Deegan, Asst. Lib. "She's cursing. Must be okay, right?"

The concerned face turned to stone. "I assume you're a new student," she said. "Sleeping is not allowed in the library. If caught again, you risk being banned from all library use."

"Sorry," I said, smoothing down my hair.

Static from the industrial carpet had my multicolored locks standing on end. M. Deegan, Asst. Lib., gave me a once-over, and I could tell she didn't care for my particular coed look, which might be called drugged calico cat.

"Well," she paused, and then glanced over at Coop who had a shit-eating grin plastered across his face. "Clean up here, please."

"Yeah," I said. "I mean, yes. Of course."

With that, M. Deegan, Asst. Lib., turned and blended into the library, like a boring book being shelved.

I bent to grab my English Comp book, but Coop had already retrieved it and added it to the stack on the desk.

"I've got these," he said, hoisting them in his arms.

"No," I said. My arms brushed against Coop's as I fumbled to take my books away from him. When I first met him standing next to my Geo, I thought he might be an inch or so shorter than me, but maybe major family drama had taken a few inches off my height. Now Coop had a few inches on me.

I blew the flyaway hair out of my face and reached for the stack. "I'll take those."

Coop still didn't hand over my books. "Were you dreaming of me?" he grinned.

"What?"

"The way you were thrashing around on the floor there, you must have been having a sexy dream, right?"

Coop's arrogance gave me the drive to yank my books out of his arms, and I stamped on his foot, using all of my weight.

"Shit!" Coop cried out.

A sudden bout of shushing echoed around us, and M. Deegan's shrill voice came over the library speaker. "Reminder: This is a library. Inside voices required at all times."

I left Coop behind and walked toward the library exit. Sun filtered in through the windows. A quick look at a clock above the door woke me up more than Coop had managed.

"No!"

"What's wrong, Girl-who-sleeps-on-floors?" Coop had caught up and held the door open for me, and flashed one palm up, old-school-Indian style.

I looked around, trying to get my bearings. I had a class to find.

"The Radioneers meet tomorrow at noon," Coop said. "Same door you leaned against on Monday."

"Okay," I said, half-listening.

"It's not as fun as sleeping on the floor, but we do our best."

I took off running.

"Hey!" Coop called after me. "What's your name?"

I left him and his question behind and raced as fast as I could while holding a giant pile of textbooks. I didn't have time to dump any in my car. I hoped I hadn't missed the entire poli sci class that I'd already missed on Tuesday. I spotted another clock when I rushed into the main campus building. 9:24. Shit! Nothing like walking in at the end of class to face a new professor.

A few elevators and zigzagging halls later, I wound up in Room 4378A, as if all those numbers meant something to someone somewhere. A tall guy stood near the chalkboard erasing what must have been the assignment. He was the only person in the classroom.

"Wait!" Maybe I'd already missed two classes, but it was too early to embrace loser student status yet. College cost money—my own money—unlike high school. I refused to slide through with Ds, like I'd done in math at Titusburg High.

The tall, lanky guy stopped miderase and turned to me. He had a red splotchy birthmark covering part of his forehead right above his nose. I willed myself not to stare at the thing. Not an easy task.

"Class is over," he said.

"Sorry." I began my spiel, "I've had family issues and missed the first class and I know I'm late today, but I'm here now."

"I'm the TA. The prof had a doctor's appointment."

"Oh," I said, not sure what TA meant. Paid professor's pet? Teacher's ass? "Well, can I get the assignment for next week?"

The guy scratched his birthmark and I tried to avert my eyes before he caught me looking.

"I could, but since you missed two classes, you're out of luck."

I guess he noticed my frown. "Come on. I told you I've got family issues."

"If you say so." He grabbed a backpack off the floor and began walking out of the classroom. "Rules of the class. No note-sharing."

Yes, the dreaded note-sharing rule. I'd heard it already, from every Hinkney professor I'd met so far. "I just want the assignment. I'm not asking for anyone's notes." I followed him. "I'm not lying. My family's wacked."

He and his birthmark had already turned the corner, zigzagging away from me. I heard him say, "Not my call, but tell the professor next week in class. He's cool."

Unlike you, I wanted to yell but kept quiet. God knew how much clout this TA had with the professor.

With no class and just a little time before I had to get to work, I headed to the Student Center to use the one and only pay phone. The old relic was housed inside a carved-out statue of a giant squirrel, painted bright purple and gray, the Hinkney school colors. This phone might have been circa 1980, same as the date carved on one of the squirrel's giant paws. I'd be cheering for the Hinkney Squirrels about as much as I'd cheered for the Titusburg Titans after Matt graduated and stopped playing. So that would be never.

Unlike me, most students had unchewed cell phones, so no one bothered me as I sat on the old stool next to the black pay phone. Graffiti filled every inch of the squirrel's interior. A few graffiti gems caught my eye: *Don't ever get caught without your soul* and *Get hard with a Hinkney Ho*. One blurb in block letters seemed written especially for me today: *WHO'S YOUR DADDY?*

Sitting in the belly of a giant purple squirrel helped me look at life a bit more clearly—or maybe it had been the night I'd spent on the floor of the library. Whichever, I made a few life decisions in that inspirational spot. While chatty students rushed by the little cave where I huddled, I pulled out a pen and a notebook from my book bag. I began writing a life list, in no particular order:

Find a place to live

Never see my family again!!! Except Matt, to make sure he's really alive

Make money! Find a job that pays more, or get an extra job

Get new cell phone

Sneak home and take clothes I forgot when I left

Don't miss any more classes! Ace college!

Go see Brady, the one person who's never lied to me

I reread the list. Exclamations and all, it felt right, and somewhat satisfying to get these thoughts on paper. "A regular adult to-do list," I said to the belly walls of the squirrel.

I wrote one final note and then traced over it again with my pen, until it was dark and bold. I hoped this note would make me bold.

Never see those who were my parents again.

Then I added—

Never call that man "Dad" or give that woman the pleasure of hearing me say, "Mom."

Seeing that thought in print made me feel both sad and powerful. I closed the notebook and put it out of sight, moving onward.

With only a quarter and a dime in change, I tried to make a collect call to Brady. His voice-mail picked up and the operator cut off the call. She didn't even wait to hear me beg. So I looked through the well-thumbed local phone book and found Stuart A. Raymond's number and dialed.

"Hi, the Raymonds aren't here," Helen's voice recited, as Sly barked in the background of the recording. "Leave a message after the beep and have a fantabulous day!" My day was far from fantabulous, but her exuberance through the phone lines made me grin.

"Hi, Helen. It's Twigs." I paused, realizing I hadn't planned out what I wanted to say. "I guess you're at the Senior Center. I might drop by after work. Well . . . I hope you're around." I paused again. "You have a—" *beep*. The phone cut me off.

I hoped Helen was having her own fantabulous day somewhere and that she'd let me crash at her pink house again tonight.

Chapter 22

"Well, aren't you a sight?" Helen said, opening her door to me. I'd driven back to her house in Hinkney after work. Sly stood at her side and bared his teeth and barked. "Sly thinks you're a trick-or-treater and he hates Halloween."

I was so tired that I'd forgotten that I wore a giant Uptown Pharmacy smock, which Dink had loaned me after yelling at me for not being in work attire. My lovely dye-stained smock probably sat crumpled on the floor of my room where I'd left it before the shocking-family-truth explosion. I'd been wearing the same ratty jeans for two days now, but the missing smock had gotten Dink's mustache bouncing. He'd only had an XXL, which reached below my knees. I looked like some kid playing dress-up.

"I look ridiculous," I'd said to Dink when I first put it over my head.

He didn't care. "We have a store image to uphold, Twigs. Wearing an Uptown Pharmacy smock is part of that image."

I wondered if being a bald prick was part of the store image, too, but I kept that question to myself.

Now, after a generally crappy day and utter fatigue from my restless night on the library floor, it was good to see Helen. Life seemed brighter around her, even beyond her shining yellow hair and hot-pink clothes.

"I don't want to bother you," I said to Helen.

Sly let out a combo growl-arf at me.

"Sly, calm yourself. It's Twigs."

"Hey, Sly." I put out a hand, and the mutt cocked his head and sniffed at me.

"Twigs, you can bother me any time. I was happy to get your call."

She ushered me into the dining room and motioned for me to sit. I'd barely got my butt in a chair when she placed a drink on the table in front of me.

"Piña colada." Helen smiled and I marveled at how she seemed ready for my arrival.

The tall pink glass had one of those curvy straws that Mom always used to put in chocolate milk when I was little. I traced my finger along the straw, trying to remember the name.

"You can't help but enjoy a drink just a little more with a crazy straw," Helen said, as if reading my mind.

Hadn't Mom said something like that once?

Just like that, I began wailing, right there in Helen's pink dining room. She didn't speak but left the room and came back with a giant box of tissues, which she placed in front of me. She patted my back while Sly rested his head on my feet. Helen remained still and let me spill until I couldn't weep any longer.

"I don't need crazy straws, Helen," I cried at one point. "I need anticrazy, normal things in my life." I blew my nose. "But I have no clue what normal means."

"It's exactly this," she said, patting my hand. "Normal is crying and laughing. Living life." Helen picked up the drink and held it out to me.

"No thanks. My stomach has a good memory." The last thing I wanted now was more puking.

Helen shrugged and took a big sip of the white creamy drink. It swirled up through the crazy straw. Helen wiped her mouth against the hem of her floral blouse, as if she'd just swigged down a cold beer on a sweltering day.

"Twigs, you feel life . . ." Helen paused. "I mean, you take things in and really feel what's going on around you. That's a good thing.

It's also good to get mad or sad or whatever it takes to get over the stinking awfulness that happens."

Helen stood and began pacing around the room, stopping at a tall glass cabinet filling one wall. Inside were a number of china pieces, each one trimmed with an ornate pink and gold pattern, all lit up and displayed. Nothing like the mishmash of dishes and plastic plates Mom kept in our kitchen.

"You know what I did today?" Helen asked.

I shook my head.

"After I left the senior center, I went to see a divorce attorney—the best in the state, or so I've heard."

Helen opened the cabinet and took out a delicate cup and saucer from the top shelf. Sly lifted his head from my foot, and we both sat on alert. A split second later, Helen's arm reared back, baseball-pitcher style, and a bomb of china exploded on the far wall of the dining room, knocking a frame of dried pink roses off the wall.

"Helen!" I leaped from my chair.

"Whew!" Helen shouted. "That felt damn good."

Sly began arfing and spinning like a crazy straw dog. I backed up, ready to run out of the room. Helen threw another piece of fine china and whooped when it cracked into pieces.

"Helen, why are you doing this?"

"I spent the afternoon crying, Twigs. Just like you were now. This is about feeling alive. I've been feeling dead for a long time." She reached into the cabinet, grabbing another piece of delicate porcelain. "Wedding china won't save my marriage. Nothing will, if Stuart doesn't love me anymore." Helen paused before heaving a gravy bowl across the room.

She didn't whoop this time but turned to face me. "The thing is, Twigs, I'm not sure I love him anymore, either."

Her revelation surprised us both. Helen dropped her throwing arm and seemed dazed. She slumped in a chair and laid her head on the table, one cheek against the glossy dark wood.

"Helen." I put a hand on her shoulder. "You okay?"

Helen lifted her head. "It's always bothered me, Twigs. Stu never wanted a baby as much as I did. I didn't want to accept that." She smiled. "Listen up. I don't love Stuart." She let out a huge sigh. "Oh, it feels good to say that. I just wished I'd realized it sooner."

Helen made my brain swirl. "But the credit card and the car? Why do all that if you didn't—don't love him? Why trash your wedding china?"

Helen laughed. "Because you inspired me, Twigs."

"Me?" I gaped.

"Without you, I would've murdered the bastard," Helen said. "Or worse, hurt myself. This is better, don't you think?"

She jumped up and grabbed a serving platter and flung it like a Frisbee across the room where it gashed the pink floral wallpaper and cracked cleanly in half, before hitting the floor.

"Here, try one for yourself."

Helen thrust a dainty teapot into my hand. "One of my seniors is a retired therapist. She told me to imagine throwing something at someone you'd like to smack in the head."

"She told you to throw dishes?"

"No, pillows. But this is more fun, don't you think?" Helen gave my hand a nudge.

Turning the teapot over in my fingers and holding it by the spout, I closed my eyes. Mom's face filled my mind for a moment but was replaced by an image of the man I had always called Dad. Lifting the teapot over my head with both hands, I heaved it better than any Olympic discus thrower, and the lovely wholeness shattered into tiny shards. Sharp and brittle now, just like me.

"Yes!" I fist-pumped the air, proud of my great throw.

"Damn fine," Helen said. "Here, Twigs. Go, go, go!" She pitched a teacup my way and we flung together, synchronized smashing fun. Nothing like teamwork for mass destruction of fine china.

My tears dried. The pile of china pieces Helen and I created resembled one of those bizarre pieces of modern art that makes you question what the artist meant.

Helen raised her drink and toasted before taking another draw through the crazy straw. "Freedom and future!"

"Freedom and future," I repeated.

I said those words again and again, my mantra. They filled my mind before I drifted off to sleep in the pink guest room, where I clung to the pillow embroidered with the name of Helen's lost baby.

* * *

"Make yourself at home," Helen said, before leaving for the senior center the next morning. "Just leave by the back door so Sly's not confused."

Helen had given me a house key on a pink heart keychain and made me promise not to look for another place to stay. "You're staying here. No arguing about it. Besides, I need your help to melt down Stuart's golf clubs." We'd laughed. "Only joking, Twigs." But I wasn't so sure.

Helen had even made scrambled eggs, which I gulped down with some almost-burned toast, exactly the way I like it. I couldn't remember the last time Mom had made me breakfast, and I kept thanking Helen until she threatened to slap me if I didn't shut up. I did feel thankful, but not only for the food; a solid night's sleep and a good meal had made me feel better than I had since Brady had left.

I used Helen's phone to call Brady before our Friday classes.

"Twigs, my Twigs," Brade said, when he answered. "Where in Titusburg or Hinkney have you been?"

"Brady, there's been a lot of shit this week. First Matt, and then my dad—" I gulped on the word, already forgetting not to call him my father anymore.

"Hold on, Twigs," Brady said.

I heard background noises. I kept pacing around Helen's kitchen chewing my nails. Sly stood with his front two feet up on the kitchen table licking my breakfast plate.

"Down, Sly!" I yelled.

Brady's voice returned. "Who's Sly?"

"A dog, Brade."

"A dog? Where are you?"

Why did he sound annoyed? I'd been the one waiting on the phone. "I'm at Helen's house. The lady I told you about. At least, I thought I told you." I couldn't remember what had happened since I'd last spoken to Brady.

"Is Matt okay?"

"We don't know yet. I mean, he's alive."

"Your mom said he's in the hospital."

"My mom?" I stopped pacing.

"She called me looking for you."

"My mom called you?" My mother barely knew Brady. His house was a nicer place to hang out than mine. I'd rarely brought him over when she was around.

"Where've you been?" Brady asked again.

"Nowhere. Only school, work, and here." I didn't like that Mom had called Brady or that he kept questioning me as if I'd done something wrong. My lying family had done the wronging, not me. I changed the subject. "Brade, I have to get to class. Where do I meet you tonight? I'll leave after work, so I'll be getting there late."

I heard something in the background again.

"Noon at the quad, northeast corner," Brady said.

"I won't be there at noon, Brade, more like midnight."

"What?" Brady asked. "Oh, Twigs, sorry. That was Lee. I'm meeting him after morning classes. His girlfriend's sorority is doing a weird performance-art thing and Lee needs me to hold a sign or something."

"Sounds cool," I said, though it sounded lame, but I went to Loser College so maybe real colleges did stuff like this all the time.

"Okay, time to get to class," he said, with a sigh. "How am I going to concentrate, thinking about you arriving later?"

Brady always knew what to say to make me smile. "You and me both, Brade."

"Okay, see you when I see you and kiss you all over then, Twigs."

My legs wobbled a little beneath me and I leaned on the kitchen counter. If a person can really swoon, that's what I thought I might do, thinking of Brady kissing me all over.

"Same here," I replied. "See you tonight, Brade."

He hung up and I did the same and gave Sly a good rub, making his tail slap side-to-side. It irked me that Mom had called him, but I loved how much Brady wanted to see me tonight. I decided to ignore the annoying part of the call and focus on Brady's kisses. That thought energized me more than any cup of coffee and I bounced around Helen's house, getting ready for class. She had even washed my stinking clothes and Uptown smock for me. I gathered my books for the day, and it wasn't until I was halfway to school that I realized I hadn't asked Brady where we should meet. I didn't even know the name of his dorm, much less the way to Duncan University.

* * *

After morning classes, I sat in a corner of the Student Center, drinking vending-machine soup, and focused on reading as much as possible in the half hour before I had to leave for work. I had to read three critical essays and write a comparison for English Comp, all due first thing next week. This hadn't been part of my upcoming weekend plans. Could I write while lounging in bed with my boyfriend, whom I'd planned to assault several times to keep from going completely bonkers? Only one way to find out. Brady might have a freshman comp assignment, too. We could study together like we'd done in high school, plowing through our work to leave more time for fun.

I needed that fun with Brady. I gulped down more watery fake chicken swimming in mininoodles and willed myself to digest the boring essay about technology's effect on the world's developing nations. Digesting the food was easier right now.

"Come on, Twigs," I whispered to myself. "Focus."

I imagined Helen cheering me on. It would be her way, I think, unlike Mom. And just like that, my thoughts wandered again—away from the page and back to Mom, Dad, Matt, and the whole Henry family saga.

I tossed my soup container away and gathered my books. Maybe if I got to the pharmacy early, Dink would let me leave work a little earlier than usual. I had a long haul to get to Brady tonight. I'd rushed by the library before classes and Googled a campus map of Duncan U. There were eight student dorms at Brady's school. If I didn't reach him on the phone before I got there, I'd just start searching at the first one and hope my lust would guide me right to his room.

I hustled toward the exit and got caught in a big group milling around the entrance to the Radioneers club. It was now covered with a door-size sign: WHNK RADIO, WINK HINK!

Laughter rippled around me as I tried to maneuver my way through the crowd. A girl with at least ten nose rings turned to me. "Did you hear him?" I did a double-take, not sure if she was speaking to me or to someone else. "Loser pride," she said, pointing right at me.

"Huh?" I asked. "What's that?"

"Girl, shut it and listen," said a guy standing next to the pierced pointer.

My "I'm eighteen" got lost in the noise.

I heard a voice I recognized. Everyone in the crowd stared at a speaker mounted over the Radioneers entrance, mesmerized by that voice.

Coop.

"I'm saying, take pride in yourselves as losers," he said. "If we were winners, we'd be at Duncan University or Harvard or one of those colleges made out of brick instead of concrete like this dump. But we're here, aren't we?"

"Weren't you kicked out of Duncan, Coop?" another voice from the speaker asked. It sounded like the grouch who'd busted me for leaning against the radio station door.

"Kicked out and proud, Benno. Duncan U is full of assholes." That got another laugh from the people around me. "You're expected to be brilliant, or at least act like you're brilliant. Here at Hinkney, you can suck. You won't get kicked out. Fact is, the dumber you are, the more Hinkney promises you an education."

Laughter rolled across the crowd and more students filled the space surrounding me, all stopped by Coop's voice. He had to be the king of BS, but the way he sounded made you think that if he'd pulled up a chair in a coffee shop, you couldn't help but buy him breakfast.

"You've been sucking here for years, haven't you, Coop?" Benno asked.

"Oh, definitely," Coop said. "I'm one proud sucker!"

Someone behind in the crowd shouted, "Coop sucks!" It turned into a chant, as if everyone was cheering him on in a big game or a political rally.

Coop spoke again over the chanting, "Thank you, fellow suckers. Afternoon classes begin shortly, so WHNK Radioneers will put a kick-ass CD on repeat while we all go attempt to learn more useless knowledge."

Benno spoke up, speed-talking now, "Remember, if you suck, too, and want to join me and Coop here on WHNK, please e-mail, phone, or grab one of us."

"I love being grabbed," Coop said.

The crowd had begun dispersing during this bit. Everyone stopped at once when Coop shouted through the speaker, "Hey, you! Look, that's her, Benno. Library sleeping girl! What's your name?"

I felt hot and trapped in this crowd. People glanced around at each other in confusion, but I kept moving, trying to leave. I stepped on the pierced girl's foot.

"Watch it," she said.

"Sorry."

"You there!" Coop shouted. "Short girl with the wicked hair!"

I looked up at the speaker and noticed the camera mounted next to it, pointed at the crowd. At me. Coop and Benno could see us.

"You there," Benno said. "You're just Coop's size." He made a kissing sound through the speaker. People burst out laughing, except for me.

"Is he talking about you?" asked the guy who'd called me girl.

"I'm no girl," I said, and turned and marched out of that crowd, away from that camera. Coop's captivating voice echoed throughout the Student Center. "Hey, come back. What's your name?"

For once, I was glad to be short, because most people looked right over me, searching for the girl Coop wanted to know.

Chapter 23

At work, Dink rushed around in a tear, hounding me over every little thing. He hated that I'd be gone the next day and that he'd actually have to man the register. We'd barely had any customers, but he managed to berate me in front of a horny couple buying condoms.

"Try smiling at our customers, Twigs," Dink said, standing next to me as I rang up their Trojans X-Licious.

The woman wore a sleeveless tank, making sure the world didn't miss the hissing purple snake tattoo that covered one shoulder. The guy kept tracing the snake with his middle finger while she paid. She could barely suppress her moans. I forced a grin, but it didn't mean squat to this couple.

"You'll have to step it up, Twigs," Dink said, after they'd gone. "We've got a lot to do if you expect to take off tomorrow."

I bit back an urge to knee him in the balls. "Sure, Dink, just tell me what you need. I'll finish up before closing." Pride didn't matter if it meant I'd be on my way sooner to see Brady.

After ridiculous hours dusting Ex-Lax, Maalox, and assorted diarrhea/heartburn boxes and bottles, and with only a few minutes until closing, I heard my name over the PA system. I hoped Dink hadn't planned some other inane task, like cleaning plastic cola bottles, which I usually did on Saturdays. Even the lure of overtime couldn't stop me from getting to Brady as fast as possible tonight.

"Hey there, Twigs!" Helen shouted, when I reached the front of the store. She held a suitcase and stood near the counter, where Dink was twitching. "I thought you might need these before your weekend."

Helen shoved the suitcase toward me. I glanced at Dink, whose eyes kept shifting from Helen's cleavage to her headache-inducing pink-and-purple-checked pants.

"What is it?" I didn't recognize the big black case.

"It's your clothes and stuff from your house. Bob let me in. He's such a nice guy."

"Bob?" Had a new guy replaced Deaf Lou?

"Your neighbor," Helen said. "He had a key to your house, said your dad gave it to him a long time ago."

I grimaced at the thought of my non-dad giving Mr. Platton a key to our house. No wonder he knew so much about us. He could come in anytime he pleased.

Dink came out from behind the register and placed his hand on my shoulder. If Helen hadn't been grinning at me, I might have fallen over in shock.

"Twigs," Dink said, "Mrs. Raymond here—" Helen cleared her throat. "I mean, Helen, reminded me about your weekend plans." I had reminded him about eighty times. Dink continued, "You've dealt with your brother's situation and starting school over the past few days, so you can leave now." He waved me toward the door. "I'll see you at your regular shift on Monday." He gave Helen a half smile.

I was too shocked to move. "Really?"

Helen took charge. "Dink remembered that extra work you did, cleaning up the hair stuff, when I paid all that money last week. So, he agrees you need a day off." She gave Dink's arm a playful tap. "He's even going to pay you for tomorrow."

Dink swallowed hard and barely nodded.

Stuart Raymond's thousand bucks had just guaranteed me a free weekend with Brady.

Dink's gaze slid down Helen's cleavage. "Okay. Nice seeing you again, Mrs. Ray—" he cleared his throat and forced himself to look into her eyes—"I mean, Helen." Dink tugged on his collar, clearly uncomfortable. "I've got to count out the drawer. See you Monday, Twigs."

"Thanks, Dink."

Helen and I dragged the suitcase out to my car in the parking lot. She let out a huge sigh. "What a sleaze! We've got to find you another job."

"Thanks for getting me a paid day off."

"You deserve it!" Helen pulled a small note from her purse. "That sweet beau of yours phoned."

I took the paper from Helen and read a note written in pink ink.

MEET BRADY AT REEB'S, 124 SOUTH COLLEGE AVE.

Hallelujah for caller ID and that Brady had called back with this info.

"His message said he'll be there with Lee and some other friends," Helen said.

I frowned.

"Is that bad?" Helen asked.

"Well, I really want to be alone with him, you know. I miss him."

"I'm sure he wants to be alone with you, too, Twigs, after he shows you off to all his friends."

I laughed. "Wait until they see my hair."

Helen smiled. "You're gorgeous."

It was one of those exaggerations you'd expect from your mom. But it made me feel good.

"I packed a cute red tank I found right on top," Helen said. "You need some color on you and I guarantee Brady will love it."

I didn't own a red tank, as far as I could remember, so Helen must have bought me something new.

"Thanks, Helen."

The big case filled the back of my Geo and I gave Helen a wave. "See you Sunday night."

"Drive safe and don't do anything I wouldn't do."

She gave me a wink. From what I knew about Helen, I doubted there was much she wouldn't do.

I started my car and pulled out, thumping backward. Either the suitcase weighed too much for the Geo or I'd run over something.

"Stop there, Twigs," Helen called from the sidewalk. "Something's not right. Your car's tilted, I think."

I got out. Helen and I walked around my Geo.

"Shit!"

"Ditto," Helen said.

The tires on the passenger side of my car were completely flat. Although it was getting dark outside, I couldn't miss seeing the slashed rubber.

"Damn it!" Tears sprang to my eyes. Crying topped my new hobbies lately. "How will I get to Brady?"

Helen crouched down for a closer inspection. "Twigs, why would anyone slash your tires?"

"The world's pissed at me, I guess." I started sobbing. "I don't know and I really don't care. I just need to see Brady."

"Do you have a spare?"

"Just one," I whimpered. "A lot of good that'll do."

Helen gave me a comforting squeeze. "We'll figure this out."

"Maybe your husband did it." I glanced around the parking lot. "He knew my car from that first day of school. It could be a way to get back at you."

"No, Stu wouldn't dirty his hands like this—he'd come after Sly first. He knows how much that dog means to me. That why I have Pat and Chris on watch when I'm not home."

Then I remembered Jerkboy AKA Brian and Bobblehead. They'd already threatened me, especially Jerkboy, but I didn't believe they'd actually do anything. I decided not to mention them to Helen since I couldn't be sure. I sniffled, trying to figure out what to do.

"Helen, will you take me to the bus station in Hinkney?" There had to be a bus that went somewhere near Brady's college.

"Nope, but I'll give you my car." Helen pulled her keys out of a pocket and tossed them at me. "It's parked on the street, right in front of the store."

I caught the furry pink keychain. "I can't take your car."

"Why not? I know you can drive, you've slept in my house, and you maimed my soon-to-be ex-husband. I trust you."

"What about you?"

Helen paced around my car. "I'll call Bob over here and we'll get some tires." Helen paused. "There's got to be a tire place somewhere around here. Then I'll drive your car back home."

"Bob?"

"We were going to meet for a bite, anyway," Helen confessed. "I'm sure he'll help."

Of course Mr. Platton would help. I was just surprised. "You're meeting Bob?"

The look in Helen's eyes made me regret my question. Except for chucking hair dye at my head, Helen had been nothing but nice to me. "Please forget I asked that. I'm sorry."

"Forgotten," she said. "He's nice, Twigs. Loves pink flowers, too. You've seen his yard."

"Yeah." Mr. Platton must have been doing the gardening all along, though I'd believed it had been the Mrs. "He knows Bell's Garage and they'll discount the tires. My—" I coughed before the word *Dad* came out. "Matt worked there before he enlisted."

A car squealed into the parking lot, and there were Mom and Deaf Lou. That huge item on my life list about never seeing her again had just been nixed. She careened into the spot next to where Helen and I stood, barely missing us. I could hear her shouting before she even lowered her window.

"You might want to know your brother's half-blind!"

"Well, hello again to you, too, Eve," Helen said.

"It's okay, Helen." My mom's behavior didn't matter right now, or my wish never to see her again. Matt mattered. I stepped closer to Mom's car. "Matt's blind?"

Deaf Lou tapped on Mom's arm and began signing.

"Okay, Lou," Mom said, "I'll tell her. Dale promised to find you today and explain everything. As usual, he's avoided all responsibility."

"Responsibility?" I nearly choked on the word. "You're one to talk about responsibility, Mom. He's not my dad anyway, right? You told me that. Or was that another Henry family lie?"

Helen placed a hand on my shoulder. Perfect spot to give me a push when I attacked Mom or pull me back, depending on how this went down.

"Twigs, the man raised you. He loves you, whether you want to believe it or not. He always has." She rubbed her temples. "He's sober now. It's time that you two talked."

"Wow, all of this honesty is gripping. Thanks, Mom." I backed away from her and slumped against my car.

Helen asked, "What's wrong with Twigs's brother?"

I corrected her, "Half-brother."

Mom jumped out of the car and Deaf Lou followed, the way a dog shadows his master.

"Don't you dare disrespect your brother, Twigs." Deaf Lou massaged her shoulders, like a prizefighter's lackey before the final bout in the ring.

Mom continued, "Matt's gone through hell and more over there, but he loves you, and you know that's true." She shrugged off Deaf Lou and stepped closer to me. "He never would have left his unit if your father—"

"He's not my father!"

"It's okay, Twigs," Helen said. "Don't place blame, Eve. That boy chose to leave his unit on his own. No one made him leave, right? And aren't you and Dale to blame for lying to Twigs all this time?"

Deaf Lou started yelling with his fingers, his way of standing up for Mom. Helen screamed back about how mistreated I'd been by everyone, only he couldn't hear her. Mom and I stood in a painful silence, watching them.

Then Mom's words cut through Helen's rant. "Twigs, a piece of shrapnel flew into Matt's eye. It came close to piercing his brain, but he was lucky." She took a big breath. "He left his unit because he couldn't handle the news that your father and I are divorcing and that you aren't his full sister."

My heart tilted, or at least that's what it felt like. "Divorcing?" This made as much sense as anything in our family, but I was still surprised.

"What did you expect, Twigs? It's been done a long time. The rest is just paperwork."

What I'd expected was for Mom and Dad to ride off into the sunset together, taking us kids along, just like in the movies.

"You know Matt's sensitive, Twigs. He's not as strong as you." I shot Mom a look and she knew it. She continued, "The news got to him. He needed time alone to vent and walked away from his unit—and almost got killed." She paused and reached for my face. Helen and Deaf Lou had stopped their lopsided argument. Mom pressed the palm of one hand onto my cheek. It felt strange, this intimate touch, especially in a pharmacy parking lot being watched by Deaf Lou and Helen. "So you think this is my fault, and a lot of it is, I guess."

I blinked a few times, watering down the moment to make it bearable.

"I'm so sorry, Twigs." Mom's hand lingered on my skin and then she pulled it away.

Swirls of retorts cruised through my mind. *"Too little, too late. Sorry for what, Mom? For having me? For not knowing whose sperm made me?"* But I said nothing. For some reason, the anger didn't seem important now. I jiggled Helen's keys.

"Okay, Mom," I blundered, unsure what to say or do next. A hug that gave any hint of forgiveness would be another lie. So I escaped, like Matt. "Well, I've got to go." I turned away from her, from Helen, and from Deaf Lou, to find the pink ride that would get me away from reality for a few days.

"What? You can't leave." Mom's soft tone disappeared.

"Tell Matt I'm glad he's alive!" I yelled over my shoulder.

"Go, Twigs, go!" shouted Helen, my personal cheerleader. "See you soon! Now, go!"

"Your family needs you, Twigs!" Mom screamed. "I'm still your mother!"

I hesitated at Mom's pleas, but so much had happened. I had to go. I waved and kept moving. "Thanks for telling me about Matt!" I meant it. Mom knew I loved Matt, and it meant something that she'd bothered to come and tell me about him.

I ran around the corner out of the parking lot. The light on the sidewalk from Uptown Pharmacy spotlighted the shiny pink VW next to the curb. I could see Dink through the store window sitting behind the register munching Pringles. He'd throw a fit if I had been doing the same thing. It struck me how lonely he appeared. He was a bully stuck in an unhappy career. I vowed right then to find a new job.

I beeped the remote to unlock Helen's car. It smelled clean and new, unlike me—and it started right up, unlike my Geo. I adjusted the seat and sped away from Titusburg and everything I knew as fast as possible. Mom stood there with Deaf Lou and Helen, watching me go. Maybe non-Dad was there, too, lurking in the shadows. I didn't look back. The past was over. I kept my eyes forward.

Chapter 24

The anticipation of seeing Brady and the thrill of driving a new car, which I'd never done before, had me singing on the way to Duncan University—sometimes along with the radio, but mostly my own silly tune over and over. "I want you Brady, oh yes I do, I don't want anyone as much as you . . ." My singing isn't even shower worthy, but it felt great to belt out my desire. I sped through Hinkney and onto the highway heading north in record time. The traffic lights all burned green for me, and I heard Helen's voice repeating in my head, "Go, Twigs, go!"

Matt's voice was in there, too. "Rock the road" had been his mantra when he taught me to drive. Thank the desert gods he hadn't been killed. I hoped that what Mom said was true, that Matt still loved me, even as a half-sis. "Rock the road."

About twenty miles into the trip, it hit me. "Holy shit!" I'd left the directions in my Geo, along with that suitcase full of clothes and a new red tank top. Even worse, my book bag containing my ID and money were left behind, too. Two eighteen-wheelers flanked me in the middle lane of the highway, so I couldn't even pull over to take the upcoming exit to turn back. I let out a stream of curses. Was the world conspiring against me in my quest to see Brady, as it seemed to do in every other part of my life?

I pouted for a bit, wondering what to do. A trucker blasted his horn, making me jump. When I looked up to my left, wondering what I'd done, a red-capped, unshaven passenger in the big rig blew me a kiss. The trucker and his flirtatious friend gave a few friendly toots and pulled ahead.

Instead of being annoyed, I howled with laughter. It sure felt better than crying.

"Yep, you win world!" I screamed over the radio and the road noise. "You win! So, what? So fucking what? You're not stopping me!"

I pressed on the gas, edging the VW's speedometer up to seventy-five, which would have torn my Geo apart. It went into spasms at the top speed of forty-eight. The thought of arriving at Brady's with only the clothes on my back somehow made me want to get to him even faster. I had the pink-ink note with the address for Reeb's in my pocket and a nearly full tank of gas. Thank you, Helen. Brady would feed me and give me money to gas up for the return trip. So what if I had to pull an all-nighter doing homework when I got back? Nothing would stop me from getting to Brady. "I win this time, world."

A pit stop at one of those trashy roadside fast-food/gas station rest stops was all I needed. There, a huge map with a YOU ARE HERE thumbtack helped me figure out the exit to take for Duncan U. I reached College Avenue before midnight.

Sandwiched between Teddy's Adult Magazines/DVD store and the Long & Sleek Nail Shack, Reeb's looked exactly as I'd expected a place named beer spelled backward to look—dark windows, Budweiser signs, and a placard on the sidewalk with an oddly spaced announcement, *Welcome Duncan Stud ents*.

The smell of beer wafted out onto the sidewalk. I made my way among the smokers leaning against the building, pulled open the old wooden door, and walked right into the belt buckle of a giant.

"ID," he demanded.

I looked up into the giant's face. This guy had to be a football player, or maybe he just stood on the field as a goal post. He wore his hair in a ponytail, so there was no missing the massive neck holding up a head the size of a boulder. Marlee's beloved Tower of Isaac might only reach this guy's chest.

"My boyfriend's in there." I pointed around his tree-trunk legs to the glass door behind him that I assumed led into the bar.

"Don't matter who's in there. ID."

I understood him, bad grammar or not. First, my flat tires and forgotten possessions, and now the world had to take another shot at me. This giant wouldn't budge, but I figured some honest pleading couldn't hurt.

"I just drove two hundred miles. Brady Haddon is in there with Lee . . . somebody." I didn't know Lee's last name. "Here's the message he left me to meet him here tonight." I held the note Helen had scribbled high over my head and hoped the giant would have mercy on me once he read it.

"No ID. No Reeb's."

His response irked me even more than his poor grammar. I wondered if I could slip through his legs or zip around him before he could grab me. Once I got inside, Brady could help me make nice with this giant bouncer.

A whoosh of laughter and a stronger stench of beer filled the entryway as the door behind the giant opened. A stringy-haired blonde in a belly shirt pushed in.

"Oops, sorry," she giggled. "I need the john. Wrong door."

I zipped around the opposite side of the giant and wedged through the door behind the lost blonde. The giant would figure out that I'd slipped by, but I hoped it bought me enough time to find Brady.

The few lights inside Reeb's were either burned out, deep red, or glaring white bulbs spotlighting arcade games and an old pool table half-covered with green felt. I gravitated toward the back of the bar, my Brady radar on high alert.

"Since when do they let kids in here?" I heard from a table with more stringy-haired big people. Had I entered the Land of Giants?

Maybe only tall people were allowed in Reeb's. I ignored the large red-eyed beer drinkers and kept moving.

"Watch out!" someone shouted from the far corner of the place. There was a crash of glass and laughter. I followed the sounds, sure that I'd heard Brady's voice.

He lounged on a bench against the back wall. A small bar table lay on its side in a pool of beer; broken glass from pitchers covered the area. Brady laughed in a way I'd never heard before and he sat with a crowd of six or seven others, but my eyes rested on the girl next to him. Thick black hair caressed her shoulders like in one of those shampoo commercials, and her hand seemed stuck to Brady's thigh. Her red nails lay close enough to his crotch to be on call for a handjob, if needed.

"You're out of here!" the giant suddenly bellowed behind me. His voice caught the attention of Brady's group and they looked over to see me being lifted off the ground by the back of my shirt. This guy seemed intent on tossing me out on my ass.

"Brady! Help!" I screamed, thrashing for freedom like a fish on a hook. I hit the hands locked on my shirt. "Let go of me!"

"Whoa! Whoa, Dean! Hold it." Brady had escaped the red-nailed beauty and jumped up to save me.

The giant-known-as-Dean's hand stretched my T-shirt up tight around my ribs and I kicked the air, as if that would get me released. "You know her?"

"In the biblical sense, from what I've heard!" shouted someone from Brady's group, making them all begin laughing again.

"Shut it, Lee," Brady said.

I stopped thrashing then and stiffened up, now pissed at this Lee whom I'd never met, and even more so at Brady. He'd obviously been chatting up Lee and whoever else about our private business. It zapped the fight out of me for a moment.

"You know this girl?" Dean asked again, lowering me a little. I stretched my toes toward the ground.

"I'm eighteen! I'm in college!" I kicked the giant hard—maybe in his ribs, but I couldn't be sure. He didn't flinch. I think he hurt my foot more than I hurt him.

"You're not a girl." Brady circled his arms around my waist and lifted me away from the giant known as Dean.

My anger disappeared at his touch. Though Dean still grasped my neckline, I wrapped my arms and legs around Brady and kissed him full and hard, not caring that everyone watched us. We did our version of a blockbuster-movie kiss—when perfect-looking stars who have survived hell and bad guys finally proclaim their love.

"Whoa, watch out!" Lee shouted. "Attack girlfriend on the loose!" The group exploded in laughter.

Dean dropped me, and I pressed my body and lips harder into Brady, doing all I could to ignore the world around us. Perfect. Except for a few distractions.

As the kiss progressed, I became aware of how strange Brady tasted and smelled. Strange, because I smelled and tasted beer, and it reminded me of my dad, or un-dad.

I pushed away, setting my feet on the ground. Brady's eyes widened, surprised that I'd stopped our public make-out session. We'd been to a few high school parties where Brady might have had a beer or two, maybe a quick toke, but this was different. His eyes, watery, red, and glazed, told the whole story.

"You're drunk."

"Uh, oh," Lee said. "You've pissed her off."

"Just a little celebration, Twigs, for surviving the first week of college." Brady reached out and smoothed my hair, something I usually loved him doing. Even his hands smelled like beer.

"What's up with your hair?" He fingered a lock of bright orange, where the dye had made its mark.

Lee had walked up next to us and bowed. "Hello, Twigs. Lee Davis at your service."

Something about Lee's bow gave me a chill. "Madeline's my real name."

Lee raised an eyebrow and glanced at Brady.

"You're only Twigs to me," said Brady, his beer breath warming my neck.

Lee turned to Dean who had planted himself next to us. "All is well, Dean, but you can see we've had a little accident." Lee waved his arm toward the mess, as if revealing a magic trick. "I'll pay, of course, for those broken pitchers."

"She old enough?" Dean asked and pointed at me.

Lee answered before I could speak, "Of course, she is." He pressed what looked like a fifty-dollar bill into Dean's giant hand. "Ask them to send over a few more pitchers on your way up front." With that, Dean pocketed the fifty and lumbered away.

"See, all is well." Lee flung his arms out wide. If he hadn't been standing in a dingy college bar, he'd pass for a televangelist urging his flock to send more money. I'd just met the guy but already didn't trust him or like him.

"Come back and sit, guys," the black-haired beauty beckoned.

Brady placed his hand on my back and guided me to the table. "You've got to meet everyone."

"Okay." I pulled his shoulder down, so I could whisper in his ear. "I really want to be alone with you."

Lee had edged up behind us. "Ooh, secret sex talk. Can't wait, huh?" He jumped over the puddle of beer and joined the others on the bench seat.

"Hi, I'm Mia." The black-haired beauty lifted manicured red nails in a half-assed handshake. The kind that meant she'd rather not touch me.

"Interesting hair," she said.

"Thanks." I'd take her fake compliment. "It's the style of the future."

Brady cleared his throat, something I'd never heard him do before. "Um, Twigs, Mia. Mia, Twigs. We're in econ together, and it's been a killer first week, right, Mia?"

She nodded, as if she and Brady had survived a horrific plane crash or war. I wondered if a week in econ could compare to the week I'd survived.

We sat down and Brady introduced me to all the other drunks in their group. Except for Mia, Lee was the only one who gave me a second look.

"I feel like I already know you, Twigs," Lee said, talking again before I could remind him to call me Madeline. "This guy won't shut up about you."

Brady pulled me closer, and I leaned against him, fully aware of the odd glance from Mia. Never one much for PDA, I hopped onto Brady's lap, feeling that I had to prove my girlfriend status. His hand slid up under my shirt and gently stroked my back. It felt like a hot spark zipped up my spine. God, I'd missed Brady's fingers! Though he reeked of beer, I rocked on his lap, eager to get him alone.

"Let's go, Brade."

"What? Go now?" Lee asked. "The beer's here." As if on cue, two pitchers were delivered and an annoyed bartender arrived with a mop to clear the mess on the floor.

"Twigs doesn't drink," Brady said to the group. "But I'll have one more."

That irked me. "Brade, can we just go?" Why did he have to make a statement like that about me? What did it matter?

Lee had already poured a glass and placed it in Brady's hand. "You don't drink, Twigs? Very interesting. Religious reasons?"

Before I could cut off this topic, Brady said, "Twigs chooses not to drink because her dad's a drunk."

I hopped off Brady's lap as if bitten by a rattler. "It's Madeline!"

The drinking group stopped their chatter and stared at me. "And you've never even met my dad, Brady." I crossed my arms and sucked in Reeb's stale air through my nose. Even though Brady was right, I felt suddenly protective of the man I now knew as my ex-dad. Why would Brady reveal something personal about me? The fact that he'd said it and that he was so drunk pissed me off even more.

I lifted my chin—anything to increase my height for my next announcement. "I do drink, sometimes. Piña coladas." The minute I'd said it, I wished I could take it back.

Lee, Mia, and the others roared with laughter.

"Well, you won't get those at Reeb's," said Lee.

Brady blinked his red eyes at me. He might have been drunker than he'd ever been, but he was smart enough to know he'd hurt me. He reached out, beckoning me closer.

"Please, Brade, can we go?"

"Sure, Twigs." He drained the beer he'd just been poured and clanked the glass on the table. "Later, guys."

People murmured goodbye and Lee grinned. "Have some fucking fun!"

Ha ha, I thought, as the others howled.

"Library at noon?" Mia said to Brady.

"Yep."

"Huh?" I asked.

"We've got a big team project due next Friday. Mia and I were assigned to work together."

"Oh."

"I figured you'd have homework, too, right? We can all get our work done."

I nodded, remembering all those books sprawled in the front seat of my Geo.

Minutes later, we were in Helen's car, and Brady directed me toward campus and his dorm. He was so drunk that he didn't even notice that I hadn't driven my junker. Silence surrounded us as we sat at a red light. Brady's hand slid across my thigh and he leaned over and licked my ear. I shivered, easily turned on by his touch as usual, and wondered how much farther we had to go to get to his dorm.

"God, I've missed you," Brady whispered. Then a belch erupted from his mouth, filling my ear with stale beer breath. "Sorry." He flopped back in his seat, before letting out another gigantic eruption of putrid air.

I lowered the car windows and gunned the car through the green signal.

"What's up with you, Brade?"

"Well, I burped, Twigs. Or should I say Madeline. What's up with that name?"

I bit my tongue. Who was this guy? The edgy tone didn't fit Brady, but I'd never seen him this drunk. He sounded more like his ass-wipe roommate.

We drove past a variety of fast-food places and drive-through banks, all with signs welcoming Duncan University students back to school. Brady had his hand on my leg again, resting on that spot where it always fit just right on my thigh. I wanted things to be good between us.

"So why is my perfectly sane boyfriend acting like one of those stupid party jocks at Titusburg that we always used to laugh about? You're smarter than that. At least I thought so."

Brady leaned his head out of the passenger window, and the night air whipped his dark hair around his face. He didn't answer, and that made me wonder if I'd gone too far, nagging him like an unhappy wife. I'd heard Mom do that before my ex-dad left. I had hated hearing it as much as he did, even if he did deserve it.

"Turn here." Brady fell back inside the car and pointed to a road with a sign, "Duncan University, Resident Student Parking, Lots Alpha, Beta."

"We only get parking lots with the English alphabet at Hinkney," I joked, but Brady didn't crack a smile.

"Follow the signs to Beta." Brady pulled a visitor's parking pass out of his wallet and shoved it onto the dashboard. "Take the first space you can find."

We entered through the side door of a huge dormitory and climbed four flights without a word. Brady clung to the handrail, pulling his wobbly legs upward as I trailed behind him. Dorm life buzzed all around and everyone we passed in the stairwell said "Hey!" as if we'd all been friends forever. More than a few students appeared even drunker than Brady, and head-banging music mixed with gangsta rap, hip hop, and country tunes assaulted me from all directions. Total sensory overload. Dorm life didn't exist at my loser commuter college.

We had to step around a group on the fourth floor filling the hall near Brady's door. A dozen or so guys spilled out from a room, where I could see a mass of TV screens and some sort of murderous video-game competition in full swing. I said hi to those Brady talked to, but I was mostly silent until we finally entered his dorm room. The only light came from a computer screen on a small desk. A photo flashed into view of Brady and me sitting together on the porch swing at his house. In that instant I forgave the drinking and the anger I'd felt at Reeb's melted away.

"Brady?" I asked, unsure if he was looking at me in the dark space. "I'm sorry about what I said before, in the car. Seeing you this way . . . surprised me." I needed him and I hoped he still felt the same for me. "Are we okay?"

Brady reached out, pulling me into his arms, and pressed against me, until our mouths and limbs intertwined. With every part of his body against mine, I had my answer.

Chapter 25

I awoke, confused about where I was, with a throbbing headache. I lay stuck beneath a sleeping Brady, who snore-drooled all over my naked chest. His hot exhalations, even ranker than before, gagged me and I flinched due to the weird angle of my neck. My head butted up against the wall at the end of Brady's bed, which wasn't much longer than my entire body.

Besides Carlos Martine, Matt's friend with the weird teeth who'd been my first a few years before, Brady had been it for me. I tried inching my way out from under him and wondered why I'd bothered to make the long drive after a shit week for a night of sloppy, mushy sex. He'd been too bombed to stay aroused, much less awake. Hot naked sex in a college dorm room screamed orgasm, but I only felt mauled and unfulfilled, not to mention bruised where my head had been crammed against the wall.

Once, after coming home from a blind date, Matt had said, "We didn't have sex, Twigs. We had sux. That's how bad it was. You can't make fire, if there are no sparks."

Making fire had never been a problem for Brady and me, at least not before he left for college. But tonight, even with a promising start, we'd had sux, no question. It might have been the beer or my utter emotional exhaustion, but tonight, the sparks had fizzled. Sux.

Yanking myself out from under Brady took a few minutes, but eventually I thudded to the floor next to him.

"Ow!" My elbow hit the wooden bed frame. I clambered up to standing and stretched out the numbness and kinks.

Brady didn't budge; his snoring increased as I moved across his room feeling my way around to find my underwear. Flinging clothes off in the heat of passion may be exciting, but retrieving those garments later is not so much fun. I found the switch for the desk lamp by Brady's computer and turned it on, and still he slept. I scoured the room and discovered my panties had landed on the pillow on the other bed crammed in the corner of the tiny space. It had to be Lee's pillow, which skeeved me out, thinking about the proximity of my underwear to where his head was each night. I found everything else except my shirt, which seemed to have vanished. I'd have to find it in the morning, but in the meantime, I pulled on a white T-shirt that had been draped over Brady's desk chair. It felt different than his usual T's, but I guessed he'd gotten new clothes for college. I prayed that it didn't belong to Lee. It made me shudder to think of wearing anything that had touched his body. I would have preferred more naked time with Brady, not sux, but I felt better fully clothed in case Lee walked in on us.

I'd heard that dorm rooms were small, and being short didn't make this cramped space seem any larger. It had only been a week, but already there was a stench of dirty socks and pot. I hadn't noticed it when Brady had been groping me earlier, but the intense odor of cohabitating college guys made me less envious about not attending a school where I lived on campus.

Brady had told me his room was a suite, with a shared bathroom connecting to another dorm room. I knew which door we had entered, so I took a chance on the door next to Brady's desk. Opening it, I gasped. A naked—very hairy—guy sat on the toilet.

"What the fuck! Fucking knock first!" he bellowed.

"Whoa! Sorry!" I slammed the door shut.

Brady sat up ramrod straight at the commotion. "Twigs? You okay?"

"Yeah, couldn't sleep."

Brady had already collapsed with his back to me. I sighed and considered stretching out next to him and trying to go back to sleep, but I felt edgy and uncomfortable. Instead, I sat at Brady's desk and clicked around on the computer. 3:04. Maybe I could access the Hinkney website and pull up some of my class assignments to work on tomorrow.

First, I clicked on my home e-mail, which I hadn't checked since I'd moved out. A mass of unopened e-mail appeared. Gina and Claire, two friends from high school, had written nearly matching messages. "College is fun! Hope your first week is a blast, too." Yeah, I thought, Hinkney is a real blast. I almost wrote back, giving them my brutal truth. "Dad's not my dad. Matt's half-blind, and Brady's a drunk. I'm already flunking political science, and I ran away from home, but other than that, all is bitchin'. See you soon!" Instead, I deleted their e-mails without responding. Would my life make any sense to them? If Brady seemed so different, then college probably had changed my other friends, too.

There were a few e-mails from Hinkney Community College about a payment I owed—$100 for staff services, whatever that meant, and updates about upcoming student events. I scrolled down reading mass e-mails from the Future Business Leaders of Hinkney asking if I planned to be a millionaire before the age of thirty and another from the Baptist Student Association asking if I'd talked to God recently. Maybe if I replied with a big yes to both of them, the Twigs success story could finally begin. I considered this, but my doubts about business and God—especially together, prompted my finger's hardy jabbing delete.

A message from Dgarkin@MuserMail.com stopped my e-mail trashing frenzy. I blinked a few times and leaned into Brady's computer screen, making sure I got every word.

Dear Twigs,

Your father is my friend. We met in recovery. You should know that he loves you. I'm fearful that he may not stick with the program if you don't show him a sign that you care. If you want to talk about this you can contact me, but please call your dad.

A concerned friend,

D. Garkin

(557) 545-1876

Brady's snoring punctuated the banging in my chest. My heart raced and revved, like one of those old cars Dad had always been rebuilding. I reread Dgarkin's message a number of times, until each word imprinted itself in the part of my brain where I kept every father memory. Non-father. I gripped the edge of Brady's desk so I wouldn't fall off the chair. The shock of Dgarkin's message had made me forget that bit of recent info.

Recovery? Stick with the program? How about the part of the program where you came clean with your daughter, or the girl you thought was your daughter? Was that discussed in those twelve-step meetings? I reared back from the desk and paced in the small area between the beds, feeling like a lion trapped in a cage. The pacing increased my anxiety over that e-mail, and I still had to pee. I tapped on the bathroom door, but only silence answered my knock. I slowly opened the door. The stench that greeted me marked another advantage of not living in a dorm.

I washed up and splashed water on my face, letting my skin drip-dry. Nothing could make me touch the dirty towels hanging there. If a bucket had been handy, I would have scrubbed the bathroom, already well trashed by these four guys after only a week. The overhead fluorescent light accented the tired circles under my eyes, and I had to look twice not to see my mother in the mirror. Mom had tried to apologize when she saw me—in her own way. It pissed me off as much as it did Mom that my non-dad hadn't spoken to me yet. Maybe she was right when she said he just couldn't deal.

Yeah, I had a tough time dealing, too. I whispered to the mirror and to the man who I'd always loved as my dad, "We might not share any DNA, Dale Henry, but I definitely take after you in that sense."

Anger and despair had become the norm for me lately. Could I learn to deal? Wasn't that part of being a grownup? If this Dgarkin was concerned as a friend, then what kind of person would I be not to care, even a little, for the man I had always believed was my dad. Dad or not, I didn't want to be responsible in any way for him not "sticking with the program."

The bulb above my head flickered briefly, turning my face a dull green and then back to my blanched self. Still, I felt brighter than before, more aware and even hopeful.

I hurried back to Brady's desk and wrote a quick response to Dgarkin before I could change my mind.

Dear Dgarkin,

I still care. I'm at work every day but Sunday. Uptown Pharmacy, Titusburg. He can find me there.

This time a whooshing sound from Brady's computer confirmed that my message had left my mind, the room, the building. It floated somewhere out there for Dgarkin to pass along to the man I'd written Father's Day cards to every year that I could remember, even after he'd disappeared.

I closed Brady's laptop, tired of seeing those screensaver happy photo faces, especially mine, and yawned. I'd have to squeeze in next to Brady and try to get a little sleep, although the floor might prove more comfortable. I'd managed on the HCC library floor quite well just a few nights ago.

Reaching to switch the lamp off, something caught my eye on the cork bulletin board behind the desk. I tilted the head of the lamp, so it shone on the paper tacked up next to Brady's class schedule. A bright red lipstick kiss puckered at me beneath a phone number and a note in big, swirling script: *Need help in econ? Just give me a call.*

"Mia," I read the signature aloud.

Brady turned in his sleep, moaning quietly. Had he reacted to my voice or to the name of the raven-haired goddess who'd given him this paper kiss?

I tried again, eager to feed my itch of self-doubt about my boyfriend and the girl who'd had her hand on his crotch at Reeb's. "Mia," I said loud enough for hairy-naked guy to hear through the bathroom doors, if he was still awake.

Another longer moan came from Brady. I stared at my boyfriend's naked backside and wondered if coming here had been a huge mistake.

Chapter 26

"Hey, peoples! Anybody naked?" Lee banged into the room later that morning. "My eyes are shut! I promise! Go right ahead with any and all hot sex. I'm just grabbing a few things." He held one hand over his face but peeked through his fingers.

I sat on Brady's bed. "Sorry to disappoint." I pulled iPod buds from my ears. "Brade's in the shower." I held up Brady's iPod, as if to prove to Lee that there really was nothing going on.

Lee plopped down next to me and pulled the cord, which lifted the blinds of the small dorm window. I squinted at the sunlight streaming across the room. At the same time he draped his hand across my leg, as if it was all I'd ever wanted in life.

"If you were my girlfriend, Twigs, I would've dragged you into the shower for a bit of soapy fun."

"It's Madeline," I said, swatting Lee's hand off my leg and scooting over on the bed. Brady had made a similar halfhearted shower suggestion, through his massive hangover, which I declined. The thought of stepping into the same shower that Lee and the naked-hairy suitemate also used killed any desire I might have had. Waking to Brady's horrid breath and bloodshot eyes and thoughts of Mia the man-eater devouring him had further stifled any lust.

I swatted Lee's hand away a second time, just as Brady emerged from the bathroom with a towel wrapped around his still-wet body. It's tough to stay pissed at a guy when he's half-naked and gleaming wet. Lee's presence helped though.

"Hey, Brady, the whole dorm's talking about the wild noises that came out of this room last night." Another smarmy smile covered Lee's face, just like the ones I'd loathed at Reeb's last night.

"How could they not?" I retorted. "We put mics around the bed and speakers in the hall. We didn't want anyone to miss the profound ecstasy and orgasmic heights that Brady took me to over and over again." I grasped Brady's sheets and moaned.

"Whoa!" Lee said. "Impressive girl you got here, Brade."

"I'm not a girl," I snapped.

"Damn straight. I like this one, Brady."

Brady squinted at us, two creases between his eyebrows. He opened a drawer and pulled out a bottle of aspirin. There was an open can of Diet Coke on his desk, which he jiggled to gauge the amount; then, he tossed five or six aspirin on his tongue and swigged the leftover soda. He looked over at me.

"Sorry, Twigs." Brady's teeth were clenched. "I didn't mean to disappoint you last night."

Lee gaped, abnormally silent for a moment, while I backpedaled.

"Brade, that crap I gave Lee was just to shut him up." I got up from the bed and reached for Brady, but he rubbed his forehead instead of taking my hand. I looked over at Lee. "Can you give us some privacy?"

"I could, but if you're in need of sexual advice, I'm your man," Lee said, pulling a chair out from his desk. He looked at Brady. "Women love what I do to them. Want me to show you on Twigs?"

"Get out!" I shouted.

"Oh, my! Twigs snaps!" Lee laughed. "Do you bite, too?"

The iPod in my hands seemed to fly across the dorm room on its own. It hit Lee right in the mouth. Touchdown!

"Holy fuck!" Lee yelled, pushing his chair over. Blood spouted from his mouth.

"Twigs!" Brady shouted.

"Will you please give us some privacy now, Lee?" I asked, sugary sweet, trying to mimic Marlee's normal voice.

"I think you broke my tooth!"

I wasn't sorry one bit. "Maybe you'll have to have your mouth wired shut."

"Bitch." Lee tugged at the hem of his shirt and swiped the blood oozing down his chin.

"Hey," I said, and laughed, "is that another one of your jokes?"

"Cunt." Lee's stupid grin disappeared.

"Oh, great." I smiled. "Now we'll never be friends." As if I'd ever wanted that.

"Shut up!" Brady shouted. "Both of you." He grabbed something off the floor and handed it to Lee. "Use this. Apply pressure."

My boyfriend had just given my black shirt to Lee to soak up the blood.

"Keep the shirt, Lee," I said. "It's my gift."

Lee's mumbled something with my shirt pressed against his mouth.

"You're puffing churches?" I asked.

"I'm pressing charges!" he shouted, and lurched at me.

If Brady hadn't jumped in front of Lee, holding him back, he might have punched me.

"Twigs!" Brady shouted. "Go wait for me in the lobby."

I couldn't believe what I was hearing. "You're making me leave?"

"It's my room!" Lee interjected, though it sounded like "It's ma froom!"

"Shut up for once, Lee!" Brady winced, his hangover assaulting him as hard as he deserved for all the beer he'd consumed.

Lee muffled something else and slammed into the bathroom. Through the door we heard him shout, "Thipts!"

"Shit," I guessed. He must have looked in the mirror.

Brady stared at me, his teeth clenched again. "Lee's hurt. Let me deal with him and I'll be right down."

A moment, or maybe it was a year, of silence passed. "You got it, Brade." I slid my feet into my shoes. "It's just—my coming to see you—it wasn't supposed to be like this." I turned and walked out.

Brady called out before the door closed behind me, "The lobby, Twigs. I'll be right there."

The video-game blasters were still at it, milling around outside a room down the hall. More than a dozen guys at a half dozen monitors reacted to spewing blood and guts with every finger on their game controls. One gamer yelled, "I smoked your ass!" I managed to get a nod from one of the less vocal gamers to get me headed in the right direction to the lobby.

Waiting for the elevator, I replayed everything that had happened since I'd arrived last night. I should have turned around the moment Dean, the giant bouncer, had refused to let me enter Reeb's without an ID. That had been a solid omen, one I wished I had heeded. In the old movies, there were omens everywhere. Train whistles, stampedes, tumbleweeds . . . saloon fights. I felt like I'd just been through a saloon fight.

By the time the elevator doors slid open, my mind was made up. I didn't want to stay here anymore. Brady didn't want me here, either—not really, even if he hadn't admitted it to himself yet.

A guy wearing a Duncan University jersey stood in the elevator. "Make a choice. In or out?" he asked, pressing a button to keep the door from closing.

"Oh, sorry." I rushed into the elevator. "I'm out." The guy looked confused. "I'm out of here, I mean."

He gave me a once-over. "You're pretty short, aren't you?"

"Hallelujah! You're smart enough for college!"

He didn't say another word on the ride downstairs.

The lobby held a mishmash of couches and tables and chairs. Some sat clustered in groups with several lone chairs scattered around, as if the tune had just stopped in some musical-chairs game where the furniture moved instead of the players. I strode, warp speed, head and eyes straight ahead, already on my way out of this dorm and Brady's life. I'd cry, but probably not any more than I already had in the past week. My heart would shatter from losing Brady, but life would go on, whether I wanted it to or not. Yep, being a grownup meant now I knew life wasn't perfect. But I would deal with it. I'd face my losses honestly, without secrets, unlike Mom or ex-Dad. The elevator ride down had cemented my plan to escape.

Brade's suitemate—hairy-naked guy—sat at a table near the lobby doors, though he now wore clothes. He and the guys sitting with him all munched on some fried breakfast, along with huge coffees. If I hadn't seen the guy on the toilet last night, I'd have been tempted to beg for a bite. My stomach, which had been growling since I woke up, rumbled like a T. rex chasing its prey. The last time I'd eaten anything had been yesterday at work. Four Almond Joys washed down with a Red Bull.

I needed food. The thought sent me out into a gorgeous day, leaving the dorm and Brady in the dust. I scanned the area, hoping I could figure out where I'd parked Helen's car. We had entered the building around the side last night, so I headed in that direction, when I heard my name.

"Twigs! Is that you?"

I turned to see the luscious Mia. There was no escape, no rabbit hole to jump into or door to lock out the evil. I didn't wave but stood still, making her come to me.

Mia shaded her too-perfect face with one hand and lowered her eyes to mine. "I called Madeline, but I guess you didn't hear me." She glanced right over my head. "Where's Brady?"

This isn't what I needed right now. "Brady's meeting me in the lobby," I answered, as if that made any sense now that I was outside the dorm.

"Oh. Well, I've been waiting in the library. I called his cell, but he didn't answer."

I digested the info, and it briefly curbed my appetite. Mia waiting for Brady. Mia calling Brady. Mia searching for Brady. Did I want to fight this?

"You were waiting for Brady?"

"Yes, we planned to meet and work on our econ project, remember?"

Sunlight glistened on Mia's lips as she said, "econ," and I pictured her kissing that paper and, worse, kissing Brady.

"Weren't you meeting at noon?"

"It's 12:30," Mia said, holding out her wrist to my face. I saw a diamond-studded watch that had to have cost more than my Geo, maybe even more than Helen's VW.

"Oh, I guess we overslept," I said. I had crawled in next to Brady sometime around 4:00, and he'd woken me moaning from his hangover when he'd gotten up for a shower.

Mia glanced down at me. "You really are short."

"Gee, thanks for the information," I shot back.

"No, sorry, I didn't realize it last night at Reeb's since I was sitting when I met you, remember?"

"I'd rather forget last night."

Her perfect eyebrows rose at that and I glanced toward the dorm I'd just escaped. Brady might be in the lobby looking for me. I didn't want to talk to Mia, or look at her gorgeous hair and face. I didn't want to think about her hand on Brady's leg or her lips on that note pinned up in his room. The more I didn't want to think about Mia or talk to her, the more I knew I had to. I sucked in some air and made a decision to act like a grownup and ask her to respect my relationship with Brady until we figured out if we still had a relationship.

But Mia trumped me by speaking first, "That's my shirt."

"Huh?" That's all I could come up with while my empty stomach rolled and dipped. I shook my head, trying to sharpen my thoughts.

"My shirt," Mia repeated, pointing down at me. "Why are you wearing it?"

A girl and a guy walked by. "Hey Mia," they said. "Where's Brady?"

A week of school and people were already associating her with him. I wondered how much time they'd spent together.

"Ask her," Mia pointed at me. "He's all hers. But that's my shirt."

I looked down at the white T-shirt I'd grabbed from Brady's chair in the middle of the night. In the bright sun, I could ee that it wasn't your basic cotton T.

I shivered. In Mia's shirt. The couple had walked on, but I heard them laughing and a phrase floated back to me. "Cat fight."

"That's my silk T," Mia repeated, like a parrot.

"Yes. You said that. It's your shirt. I couldn't find my shirt earlier and grabbed this one." I swallowed. "Funny, but I thought it was Brady's since it was on his chair. Guess I was wrong."

Mia bent over and her face closed in on mine, like a mom reaching down to her toddler. "That's right, Twigs. My shirt was in your boyfriend's room."

I smelled the fruit-flavored lip-gloss highlighting her perfect lips.

"Why?" I wanted a truth that would clear Brady in all of this.

"Because I left it there." Mia smiled. "We were studying. Those dorm rooms get so hot."

"So you just stripped?"

"Brady loaned me a tank to wear." Mia stood up straight and tilted her head from side to side, as if cracking her neck. "Brady's nice. I guess you know that." I held my breath, waiting for the rest of my world to evaporate. "I don't play around, but I always get what I want." Her smile widened. "I haven't decided if I want Brady or not, but when I do I'll let you know."

Little black stars darkened my vision and I gulped for air. Mia had jabbed my heart without lifting one of her manicured fingers.

"Twigs!" Brady leaped down the dorm steps and ran toward us.

Mia and I turned at the same time, and I couldn't help but see her fling her hair around and pull her shoulders back. I also couldn't help but notice how Brady's eyes flitted from me to her, lingering on her face longer than on mine. Moments before, I had been racing to leave, but right now I hoped Brady still wanted me—me, ahead of Mia and everyone else.

"Lee's better," Brady said, as he got closer. "He's heading to the Health Center."

Funny, I hadn't asked for an update.

"Mia," Brady said, "sorry I didn't show. It's been a weird day."

"What happened?" she asked.

"Lee was just being Lee. And Twigs . . . ?" Brady stared at me. "What were you doing, Twigs?"

I didn't want this scene. Not in front of Mia. Gulping back an urge to spit at this collegiate Brady, the guy I loved, or believed I'd loved, I thought of those china plates I'd smashed with Helen. That giddy joy I'd felt with every shattered piece. I wanted that feeling again.

I took off Mia's shirt.

"Brady, I need your shirt."

"Twigs! What the fuck?" Brady jumped back, surprised.

Mia began laughing. I flung her white silk T at her feet, resisting the urge to rip it to pieces. The warm noonday sun felt great against my shoulders and I spread my arms, flashing my 34A pink-lace pushup bra to Duncan University. I'd bought it with my last paycheck, with this weekend and Brady in mind.

"Twigs!" Brady tried to pull me to him, but I needed to move.

I began spinning around in the grass and remembered doing it with Matt when we were little and Marlee was still a baby. "It makes you drunk without beer," Matt had said, already familiar with our dad's drinking habits.

"Whee! Whee! Spin with me, Brade!"

A few dorm windows opened and heads popped out, watching me spin, faster and faster. Life had been whirling all around me lately, but this wild spin had been my choice. If everything kept spiraling out of control anyway, why not embrace it?

"Twigs," Brady grabbed my hand as I spun near him. "What's going on?"

"Nothing, Brade." I panted for air. "Just spinning. I wish you'd join me." I began rotating again.

Someone from one of the dorm windows shouted, "Take it all off."

"Twigs, please." Brady took hold of my shoulders and stopped me midspin. "Here." He pulled off his shirt and in one seamless move, pulled it over my head before my next breath. I slid my arms into the holes and hugged the navy blue Duncan—or as I now thought of it, Drunken—University shirt close to my body. It smelled like Brady, fresh from the shower.

"Thanks for the laugh," Mia said, grabbing her shirt off the grass. "Brady, I'm heading to the library. See you when you get there."

"Okay," Brady answered, "as soon as I can."

I wanted the last word since I didn't plan on seeing Mia ever again. "Here's hoping you figure out what you want."

She tilted her head and stared at me, eyes narrowed, before she turned and strode across the green. I noticed how Brady, even through his hangover, couldn't help watching Mia's purposeful stride, with her dark hair bouncing and her chin held high like the carving on the front of a pirate ship. No doubt Mia knew where she wanted to go. She had the confidence to face any and all storms and easily crush someone named Twigs.

Chapter 27

"Twigs, hold up." Brady trailed behind me.

I couldn't get into Helen's car fast enough. My visit to Drunken U had been a complete bust.

"Twigs?" Brady jogged to catch up. "Where are you going?"

"Where do you think I'm going, Brade?" I kept moving.

The thought of spending another minute trying to force myself to fit into some mold of the perfect college girlfriend only made me move faster. Brady ran ahead, easily turning and walking backward, so I'd have to look at him, now shirtless. A few girls passed us and checked out his body—hard not to admire, shirtless or not. Whenever we cuddled, my hand would always rest right in the middle of his chest. Once, I'd taken a pen and traced my handprint on that spot and written *Mine*. Now, with the ink long gone, I wondered if a tattoo of that image would have made any difference. Probably not. Nothing of mine ever lasted.

"Twigs, I'm sorry about last night. I told you that."

We turned the corner of the dorm and I stopped. I faced a parking lot easily the size of the entire Hinkney campus. It had been dark and late when we arrived last night. I'd been distracted by Brady's drunken state, so I couldn't quite remember where I'd parked, but I soon spotted Helen's VW. The pink car popped out about five rows in, among the shiny black Beemers and oversized trucks that filled the lot.

"Where's your car?"

"I see it," I said, without explaining that I hadn't driven my own car. Brady had been too drunk to notice much of anything last night.

I shielded my eyes from the sun and looked at him. Apart from the question about my car, he hadn't bothered to ask anything about my life since I'd last seen him. Not about school, Matt, Dad—nothing.

My whole life had changed in the past week, and it had become obvious that my boyfriend was no longer a part of it. That thought made me ache inside, along with hunger pangs. Still, compared to Dad not being my dad and Matt being half-blind, this glitch with Brady was minor.

"Brade, I need to borrow some money for gas. I'll pay you back, I promise."

Brady reached out and pulled me into his arms. "Let's go get something to eat, okay?"

My stomach growled in response, but I shook my head.

"Brade, I don't fit here."

He sighed. "That's a cop-out, Twigs."

"Maybe, but you want to hang at Reeb's. I don't. You like Lee. I don't."

Brady backed away from me. "I have to live with the guy. And Reeb's is just a place to relax."

"Yeah, you were ultrarelaxed last night," I said, getting a scowl from Brady. "That's another reason I don't fit."

One of those monster trucks roared by, with the windows down, and a rap lyric assaulted us. "I wanna do you, do you, move you, take you, shake you, bitch, and make you scream."

A blonde craned her head out as the truck curved past us standing on the sidewalk. "Reeb's tonight, Brady! Back table."

"Brade, I have to go."

His gaze followed the truck, and then he turned to me. "How much do you need?"

"Gas money. A twenty should do it."

Brady pulled his wallet out of his hip pocket and took out some bills. He pressed two twenties into my hand, catching my fingers before I could pull them away. "Just stay a little longer."

The ringer on Brady's cell erupted in a loud guitar refrain and I flinched. Was Mia already calling to check up on him? Brady pulled his phone from his front pocket and the way he glanced at the caller ID, I could tell he didn't recognize the number.

"It might be my folks. They're traveling." He tapped the phone. "Hello." He paused. "Hello?"

I took a step away, feeling as if I was eavesdropping. Although I knew it would be rude to leave without an official goodbye, I moved toward Helen's car.

"Oh?" I heard Brady say. "Yeah, she's here. Hold on."

I'd stopped right in the middle of the first row of cars, when Brady had said, "She's here." My breath caught in my throat.

"Twigs," Brady called out, "it's for you."

"Who would call me on your phone?"

"It's somebody about your brother," Brady said.

The mention of Matt made me dizzy. Had he come home already? Maybe that was why Mom and Deaf Lou had come to find me at work yesterday. Had the shrapnel that blinded him moved into his brain? I crossed back to the sidewalk and yanked the phone from Brady's outstretched hand with my shaking one.

"Hello?" I prepared myself for the worst. Easy to do after the week I'd had.

Crackling static filled my ear. "Twigs Henry?" a woman asked. She might have been on the moon or talking through a tin can, the way her voice sounded so removed from this place. "Twigs Henry?" she repeated.

"Yes. I'm here. You're calling about Matt?" Brady looked at me, but I turned, feeling protective about anything to do with my brother—half-brother.

"Yes," the woman said. "I'm glad I reached you."

Impatience set in. “Matt. What about Matt?”

“I’m Nurse Sergeant Sarah Tillis,” she said. “Your mother gave us this number. I’m calling from Baghdad.”

The words *mother* and *Baghdad* hit like a one-two punch, and I gulped to get my breath. “Is Matt okay?”

“Matt’s here and would like to speak to you,” she said. “I’m afraid I can only allow a brief call.”

“Okay, sure.” The last time Matt had called home had been about three months ago. I’d been at work and Mom had forgotten to tell me until a few days afterward.

The phone line went quiet and I thought the connection had been lost. “Hello? Hello? Matt?” Then I heard a whirring noise that kept getting louder and louder.

“Damn!” Matt said. “Friggin’ helicopters do a fly-by when it’s my turn.”

“Matt!”

“Hey, Twigs.”

Tears began falling from my eyes. Hearing Matt say my name, after thinking he’d been dead, turned the tap on my emotional well.

“Twigs?” The whirring sounds began fading. “You there?”

“Hey, I’m here. I’m just shocked to hear from you and . . . well, I’m pissed at you, too. Sort of, I think.” I didn’t make sense, even to myself, but Matt had been in touch with my non-dad and knew the truth long before I did. Mom had made that clear.

“Yeah, well, I was major pissed, too, Twigs. It cost me my eye. Look, I’ve only got a minute. Tillis is one bad-ass nurse, and I mean that in the most respectful way.” I heard a short “ha!” in the background from the nurse, I guessed. “I promised Tilly here to clean my own bedpan later if she’d let me call you.” Matt let out a hearty laugh and the nurse joined in, too.

Matt had the kind of laugh that everyone loved, from the bratty toddler who lived down our block to his gruff boss, Mr. Bell, and women of all ages. His laugh melted Mom's anger and always made me feel better, even through a scratchy phone call half a world away. I couldn't help but grin while still wiping away tears.

I jumped in surprise when Brady touched my shoulder. "Is he okay?"

I shushed him, turning away. I cupped the phone tight against my ear and crouched down on the curb to block out every sound at Drunken U, so I wouldn't miss a breath from Matt.

"Twigs," Matt said, "listen and listen good. I don't care an Iraqi rat's ass who Mom and Dad did or didn't fuck. You're my sister. Sister Twigs. You understand?"

"Half-sister."

"Don't be a twit, Twigs." Matt chuckled at this little joke. "Do you think I care about blood? I'm not related to any of the guys in my unit, but I consider each and every one of them my brother. You're smart enough to get that."

I got it, but something nagged at me, especially since Matt had always been the most honest person I'd ever known. "Why didn't you tell me that you knew the truth?"

"Dad asked me to wait, Twigs. He couldn't handle what Mom had done, but he didn't want to hurt you. I had to respect that."

I tried to wrap my head around what Matt was saying. "Didn't want to hurt me? That's a laugh." I'd been betrayed by all of them.

"Twigs, the man is a drunk, whether or not Mom fucked around. Do you get that? But he loves you, and it killed him to find out he's not your real father."

A loud voice cut through our conversation. "Wrap it up now," Nurse Tillis said.

"Keep your thong on, Tilly," Matt said, and I heard some background mumbling.

"Twigs, I may be half-blind," Matt said, "but I'm your whole brother and I see a helluva lot better than you." He laughed. "You like that saying? It took me all night thinking up that one for you."

"Good one," I said, sniffing. From the other side of the world, Matt managed to make me feel better. I wish I had an ounce of that skill. "Are you really okay?"

I heard Matt clear his throat. "Well, I'm going miss this eye. If I hadn't been so mad at Mom and Dad, I might have stayed a click closer to my unit and away from flying shrapnel. There's a priest here who's half shrink making sure I'm—" Matt deepened his voice—"'at peace with my eye.' His words." Matt sighed. "Yeah, Father, I'd like the piece back that I lost."

We both were silent until I asked, "Are you coming home?"

"Soon, I hope. Just what our effed-up family needs—a disabled vet! Couldn't hurt, huh? First, I've got to get me a fancy eye patch. Ahoy, mateys!" Matt laughed again. "I'll be the first ever pirate mechanic in Titusburg. Maybe in the world."

Matt could repair anything, probably with both eyes missing, and I had no doubt he'd still be able to work on cars.

"I've got to scoot, Twigs. Tilly's itching to give me a massage. It's her specialty."

I could imagine him grinning and pictured his nurse's face, too. "Hey, brother Matt." It came out as naturally as it always had before. "I love you."

"Hey, sister Twigs. Love you, too. See you—well, half-see you, soon."

I heard one more laugh before the crackling abruptly stopped and our phone call ended.

I kept listening. Maybe he'd surprise me with another joke or two and give me a bit of the Henry family philosophy. "We're weird as shit, but the love's still there," Matt had said after Dad left. "Just like most families."

My eyes focused on the shiny bumper of a car parked next to where I sat. What was it Mom said? "Matt knew how to love." I had never quite gotten it before, but Matt, Mom, Marlee—ex-Dad, too, I guess—were my screwed-up family. All mine. I could accept them and all that meant or walk off into a desert like Matt. He'd come back. Could I do the same?

A shadow loomed over me, and I looked up to see Brady.

"Everything okay?"

I stood and stretched out the kinks from crouching on the sidewalk. "It was Matt."

"Yeah, is he okay?"

Something about the way Brady spoke or the way he rubbed the stubble on his chin made me pause. I wondered if the reason I'd fallen for him had something to do with the way he reminded me of Matt. They both accepted people for who they were, without judgment—even asshole roommates like Lee.

I shielded my eyes from the sun. "He called to say he loves me."

"Of course he does," Brady said. "He's your brother."

Brady had never gotten the half-brother, half-sister news, and I didn't want to rehash it now.

"Yep," I said, and reached to give Brady his phone but bumped the side mirror on the silver BMW parked there. Instantly, the car alarm's jolting shriek sent me running.

"Ow!" I covered my ears. "I barely touched it!"

Brady yelled over the annoying *EEE-OOO-EEE-OOO*. "Twigs! Wait!"

I bolted away from the sound, sprinting across the lot to Helen's car where I fumbled for the keys.

"Did you get a new car?" Brady asked, catching up.

I had the VW's door open and jumped inside, anxious to block out the alarm, Drunken U, and Brady, too.

"It's Helen's. That woman I told you about."

Brady gave me a confused look and shouted over the blaring alarm sound, "The crazy woman who attacked you with hair dye?"

"She's not crazy." I'd already learned that Helen had more smarts and heart than anyone in my life.

More than ever, I wanted to leave. I gave Brady a half smile. "Bye."

He had his hands on the car door, preventing me from closing it. "Twigs, you're not really leaving."

"I've got a lot of studying—you do, too," I said. "There's so much going on with my family, and we're both adjusting to college . . . " I trailed off. I couldn't believe what I'd just said myself, but there it was. All true.

Brady's face changed about eight times in eight seconds, from shock to sadness to anger. "You're dumping me?"

"No, no." Could I really do that? "Brade, you know me. I'm a little crazy right now. Look, Mia's waiting for you." Was I really sending him to meet the dark goddess who was waiting to devour him? "We'll talk later, I promise."

He gripped the door and pressed those kissable lips of his into a tight line. I felt the heat rising from his shirtless chest and made myself focus on his eyes.

"Thanks for the money, Brade. I'll repay you."

"You know you don't have to," Brady muttered, barely loud enough to hear over the shrill car alarm, which had changed into one long beep. He stepped away from Helen's car door, freeing me to go in more ways than one.

A cloud moved across the sun and Brady's eyes, too. In one quick move, I jumped out of the driver's seat and wrapped my arms around him. I kissed him, deep and hard. My version of a passionate farewell smooch. At least, I pictured it that way. Brady kissed me, too, but then he stopped, gently pushing me away.

"What are you doing, Twigs?"

I wasn't sure how to answer that, so I got into the car. "I've gotta go, Brade."

Brade pushed the door shut and took a step back, crossing his arms over his chest. He watched me start up the car and pull away. He filled Helen's rearview mirror, his reflection shrinking as I followed the exit signs leading me away from his life and back to mine.

Chapter 28

The phone conversation with Matt replayed in my mind and kept me from thinking too much about what had just happened with Brady. I used his money to gas up the VW at a truck stop and buy myself the Eighteen-Wheeler Breakfast Special, served all day. Three eggs, home fries, greasy bacon, and, instead of toast—two cake donuts. I ate every bite and downed cup after cup of tar-black coffee to keep me buzzed for the drive to Hinkney. A full stomach, after a week of vending-machine food, made the day feel brighter, but I knew hearing Matt's voice had a lot to do with the lightness in my heart.

I hadn't had a Saturday off since I'd started working at the pharmacy, and I felt a bit wicked, speeding down the highway. Everything reminded me of Matt. How he'd read road signs backward to make us laugh. He'd howl at me cruising in this pink VW since it was more Marlee's color. That made a memory of Dad pop into mind. He'd been rebuilding an old VW engine for a neighbor and cursing through his umpteenth beer about it not working.

"Why bother fixing it?" I had asked.

"Because it's the heart of the car, Twigs. Without the heart, the rest is just metal."

Dad and Matt had that talent to make a dead heap live again. They were both part of my heart, too. I'd put my heart out there, e-mailing Dgarkin that I still cared for the man I'd always called Dad. Now it was up to him to face me if he loved me, real daughter or not.

I cruised back to Helen's in record time, even counting pit stops after all the coffee. I pulled up to her house and began yawning, as if on cue, the moment I took the key from the ignition. The craziness of the past week, little sleep, and the long drive caught up to me all at once. My Geo sat parked next to the pink mailbox and the clean black rubber of four new tires grabbed my attention. I'd only ever used retreads on the car, so the shiny thick treads made my lime green junker glisten—at least to me.

No barks greeted me when I walked into the house; it felt empty. I wondered where Helen had gone without a car but guessed she'd taken Sly for a walk. Except for driving, I hadn't been alone since the day I'd come home when we learned Matt had gone missing, before my life flipped inside out. I put Helen's keys on the phone table in the hall and just breathed in the quiet. If only I could bottle this feeling to use when I needed it.

I dragged myself upstairs to the guest room. Helen had been busy. My book bag and books were stacked on a little desk in the corner. A new *High Noon* poster like the one I'd shredded was tacked over the bed, replacing one of Helen's dried-flower arrangements. Gary Cooper and Grace Kelly looked as in love as ever, maybe more so in this pink room. The pillow embroidered with the name of Helen's lost baby, Celia, had been replaced by my mushy pillow and comforter. I opened the closet door, revealing my mishmash of clothing, all on nice pink plastic hangers instead of the bent wire ones I'd always used at home.

In front of ratty jeans and old shirts hung that new red tank, which had been in the suitcase I'd forgotten when I went to see Brady. Something about that little piece of clothing that Helen had bought just to give me something new triggered a wave of tears. No one had done much of anything for me in a long time, and Helen had done all of this. I lay back on the bed and hugged my pillow. "Thanks, Helen." In spite of the pink, this room felt more mine than anything at home ever had.

A voice boomed from downstairs. "Grab the hand truck!"

Some man was down there. I scrambled off the bed and wiped away my tears, wondering what I should do. Helen hadn't expected me back today.

"Helen!" the same voice yelled. "This is the time we agreed on." Banging thumps erupted. "Christ! Watch out, guys. Anything of Helen's gets broken it comes out of your pocket."

I stuck my head out of the bedroom door, listening. The voice called from the bottom of the stairs. "Helen! You up there? Keep Sly leashed. We'll need to move your car out of the driveway so I can pull the truck in."

Stuart Raymond. His voice hit me like the sledgehammer Helen had used on his car. My legs began shaking, and I held onto the door to steady myself. Stuart Raymond was down there barking orders and I could either hide or face him. I felt Gary Cooper's eyes staring at me and glanced at the poster across the room. He seemed to be giving me a come-on-buck-up look. I knew what he'd say, "You're afraid of a one-armed college professor?"

"Yep," I whispered.

Then I heard another voice downstairs. "Hey, Prof, doesn't that ugly green car belong to that girl who hit you?"

Stuart Raymond's voice boomed from somewhere on the first floor. "Stop wasting time, Coop. Help those guys move my desk out of the den. Box the books, too. You don't help, you don't get paid." He paused and then yelled again, "Guys, I'm going out back to see if Helen's there with her dog. Once the car's moved, I'll need help emptying my closet upstairs."

Great! Not only did I have Stuart Raymond to deal with, but Coop too. I took several deep breaths, revving myself up to face whatever was downstairs. Or I'd slip out the front door, whichever came first.

I stepped out of the bedroom and slammed into Coop, my new habit these days.

"Ahh!" He clutched at his chest. "You scared the shit out of me. What are you doing here?"

"I live here, sort of." I rubbed my arm where I'd smacked into him.

"Really?"

"Really."

Coop scratched his head and then pointed at me. "And you hit the professor with his car, right?"

"Right."

Coop paused and glanced over my shoulder into the bedroom and then shook his head at me. "You're the weirdest chicklet I've met in a long time."

Chicklet aside, something about the way he spoke made it clear that weird was a good thing. "Thanks."

Coop wore a bright red T-shirt with the word *WAR* inside one of those circles with an *X* crossed through it. The work boots he had on gave him a little more height, or maybe it was how his hair stood up, all bed-head, this late in the day. Out of nowhere, "cute" popped into my head.

"What's that?" Coop asked, pointing at my *High Noon* poster.

"A poster."

"Smart ass," Coop said, "that yours or the prof's wife's?"

"All mine. It's *High Noon*."

"I know," Coop said. He nodded at the poster. "He's my namesake."

If a jaw can hit the floor, then mine came close. "No way," I said.

"Yep. My dad was a Cooper, too. My grandma had a real thing for that guy." Coop held up one hand with a finger pointed out and gave Gary Cooper an air bullet. "Great movie, right?"

I was nodding. Hadn't Dad said that every time we watched this movie? "A classic."

Curse words floated upstairs. "Don't scratch the wall!"

Someone else asked, "What happened to Coop?"

"It blows my mind that you're in this house," Coop said. "I've got to get down there and help. The prof is paying, but I've got to earn it first."

"Wait," I said, grabbing Coop's arm before he reached for the banister. "He yelled for you to help in the den. I heard him." I paused. "Why did you come up here?"

Coop shuffled his feet and looked down at the pink carpet. "To find the den."

"Since when are dens upstairs?" I asked, dropping my hand from his arm.

Coop pulled back his shoulders and stood up as tall as he could manage. I'd done the same thing myself a lot lately. "Can you handle the truth, chicklet?" he asked. Matt liked saying this movie line, too, but without the "chicklet."

Coop had my interest, but I wouldn't play games. "I'm all about the truth, chicklet," I said, and turned away from him.

"No, wait," Coop said. "The reason I came up here?" He smiled and his soothing radio voice came through now. "To find you. I knew that was your car out there."

"Oh." I let that piece of info register and had to admit that I felt flattered. "Okay."

"You want me to help you hide from the prof, chicklet?" Coop glanced downstairs.

"Stop calling me that!"

"Sure, chicklet," he said, slowly enunciating every sound of the word. "I'll stop when you tell me your name."

After numerous encounters with this twerp over the past week, I still hadn't told him my name. Why not tell him? It would beat being called chicklet. "I'm Madeline Henry." I swallowed. "But my family always called me Twigs." That came out before I could think about it, but it felt right to tell him.

Coop's eyes widened. I'd heard in some English class that eyes are the windows to the soul, and what I saw in Coop's eyes right then made me smile because he reminded me of Matt.

"Twigs." Coop paused, closing his eyes, as if tasting my name. "Yeah, that's good." His eyes popped open and, with his arms spread wide, he announced, "Ladies and gentlemen, Twiiiiiiigs!"

I flipped him off and Coop laughed.

"Like I said, you're the weirdest chick—" He stopped himself from saying the rest of the word. "I don't know what your parents were smoking when you were born, but Twigs suits you."

"Thanks." I was smiling. "You're no Gary Cooper, but Coop fits you, too."

Footsteps pounding on the stairs startled us both. Stuart Raymond held his broken arm tight against his body. He glared past Coop up at me. "What the hell are you doing in my house?"

Who knows why, but Coop moved in front of me, stretching one arm across me, as if that would hold back the wrath of Stuart Raymond.

"Prof," Coop said, in that voice that made you listen, "cool yourself, okay? She's living here. Right?" He looked over his shoulder at me.

I nodded, as Stuart Raymond reached the top of the stairs.

"Where's Helen?" He weaved his head side-to-side, trying to look around us. "What's she up to now?"

Coop's presence helped me feel brave enough to answer, "She must have taken Sly out for a walk."

"She planted you here to threaten me, didn't she?"

The thought of being a threat to anyone made me laugh. Coop laughed, too.

"Threaten you, Prof?" Coop asked. "This lovely lady?"

Stuart Raymond's face rode the color spectrum from white to purple-red as he continued shouting at me. He slapped the banister with his other hand. "Are you planning to push me down the stairs today? Or maybe hit me with a skillet?"

"Why would I do that?"

Stuart Raymond held out his arm, plastered up over the elbow and wrapped in a navy blue sling. "Look at my arm! You almost killed me!"

"It was an accident!"

"What up?" said someone from downstairs.

I looked behind Stuart Raymond and recognized the birthmark TA guy from the poli sci class I'd missed standing at the bottom of the stairs.

"Stay out of it, Todd," Stuart Raymond shouted without taking his eyes off me.

Coop shouted, "Yeah, nothing to concern you, Toad."

"You call me that again . . ."

"Okay, you got it," Coop said, "Toad."

Birthmark guy began running up the stairs with his hands clenched into fists. Coop took a step back. His outstretched arm bumped into my chest, making direct contact.

"Oof." I clutched at my breasts.

"Sorry," Coop said to me. "Damn, Toad. You made me cop a fake feel."

Toad-Todd just raised a fist as he ran up the final few steps behind Stuart Raymond.

"Stop!" I shouted, but I'm still not certain that Toad-Todd even realized I was there.

Coop had to take another shot. "Yeah, stop, Toad!"

I shouted, "Watch out!" I tried my best to warn Stuart Raymond. It was one of those moments when you see clearly what's about to happen, but there's no way to stop the bomb before it explodes.

Stuart Raymond forgot that his arm was in a sling and lifted it, as if planning to slow Toad-Todd as he lunged for Coop's face. Todd's flying fist missed its target and hit Stuart Raymond's cast, knocking him down on the stairs, where he moaned in pain. Toad-Todd fell, too, clutching his hand and screaming in agony, "My hand, my hand!"

Both Stuart Raymond and Toad-Todd lay spread across the top ten or so steps spewing curses through a jumble of plaster and limbs. I gawked, in shock, and imagined lips against my cheek. My hand flew up to my face, and I felt the moist spot where I'd been kissed.

I jumped away from Coop, not realizing I'd been holding onto his arm during this whole stairway explosion.

"Sorry," he said. "The situation called for something drastic, so I did the first thing that came to mind."

"You kissed me?"

Coop had a goofy grin on his face and he shrugged his shoulders. Matt used to do the same thing whenever Mom asked him if he'd eaten the last Oreo, which he always had, and if he'd left the empty bag in the cabinet.

"Sorry," Coop repeated, with his hands up in the air. "It was just a peck. I swear I didn't mean to. Chalk it up to one of those out-of-body things you hear about."

I liked how nice the words sounded from his mouth. "You kissed me by accident?"

Coop shrugged again and I looked at his lips, wondering if it might be possible to kiss by mistake.

"Christ, Coop, help me up here." Stuart Raymond had turned pale, squeezing his eyes shut against the pain. "I think Todd cracked my cast."

"My hand's broken. I know it!" Toad-Todd wailed. He held up a red swollen hand. Then he got up and half-stumbled down the stairs. "Coop, you'll pay for this!"

"Todd, you're an ass," Stuart Raymond moaned. "Just get in the truck."

I didn't really know Toad-Toad, but from what I'd seen so far, I had to agree with the professor.

Coop and I both bent to help the professor off the steps.

"No, not you!" Stuart Raymond butt-scooted down a few steps to get away from me. "You're dangerous."

"I'm trying to help!"

"You broke my arm!" Stuart Raymond screamed.

"It was an accident!" He never seemed to hear me when I said this. Maybe he'd never listened to Helen, either.

Coop squeezed my shoulder and maneuvered past me. "He's just in pain and upset. Right, Prof?"

Stuart Raymond grunted and let out a yelp for mercy as Coop helped him struggle to standing. A triangular piece of his cast plunked to the floor.

"I better get you and Toad to the ER." Though much shorter than Stuart Raymond, Coop easily supported his weight and helped him down the stairs. I followed, keeping a safe few steps behind them.

"You!" Stuart Raymond said at the bottom of the steps. He clenched his teeth and looked over Coop's head at me. "Tell Helen I'll have to come back to get the rest of my stuff, when you aren't here."

"Okay," I said.

Coop gave me a smile. "Come by WHNK on Monday."

"Wink?"

"Radioneers." Coop winked and repeated each letter, "W-H-N-K."

"Coop, I'm in agony," Stuart Raymond whined. Matt had lost an eye and didn't act like such a baby. No wonder Helen had been unhappy.

Coop asked again, "Monday, okay?"

I didn't answer right away. "Does begging work with you?" Coop sank to his knees, with Stuart Raymond hanging onto him, and clasped his hands. "Oh, please, Twigs!"

"Ow! Coop, get the hell up!" the professor moaned again, sprawled at the bottom of the stairs.

It's not often a girl gets a guy on his knees for her. "Maybe," I said.

"Maybe works."

"Coop!" Stuart Raymond screamed in agony, and Coop jumped up to help him.

"That kiss, Twigs Henry," Coop said, right before going out the door with the poor professor, "was no accident."

Chapter 29

I awoke on Sunday to loud laughter. I had slept harder than I had in months, because, for a change, I knew Matt was safe. Even though he had lost an eye, he was out of the fighting zone, recovering in a hospital, and flirting with Nurse Tilly. I had no doubt that Matt had each and every nurse's attention, chatting them up, and probably the other patients, too, and beating them all at cards.

Helen tapped on the bedroom door. "Twigs! You up?" She popped her head inside.

"Hi," I said, stretching out in the queen-size bed, which beat my old twin in every way. "I came back a day early."

I'd been utterly spent from the lack of sleep at Brady's and the long return drive, not to mention the verbal lashing from Stuart Raymond. After sweeping up pieces of his broken cast, I'd crashed minutes after Coop drove off with the maimed professor and Toad-Todd.

"I guessed as much when I saw my car in the driveway last night. You didn't budge when I peeked in on you." Helen paused. "Everything okay with that boyfriend?"

I shifted on the bed, avoiding Helen's question. "Your husband came by yesterday."

"I know. That's why I stayed out." Helen leaned against the doorjamb. "Out of sight, safe from death. At least from me." She laughed. "Stu didn't bother you, did he?"

Sly came in and jumped on the bed. He walked a few tight circles and finally plopped down against my leg like it was something he did every morning. I patted the dog and wondered if I should tell Helen about Stuart's manic stair scene. I didn't want to send her on another car-murdering spree.

"He might have been a little annoyed about me being here."

"Damn, that whore lover!"

I bit my tongue, trying not to laugh. Helen's moods shifted faster than one of Matt's souped-up cars.

"I surprised him, that's all. He said he'd come back another time to finish moving his stuff."

"He has to clear it with me, first." Helen jutted out her chin.

There was a mark on the lower side of her neck, which I hadn't seen before. I'd seen marks like that before on Matt, more than once. Helen noticed me notice it. It wasn't a birthmark. She tugged at her yellow hair, pulling it around as much as possible, to cover the love bite—as Matt always called them—but her hair was cut too short to do much good. A flush of red brightened her face and she grinned at me.

"Sly, tell Twigs it's brunch time. We made French toast, loaded with rum raisins." Helen gave her dog a rub behind his ears. "Guaranteed to make your Sunday bright."

My stomach rumbled at the mention of food. "I've never had brunch, Sly."

The dog pumped his tail a few times.

"A plate's ready for you. Throw on some clothes and join us."

"Us?"

"Just a few neighbors. You know Chris and Pat, and Bob's here, too."

"Bob?"

I heard a door slam open and shut downstairs. Helen gave me a wink, and I remembered Bob now. That was Mr. Platton's first name.

"He helped me run the senior center square dance last night." Helen grinned and nudged Sly off the bed. "Bob do-si-doed with every lady in the group, even the ones in wheelchairs."

"Mr. Platton?"

"He made more than one heart flutter. Even mine, a little." Helen patted her chest, which was squeezed into a tight V-neck blouse covered in pink glitter daisies that looked more appropriate for someone Marlee's age. "Bob's a real charmer."

"Mr. Platton?" I repeated. The realization that he'd been sucking Helen's neck baffled me. Curbed my appetite some, too.

"We're on the patio. Come eat before it gets cold." Helen left with a little wave.

I dressed and meandered down to the backyard, not sure I wanted to join Helen's brunch party. Even before I'd said hello, Mr. Platton did his nosy neighbor thing.

"Too bad about Brady, Twigs," he said.

"What?" How could this man already know what happened between Brady and me?

"Something's up or why else would you have come back a day early?" he asked.

Pat and Chris both reached out and gave my arms a squeeze, and it was obvious that they'd all been talking about me.

"Take it from me, Twigs," Mr. Platton said, "and your parents realized this, too—sometimes people float apart, without even realizing it."

Helen came out from the kitchen carrying a big pitcher of orange juice. Mr. Platton jumped up to take it from her and set it in the center of the patio table.

He pulled out a chair for Helen to sit. "It may hurt, but new doors always open, right, Helen?"

"Exactly, Bob." Helen grabbed a stack of pink plastic cups from the table and lined them up in a row. "Mimosa time!"

* * *

I'd planned to spend my entire Sunday studying since I'd come back early from my Brady trip, but Helen had my day mapped out before I'd tasted one bite of rum-raisin French toast.

"You don't have to pay a cent for your new tires, Twigs, but you have to help me today." I couldn't argue with free tires.

Helen and Mr. Platton dragged me to the Hinkney Senior Center for the Sunday early-bird dinner, which consisted of mushy creamed corn, baked ziti, and applesauce.

"Soft foods," Helen explained. "Some of these people haven't had teeth for decades."

She guided me to a group in wheelchairs and began whispering to me, though I doubted any of these near-deads could hear her, "These folks never get visitors, Twigs. Their relatives did a dump-and-run."

"What?"

Helen leaned closer to me. "Family fills out the paperwork, dumps their elderly, and runs."

I gulped, remembering visits to my grandma after she'd had her stroke. Matt drove Marlee and me to the nursing home about once a month. Mom rarely visited, and when Dad did manage to get there to see his own mother, he drank twice as much as usual afterward. So Grandma had been a dump-and-run, too.

Five drooling beings surrounded the table, and they all stared into their softened food. I tried not to gag over the mishmash of putrid smells filling the air around us. It wasn't just the food.

"I can't do this, Helen."

"If you can work with that creep Dink, you can do this." Helen had a point. "It's easy if you focus on their eyes. These people just want you to talk to them."

Helen could talk to a rock. I barely spoke to my own family, but somehow talking to those seniors came easier the more I tried. The odd thing was I liked it. Everyone seemed genuinely nice, even the old man without a jaw. Or if he had one, it had fused to his neck long ago. He kept grinning at me, and from the looks of his yellow, calloused gums, his teeth had been long gone, too.

As long as I focused on his eyes, I could handle it. "Mr. Greggs," I said, "do you want any applesauce?"

He nodded, so I spooned watery mush into his mouth.

He garbled, but I could still make out his words, "That's fine hair."

"Thank you."

"You fall in a paint vat?"

That got a big laugh from those near-deads who could still hear.

I played along. "Yep, I couldn't decide on one color, so I chose them all."

Then another near-dead, Miss Tranico, spewed a choice word about her nephew, who must have been her dump-and-run relative. "Petey's a cocksucker," she mumbled as a bit of creamed corn slid down her chin. When a toothless, wrinkled woman with cloudy eyes and only four or five white hairs on her head begins cursing, you can't help but laugh.

"I am not!" said Mr. Greggs.

"Not you!" Miss Tranico shouted. "My dead sister's son. Cocksucker!"

Everyone's alert level jumped from near-dead to barely alive and they all began cursing at Petey and the world.

Helen was busy leading a game of bingo in one corner of the large open room. She looked over at our noisy group and waved at me.

Mr. Platton appeared at our table. "Twigs, you've got them going! That's great."

They might have been cursing, but those near-deads were smiling, too. Some even seemed happy. Mr. Platton took Miss Tranico's hands and she relaxed back in her wheelchair, squinting up at him.

"You were some dancer at the square dance last night." Mr. Platton grasped the handles of her chair. "Let's go for a spin right now, okay?"

The cursing died around me, and we all watched Mr. Platton moving Miss Tranico's chair in slow curves. He bent over and gave the old woman a light peck on her wrinkled cheek. If it's possible for your heart to ping, then mine did, like a harp string being plucked. I kept blinking to keep from crying and dropped the spoon I'd forgotten in my hand. A spray of applesauce splashed on Mr. Greggs's wheelchair.

"Oh, I'm sorry, Mr. Greggs." I reached for a napkin to wipe the spokes clean.

"Doesn't matter," Mr. Greggs said. Then he asked, "You crying?"

I touched my cheek. "I guess I am a little." These near-deads probably had more control over their bladders than I had over my emotions these days.

"Want to dance?" Mr. Greggs smiled the best he could manage with a sunken jaw.

I hesitated, not sure how to answer.

"I'll only ask once," Mr. Greggs persisted.

Across the room, someone shouted, "Bingo!"

"We have a bingo!" Helen shouted.

"I'd love to dance," I told Mr. Greggs. I'd never said anything like that in my entire life. I felt the same way I'd felt throwing those plates with Helen and spinning around Brady. I felt joy.

I pulled his wheelchair away from the table and rolled Mr. Greggs around to face me. I placed my hands on his armrests. I didn't know how to make the smooth curves Mr. Platton accomplished as he moved with Miss Tranico, but we managed.

"Don't change that hair," Mr. Greggs said.

"I don't plan to."

"Are you a one-timer?" he asked after a slow spin.

"A one-timer?"

Mr. Greggs let out a grunt and I sucked in a whiff of him. New cars have a special smell, and old people have one, too, only not appealing whatsoever. I breathed out through my mouth.

Mr. Greggs said, "One-timers visit once and never again."

Helen appeared next to his wheelchair and rubbed Mr. Greggs's head. "Twigs'll be back." She wrapped her arm around me. "Right, Twigs?"

If it had been my mom deciding my life's agenda, I know I would've kicked and screamed, "No way in hell!" But Helen seemed to know more about me than I did myself. I nodded in agreement.

"Good thing," Mr. Greggs garbled. "They need more help around here."

"You said it," Helen said. Then she whispered to me, "I bet we can pay you more than that troll Dink does."

Not one of us had noticed the man in cowboy boots standing a few feet away.

"Excuse me," he said. "Are you Twigs?"

I turned from Mr. Greggs. "Yes?"

"Petey!" Miss Tranico said, reaching out to him.

The cowboy-booted man turned to Miss Tranico. "No, ma'am, name's Don, not Petey." He held out a hand to me. "Hi, Twigs. I'm Don Garkin. I e-mailed you a few days ago."

"You look like Petey," Miss Tranico said.

Dgarkin. Dad. My brain clicked away from the near-deads surrounding me to that e-mail I'd read on Brady's laptop.

"Nice to meet you." Helen stepped up and shook Don's offered hand. "I'm Twigs's friend, Helen."

"I'm Bob, another friend."

Mr. Platton and Helen flanked each side of me. Whether they had planned it or it was a weird coincidence, I felt protected and thankful, since my legs were wobbling along with my nervous stomach.

"Twigs's sister sent us to your house," Don said, looking at Helen. "A neighbor said we'd find you here."

"Sure," Helen said. "If I'm not home, I'm usually here."

Don smiled and turned to me. "We came to see Twigs."

I scanned the room, wondering if my non-dad lurked nearby. I looked back at Don, who wore a blue work shirt over jeans. He just needed a cowboy hat to complete the look.

I couldn't get any words out. Had Dgarkin brought Dad for an emotional showdown right here at the Hinkney Senior Center?

"He's outside," Don said.

"Who?" Helen asked.

Mr. Platton used his special know-it-all-neighbor powers to explain, "Twigs's Dad."

I swallowed one or twenty times.

"He wants to see you," Don said.

Helen grasped my shoulders tighter. "Well, Twigs is right here. Send him in. They can find a quiet corner somewhere."

Quiet wouldn't exactly describe the senior center. Near-deads mumbled nonstop, and other hard-of-hearing folks shouted bingo numbers at each other.

I heaved a sigh, short of breath, since I'd been holding it.

"Your father's waiting for you in the truck. It's better if you come out." Don held out a hand, offering to lead me away. My heart thumped on high, but my feet remained planted. Matt told me how much this man loved me. This is what I'd wanted, but I felt chewed up by all of this hurt.

"I've been waiting for him, a long time."

Miss Tranico summed up my feelings, "Cocksucker."

Mr. Platton gave her wheelchair a quick spin to distract her or make her dizzy or both.

"Don," Helen said, "if he wants to see Twigs, please send him inside. No one wants a family reunion in a parking lot."

"Yeah!" I surprised myself, and the near-deads all joined in, chanting with me, "Yeah, yeah!"

Mr. Greggs spoke up. "Is he afraid we'll bite?" He snapped his toothless yellow smile at Don.

That set the whole group laughing and snapping their gums and I laughed along. Something about these people in this place, with Helen and Mr. Platton, set me off.

"If he wants to see me, send him in!" I waved to an empty chair. "There's plenty of ziti and we can even play bingo."

Don turned, as if to leave, and then snapped his head around. "Twigs, this is really tough for your dad."

My laughter stopped cold. "He's not my dad." I took a breath, willing myself to say what I needed to say, "I've spent nearly every waking moment since he left dreaming of seeing him again—" I almost went on, but stopped. Why did I need to waste words on this stranger? A ball of hurt swirled in my gut, and my fingers curled tight. I could have squeezed Mr. Greggs's wheelchair handles in two.

Don sighed. "He's doing his best. He wants to stay with the program, but this stress is tough to handle."

I began shaking and Helen's arm pulled me closer. I'd never stuttered before, but getting words out now seemed impossible. "S-s-s-stress?"

I pushed Helen away and ran, but I wasn't running away from anyone this time. I wanted my father or the man who had held that title until a few days ago. The food helpers looked up from ziti pans as I flew past. I swerved through wheelchairs and past the bingo crowd. Someone shouted, "O-27!" and it echoed across the room. Everyone repeated it aloud, as if that would make the number magically appear on their card.

Behind me, I heard Mr. Greggs call out, "Don't be a one-timer!"

Pushing through the glass front doors, and past a few near-deads basking on the front porch in the September sun, I raced down the wheelchair ramp into the parking lot. A black pickup truck idled in one of the handicapped spots. I rushed toward it and the man sitting in the driver's seat. Sunlight glinted across the truck window, preventing me from seeing his face, but the way one arm draped over the steering wheel and the other elbow rested on the driver's door made it clear that I'd found the man I'd hoped to find.

"Hey!" I yelled, stopping in front of the truck. Both arms in the truck tensed and I knew that he saw me. "Hey, Dad! Or whatever I should call you—I'm right here."

Our eyes locked and my face muscles moved. Without meaning to, I smiled at the man I'd missed so much. But he didn't return the smile.

I heard him say, "Twigs," through the open window.

My heart seemed to erupt; words spewed from my mouth, "Mom screwed around, but if you hadn't been a drunk, she might not have done that—" I gulped, unable to stop—"but since you're not my real dad, maybe that doesn't matter."

The man's head dropped. The brief connection between us disappeared. Don had caught up and opened the passenger door of the truck. He murmured something to my ex-dad.

Don turned to me. "I thought he was ready, Twigs. He did, too, but I guess not. Sorry this didn't go smoother. Sorry for both of you."

With that, he jumped into the truck, and they sped away. My ex-dad didn't even give me a second look. I really was fatherless. My legs gave out and I sunk down on the curb next to where the truck had just been parked. My heart seemed to swell in my chest. Even with Helen, Mr. Platton, and all the near-deads to console me, this hurt—this emptiness—made me feel more alone than ever.

Chapter 30

Labor Day started with a bang, literally. Stuart Raymond banged on the front door of Helen's house, screaming at the top of his lungs, "Helen, open up!"

Sly whimpered, with his nose at the base of the door, but Helen kept bustling around the kitchen, making coffee and pretending no one was there.

"I know you're in there." Keys jangled and Stuart Raymond yelled louder, "You changed the locks?!"

Chris had already installed new locks for Helen before we got back from the senior center on Sunday.

"Twigs, would you like some coffee?" Helen asked.

I nodded. Caffeine was a must today. Images of my ex-dad in that truck pulling away without a second glance had kept me up most of the night. Around midnight, I'd forced myself to read my comp assignment, and when I'd finally slept, it was only for a few fitful hours.

Stuart Raymond pounded hard enough to make Sly start arfing. "Helen, open the goddamn door!"

She sat at the kitchen table next to me and flipped open the paper. "Want to hit a Labor Day sale later? You could use an orange shirt to match that streak of hair." She pointed to the bright streak across my shoulder. "And I always need more pink."

"Sure." Helen's fashion sense eluded me. Pink didn't match her yellow hair, so why would I need orange to match mine?

The kitchen door leading to the patio suddenly rattled, and I splashed coffee across the table, but Helen didn't flinch when Stuart roared, just like a big bad wolf, "I'm calling my lawyer if you don't let me in!"

Sly had raced into the kitchen and scratched at the floor, trying to dig a way outside. Helen calmly sopped up my spill with napkins, and Stuart Raymond's silhouette appeared through the gauzy pink drapes covering the glass-paned door. I wondered if he would huff and puff and blow the house in, but he just kept yelling.

"I'll break a window, Helen. I swear!"

I gulped down a bite of the giant pumpkin muffin Helen had placed in front of me. "Do you want me to let him in?"

Helen squirted a huge glob of honey on her muffin. She gripped a butter knife and spread the honey. She slowly licked the blade clean. Helen was holding it in—barely.

I'd faced Stuart Raymond before, and after being dumped by my ex-dad, I figured I could handle a raving soon-to-be ex-husband—or anything else life wanted to shove at me. "I'll deal with him, if you want me to."

The phone began ringing and we both jumped. Helen grabbed the cordless off the kitchen counter and nearly sang into the receiver. "Good morning! You've reached the home of powerful women who won't put up with loser men."

Outside, Stuart let out a fresh round of curses and pounding, which made Sly arf louder. I washed out my coffee cup while Helen chatted.

"Oh, hi, Pat." Helen paused. "Yes, I bet everyone on the street can hear him." She paused again, listening. "No, I won't interfere. Thanks, Pat. Oh, and Pat? Tell him that after we settle this, I hope he has enough money left to get that penis enlargement he's always needed."

Then she clicked off the call.

Helen didn't speak, but when she opened the freezer and threw her phone in the icemaker, I knew she was upset. The pounding abruptly quieted, and we both strained to hear the conversation through the door to the patio, as Pat spoke calmly to Stuart.

Helen leaned her forehead against the refrigerator, and tears started falling down her cheeks. Though it was something I rarely did with Mom or Marlee, I felt compelled to reach out and comfort her. Helen returned my hug and held me so tight, I almost couldn't breathe, but it was a good kind of suffocation.

She wiped at the tears and runny mascara clinging to her face. "Life can be putrid black, can't it?"

I nodded. "It's not pretty pink." We both laughed at my lame joke. The voices outside had stopped. "I think he's gone."

"Pat's the Dr. Phil of our street. She could tame a charging bull on steroids," Helen said. "I owe her a pitcher of piña coladas."

After a glance outside to ensure Stuart wasn't there, Helen grabbed her purse. "Make sure Sly does his business before you go anywhere."

It took me a second to understand since I'd never had a dog before. I pictured Sly making calls and slobbering over a computer keyboard checking e-mails.

"Tell Mr. Greggs hi for me."

"Stop by and tell him yourself." Then Helen imitated Mr. Greggs's garbled voice, "Don't be a one-timer."

"I've got to study and then go to work. It's not a holiday for me."

"It's up to you, Twigs, if you'd rather be with Dink," Helen said. "Mr. Greggs won't be going anywhere, until he dies."

Guilt washed over me. I had enjoyed being with those near-deads until Don Garkin and my ex-dad ruined the day. Being considered a one-timer made me feel like crap.

"I'll try to stop by later."

"Great. We're doing a Labor Day Luau. Beach Boys and Elvis *Blue Hawaii* music all day. That poi goop is already mushy, so it's the perfect food for my sweethearts." Helen grabbed a huge shopping bag by the front door overflowing with colorful leis. Before leaving, she said, "I wasn't kidding. We're always short-staffed."

The intense pain of watching my ex-dad fleeing from me yesterday had made me forget about Helen's job offer. It was something to consider. Hanging out with Mr. Greggs, Miss Tranico, and the rest of the near-deads had to beat working for Dink.

* * *

After Helen left, I gathered my books and made use of a free Labor Day morning to get some studying done. Got to love school holidays. I'd just settled in at the kitchen table to work on an essay when Sly began arfing in that insane way that could've meant Stuart Raymond was still out there. He raced out of the kitchen and leaped at the front door.

"Okay, okay. Settle down, Sly," I pleaded, hoping that it wasn't Stuart Raymond but only Helen who might have forgotten something she needed for the day.

I peeked out of the living-room window to see my sister and Tower of Isaac sitting in his car in Helen's driveway. I opened the front door and Sly burst outside, a rocket on legs. I followed as he jumped and barked at the strange car.

"Sly! Quiet!"

The dog ignored me, of course. Tower of Isaac reached one of his big hands out of his window and allowed the dog a whiff. Sly settled a bit.

"Hey, Twigs," Marlee called out, "you're on the radio!"

I wasn't sure if I'd heard her correctly. "Huh?"

"This guy, the funny one, he's talking about you."

"What?" I walked over to Tower of Isaac's car.

"Are you doing the horizontal with him?" Marlee grinned.

It's nice that my sister thinks so much of me. "Marlee!"

Tower of Isaac continued to pet Sly's head and let out a nervous chuckle. "It's none of our business, but this dude is into you, Twigs. He's been talking about you for a while now."

I didn't trust my sister for a lot of reasons, but I knew she liked pulling pranks just like Matt did. "What is this, Marlee?"

"Listen." She turned up the volume on the car radio and Coop's voice floated out of the car.

"She's small, but strong. Fierce," he said, "and she doesn't put up with my mouth or my act." There was a short pause. "You Hinkney losers and chicklets know what I mean."

"He's not talking about me." Still, I leaned into the car to hear better.

"Ssshhh!" said Marlee.

"So, wherever you are on this Labor Day, Twigs, this is Coop at WHNK. I told you I'd be here today, and I want you to know that I've got you on my mind."

I let out a gasp at hearing my name coming out of the radio, even if it was on a loser college station.

"See!" Marlee said, taking me back to one of our childhood fights. "See, Mommy, see. Twigs did it." Whatever "it" was, I had always been blamed and Marlee's cute factor won every fight we'd ever had.

"She's right," Tower of Isaac chimed in, giving Marlee's leg a rub.

"Yeah," I agreed. "Sshh." I wanted to hear Coop.

"Twigs, I hope you're out there listening," Coop said. "If we were at a school for smarties, we'd be out on our yachts enjoying Labor Day. But we're Hinkney losers and I bet there's a lot of us just hanging out today because we've got no money to do anything else."

"This guy is wonked when he comes to choosing music," Tower of Isaac said. "But he talks a good talk." He got out of the car to pet Sly.

"He sounds hot," Marlee said, low enough so Tower of Isaac couldn't hear. "Is he?"

I slouched into the driver's seat next to Marlee and noticed a shiny condom package in the side pocket of the car door. I picked it up, thrusting it in my little sister's face.

"What's this?"

"If you don't know, I'm not telling you," Marlee replied, tart as ever.

Coop's golden voice grabbed my attention, "You Hinkney losers wouldn't know about Gary Cooper."

Tower of Isaac plucked the condom from my fingers and thrust it into his pocket. "That's for when God tells us it's time."

I thought God had already given them a thumbs-up. I stared at Marlee. "You haven't . . . ?"

Marlee shook her head. "We've done some stuff, but not real sex."

"Real sex? Whose dictionary have you been reading?" I pointed at Tower of Isaac, now sprawled on the grass doing one-armed pushups, switching from left to right. "His?"

Marlee shrugged, and it struck me again how much she looked like Mom, but my ex-dad's genes were there, too. Marlee got the best of both of them. I had to stop myself from reaching out to smooth back her hair so it didn't hide so much of her gorgeous face. Coop's voice interrupted my thoughts.

"Gary Cooper's this old, dead movie dude who women adored." Coop let out a laugh. "And Losers, here's a little known factoid. I'm named after him. Yes, and we all know the females of Hinkney adore me. See, Coop is a hot name. In his movies, or the good ones anyway, Cooper always rode off with the most gorgeous chicklet on the prairie."

A sound effect of wind blowing and wolf howls clicked on behind Coop's voice.

"Twigs, my heart, and some of my other oh-so-manly organs, tell me that you're listening. Won't you ride off into the sunset with me? Or at least go out for a burger? Here's a little Labor Day Cooper love scene just for you."

My hands gripped the steering wheel and I held my breath.

"Are all the guys at HCC like that?" asked Marlee. She'd been drumming her fingers on the dashboard but stopped to listen. "Hey, it's that movie you and Dad . . ."

"Ssshhh!" I swatted at her to be quiet. We both sat mesmerized by the dialogue coming from the radio. Gary Cooper's voice filled Tower of Isaac's car. I mouthed along with the words that I knew so well.

A few seconds later, Coop's voice cut in again, "Losers, that was a clip from *High Noon*. The kick-ass blonde jumps off the train to help her man, the Coopster. She even shoots an asshole cowboy, which is against her religious beliefs. Ask yourself, would you go against your beliefs for someone you love?"

Coop paused, and I could picture him, behind that door with the WHNK poster, sitting at a microphone. I caught a glimpse of myself in Tower of Isaac's rearview mirror and saw the foolish grin plastered on my face.

"Twigs—" Marlee leaned into me, close enough for me to smell the watermelon shampoo scent of her hair—"I need some advice." She glanced out the window, watching Tower of Isaac play in the grass with Sly.

Coop said, "Losers, I gotta take a break to drain my hose. Here's a weird song for the chicklet who made my boring dream moist last night. She's definitely weird, and that beats normal in my book."

"Tweeeeggggsaaaa!" filled the car. Marlee scowled. "You like this?"

"Not really." I laughed hard enough to make my eyes water.

It was the same freaky song that Brady had put on my iPod. As far as I knew so far, Coop was nothing like Brady, but he picked the same song for me. I touched my cheek where he had kissed it. More than anything, I wanted to give Coop a long kiss, to see if it was as good as I hoped it would be. I sang along with the Tweeeeegggsssaaaa chorus filling the car.

"He's right. You're weird." Marlee smiled. She nodded toward Tower of Isaac, who now raced around the yard with Sly. He had a graceful way of running for such a big guy, and I wondered if the football coach made his team take ballet. I could picture Tower of Isaac in those clingy guy tights, lifting Marlee over his head.

"He wants to marry me." Marlee gave me a sheepish grin.

"You're fourteen!"

"Yeah, I know." She sighed and gazed out at Tower of Isaac, now lounging on his back, with Sly licking his face. Tower of Isaac's perfect black skin glistened in the sun. He looked over and smiled a shining smile at my sister.

"Mom said the same thing. 'Honey, you're only fourteen!' But what does she know about love?" She gave my arm a playful jab.

Marlee's imitation of Mom set me off again. We both began howling. Mom may know men, but it had nothing to do with love. It felt good to laugh with Marlee. We were so different from each other, but we had our wacked family in common. Same as Matt.

I held my belly, sore from laughing, and sputtered, "Well, Mom keeps trying. Deaf Lou seems nice."

"Yeah," Marlee said, "I think she might keep him." She'd stopped laughing. "Twigs, you found Brady. And you're both so cool together. That's why I'm talking to you about this."

It flattered me that Marlee thought me cool in any form, so I didn't interrupt her with the sad Brady truth.

Her eyes widened and she held her hands together on her chest, as if taking an oath. "I'm young, but Isaac wants to be with me forever and ever, even after death."

If Tower of Isaac could guarantee love in the afterlife, then he might be a keeper, but I kept that thought to myself.

"Every guy at Titusburg High is going to want you, Marlee. You might try dating a few, before deciding your whole life right now."

Marlee chewed her lip. "Yeah, Isaac said I could date if I want."

"Really?"

Tower of Isaac's shadow crossed the window of the car. "I read you," he said, leaning down on my side of the car. "Marlee can check what's out there. I'm cush with that. I prayed about it. God made it clear. She'll come back to the man who loves her the most."

I went all mama bear, defending Marlee. "I don't care if God tattooed his message on your ass. Don't fuck with my sister." I may have growled, but I know Matt would've said the same if he were here.

"Twigs!" Marlee said.

"Hey, Twigs!" said Tower of Isaac, taking hold of the finger I'd been jabbing at his face. "Whoa! I honor your sister. I love her. And I knew it the first time I saw her."

"Twigs, chill," Marlee said. "We won't do anything until I'm eighteen. We signed a Teens for Jesus contract at Isaac's church."

Tower of Isaac nodded in agreement.

The church nuts I remembered at Titusburg High were screwing more than anyone else. But something about the way Tower of Isaac looked at Marlee made me bite that thought back inside. I had a quick vision of a future family photo with Marlee and Tower of Isaac surrounded by a pack of beautiful kids.

Marlee reached over, turning my face to hers. "What's all this super-sis act? You never cared what I did before."

She was right, but something Matt had said stuck.

"We're sisters," I said, "well, half-sisters, so I'll care about you fifty percent and you do the same for me. Maybe it'll even out."

A smile spread across Marlee's face. "Did you learn that in high school math?"

"You should know since you did most of my work," I retorted, our sisterly sparring back on track.

I got out of the car and stretched, standing as tall as possible to talk to Tower of Isaac. The fact that I only came up to his waist, made his penis my target when I said, "Don't love her into an early pregnancy, okay?"

Tower of Isaac held up one hand, as if swearing on a Bible. He held the other on his chest. Sly put his front paws up on Tower of Isaac's giant legs, stretching up for more attention.

"Dogs and kids love him, Twigs," said Marlee. "You will, too."

Coop's voice came out of the car speakers again, "Freakin' stoner song, huh? But good. You losers calling or e-mailing to complain, eff you. For the rest of you, I'll post more on the podcast and extras about Gary Cooper, too. All for Twigs. It's Labor Day. Get out and take one last crack at summer. It's eleven oh two, WHNK time."

"Shit!" I cried. "I'm supposed to be at work right now."

I ran across the yard to the house to grab my keys and Uptown Pharmacy smock. Sly passed me, running ahead to the front door.

"Twigs!" Marlee shouted at my back.

"Yeah?" I turned.

"Mom wants you to come over later," Marlee said. "After work."

"Why?"

"I don't know, but she didn't want to leave a message. She asked me to come here and tell you in person."

I was in such a rush, that I answered in a way I'd never done before when it came to anything to do with my mom. I didn't argue. "Okay."

Mom might not have been a perfect mother, but at least she wanted to see me. Since she was the only real parent I had, that must count for something.

Chapter 31

When I finally arrived at 11:35, breathless and late, Dink blustered and blew his way through the store, a tornado with a mustache. He berated me for a solid five minutes, "This won't do, Twigs. You already had Saturday off. This is an official warning."

"How about an unofficial one and I come an hour early tomorrow?"

Dink smirked at my halfhearted bargaining plea.

I looked around. The register hadn't even been unlocked. "Everyone's enjoying the holiday. Have any customers been in here at all today?" I'd never spoken back to Dink, but it was obvious that the store had been empty.

"Doesn't matter, Twigs." He pointed at his eyes with two fingers and then down at me. Universal sign language for dorks.

"Yeah, I'm watching you, too, Dink." Oh, it felt good to say that aloud. I gave him the same two-finger sign, just pointing a little more than needed with my middle finger.

Dink's nostrils enlarged as he puffed air over his mustache. I thought he might explode, but he turned and looked at the clock over the pharmacy counter. It was almost noon. He glared at me but then hurried out for a lunch date. I watched him walk across the town green while twiddling the ends of his mustache. He hitched up his pants, too, and I noticed his socks were different colors, one gray and one black. Maybe he was meeting someone, but more likely, one of the waitresses over at TBGs was in for a major Dink flirt attack. Fine by me. Life at work was far easier when Dink disappeared.

Fifteen minutes on a lonely Labor Day in Uptown Pharmacy felt like eight hours. Not that I wanted Dink back in the place with me. Mr. Franks had taken the holiday off and I hoped no one came in needing medicine. I yawned and wished for a radio to listen to Coop. To hear that voice. Maybe I'd stop by WHNK tomorrow after classes.

I picked up a new rag mag and noticed the same blonde-of-the-moment that had been on the previous week's cover. This photo was blurry but clear enough to see the starlet's tummy hanging over her micro two-piece bathing suit.

Giant letters filled the headlines. *PREGNANT?!!!* Underneath, in slightly smaller print was another large question, *WHO'S THE FATHER?!!!*

"Yeah, I'd like to know that, too," I wondered aloud. "Who's my father?"

No one answered. No fairy godmother. No angel with messages from the Big Guy. Maybe that's what Mom wanted to see me about later. Maybe she'd figured out whose sperm made me happen. More true confessions.

With Dink gone and no customers, I gorged on Twizzlers. I opened a new giant container of the red licorice sticks after I'd emptied the first one. A half-eaten Twizzler hung out of my mouth when the main door of the store opened and a familiar person walked into Uptown Pharmacy. My ex-father.

If air can be sucked out of a place, it happened when I saw his face. I felt it inside, too, my body caving in for lack of oxygen. The big red neon clock in the back of the store might have blinked, adding a few extra seconds. It was noon, or close to it. Time seemed to stumble and stop for additional effect. The headline on the rag mag might have rearranged itself in my blurry vision—*TWIGS'S HEAD IMPLODES!!!*

"Hey," he said.

The way he spoke reminded me of Matt. Then I realized it was the other way around. Matt could have been my ex-dad's clone, except for the gray streaking his hair. That streak hadn't been there before he left us. That night he'd passed out on the couch next to me and a stack of empty beer cans. Something that happened a lot. We'd been watching a John Wayne movie. I'd left him snoozing there when I'd gone to bed. But we'd all been awakened when Mom had finally rolled in past midnight. "A meeting," she'd said, but even I knew deaf school secretaries don't work that late.

They'd had the fight of all fights and the next morning Dad was gone. "Early to work," Mom had told us, her eyes still puffy from crying. Maybe she believed that, too. We all believed her when we trudged off to school that day. There had been a lot of fights, so Matt, Marlee, even me, especially me—we all expected Dad to be home later.

Now, I looked at him and waited for my head to implode or maybe it'd hit him instead. There'd be an explosion or vaporization in this Twigs movie where ex-dad melts into the ground, like that witch in Oz. But nothing happened. He stood there, with his hands tucked in his jeans pockets. The way his shoulders hunched forward, it was clear that being with me took a lot of effort.

He stepped toward the counter, where I sat on a high stool behind the register. My hand let go of the rag mag, which I let drop to the floor, and I stood to face him, the Twizzler falling from my mouth. Once my feet hit the floor, I felt rigid, like a stake nailed me into place. I put my hands flat on the counter, thankful for the buffer between us.

"I almost had a beer," ex-dad said.

I still couldn't speak. I feared what I might say to this man, the stranger who had been my father.

"There's a bottle in my truck." He nodded his head toward the front windows. I followed his gaze to the truck I'd seen at the senior center. "It's unopened. So far." He took in a big breath. "I really want it. I can't, though. I've learned that much."

Ex-dad paused as if waiting for me to say something, anything, but I only blinked. I kept blinking, willing him to disappear, or to reappear the way he'd been before all this had happened. But he didn't.

"Twigs, it's not your fault." He glanced around the pharmacy as if looking for someone to help him. He wiped his face. Sweating or crying, I couldn't be sure.

I wanted help, too. But this was just between us. We stood there, a silent showdown between two members of the Henry gang, although I wasn't a true Henry anymore. A nerve pulsed on the side of his head near the gray streak, and he squinted at me, into me. Maybe he had learned mind control in those AA meetings. My head began pounding, a regular drum solo with no sense or rhythm, but painful enough so I clamped my eyes shut. I tried blocking the world out, but the pounding continued.

"You okay?"

One of his fingers lightly touched my hand on the counter. A shiver raced through my body, but then changed to intense heat, as if I'd touched something so cold, it burned. His touch hurt. It wasn't mine anymore. The meaning of everything Dad and daughter between us had been erased.

For the thousandth time in a week, I cried. Swift, sad tears slid down my face, onto his hand and mine.

"You're not my dad," I barely whispered.

"Yeah," he said, "but I am. I have to be."

His Matt-blue eyes gushed with tears, too. He reached across the counter and tugged on my ear. That soft earlobe pull had been part of our routine when he tucked me in at night—unless he'd passed out drunk before my bedtime.

"Oh! I remember!" I exclaimed, not in pain but excited. My ex-dad's eyes widened. "Did you pull my ear before you left that night?"

He nodded.

A sudden memory from the night he'd left home flooded through me. I'd heard him fighting with Mom. "Not mine?" Dad had screamed over and over. I'd fallen asleep with those words filling my head, never knowing until now that it was all about me. It had been deep and late that night, or in the early dawn, that I'd felt it. That tug. He'd come into my room and tugged my ear. He'd planted a mushy, beery kiss on my forehead, too. I'd turned over, ignoring him, eager to stay asleep.

"The blood thing hurt me, too," ex-dad was saying, pulling me from my memory. "It was plain silly pride that sent me on a binge to end all binges, but it's what happened. It doesn't mean that I don't love you."

A sound at the back of the store made us both turn. I was just tall enough to make out someone jumping over the pharmacy counter.

"Hey!" I yelled. "You can't go back there!"

"What's going on?" Dad asked. I thought of him that way again. Ex-dad, Dad, what difference did it make if he cared? I believed he did.

"Hey!" I screamed again and came around from behind the front counter. "The pharmacy's closed today!" I shouted like it would make a difference.

Pill bottles clattered. I could see row upon row falling from the shelves that reached the ceiling in the pharmacy. Someone was operating in destroy mode, unless an earthquake had just struck that part of the store.

"Mr. Franks?" It was a stupid question. I knew the minute I said it that it wasn't the pharmacist back there. Even if he had been there, given his lack of a hearing aid, he wouldn't have heard me.

I started toward the pharmacy, but Dad grabbed my arm.

"Call nine-one-one," he said and took off toward the sounds before I could stop him.

"Dad, wait!"

I watched Dad's head bobbing down Aisle 7, the memorable hair-dye aisle, and then he disappeared from view. The crashing sounds abruptly stopped in the pharmacy. The sudden silence was not golden. There was no calm in this quiet. My stomach lurched with the overload of Twizzlers churning inside, and I hoped that Dad had just crouched down out of sight.

"Dad?" I called out. Who cared if the pill robber heard me? The thought of losing my dad again, even if we weren't related, made my chest ache. My heart seemed to squeeze in on itself. "Dad! Come back!"

The call forgotten, I raced down Aisle 5, glad to be short for once. I pushed the Stay Fresh cardboard lady out of my way. I'd make my way around the far end of Aisle 7 and find Dad.

Instead, as I curved around the end of Aisle 5 and stopped short, a bloody knife was thrust at my chest.

"Don't move, bitch."

Jerkboy. He held a knife. Not an ordinary steak knife, but a whopping monster with a short handle and a blade as wide as my hand. One of those horror-movie head-chopping weapons, complete with blood dripping off the edge of the glinting metal. Was it my dad's blood?

Jerkboy waved the chopper in front of my face like a magic wand. Abracadabra.

I screamed, "Where's my father?" I tried to jump around this kid. Yeah, there was plenty of fear but there was rage, too. I couldn't let anyone or anything get between us again.

"Some ass-wipe got in my way." Jerkboy sliced his chopper, ninja style, and sent a *swoosh* of air my way. In his other hand, he held a plastic garbage bag, which rattled with pill bottles.

Knife or not, I flung myself at Jerkboy, startling him. I shoved him to the floor and nearly flew over him. My bones seemed to have turned into noodles of fear, and I wobbled as I ran. I raced up Aisle 6, past pink kids' Tylenol bottles and two shelves full of nose sprays, one of Dink's favorite products.

"Dad!" I kept calling him. I heard my name, one aisle over.

Jerkboy had gotten up and charged me, a raging bull on attack. If I hadn't been terrified, I might have laughed. His crazed face and the chopper pointed at my head could have been straight out of one of those ridiculous video games those guys were playing in Brady's dorm.

Channeling a bit of Helen, I whipped my hands along the display shelves. Containers of aspirin and cough-syrup boxes flew off the shelves and onto the floor to slow Jerkboy's chase. He was still about half an aisle away from me. I spied a lone Listerine bottle on the bottom shelf. It gleamed in the fluorescent store lights, as if flashing me a rescue signal. I wrapped my fingers around the dusty bottle. It felt as heavy as my pile of college books. I suspected it might be the only glass container left in the store, since most every liquid item I'd stocked had been plastic. I'd never seen a discus toss, but I twisted my body, pulled back my arm holding the hefty bottle, and let it fly.

I missed. My target landed short of Jerkboy by a good two feet, but the bottle smashed, sending a spray of gold liquid and glass shards right at him. It was enough to make him slip.

"Bitch!" he yelled.

I left Jerkboy screaming and cursing as I continued my search.

A trail of blood led me to Aisle 7. Dad lay about halfway down the aisle, leaning against the Clairol display, right where Helen had sat a little over a week ago. He was clutching his thigh, and panting. A deep red liquid circle dotted the floor where he sat, as blood pooled underneath him.

"Dad?" I ran to his side. I wanted to lift him, hug him, hold him, and love him—whatever it took to make him okay.

Dad reached for me with bloodied hands. "He didn't hurt you, did he?"

"No." I knelt next to him and noticed how gray his face appeared.

"I think he got an artery." He winced.

I realized I hadn't called 911. I yanked my smock over my head and wrapped it around Dad's leg, trying to make it as tight as possible. The white smock turned red in my hands.

"Whoa, that's a lot of blood." Jerkboy stood at the end of the aisle, in the same spot where he'd been before, staring at Helen Raymond.

"Call nine-one-one! My dad needs help!" I screeched. I guess I expected the villain to help his victims.

"Who cares?" Jerkboy said. The chopper dangled from his hand. He hoisted the bag of pills over his shoulder and headed toward the back door. His rage spent, it seemed, as if it had never existed.

Somehow this reminded me of his father in that IHOP parking lot when the mom begged him to stop scaring his kids. What had she called him? Not Jerkboy. What? His name popped into my head, and the feel of my father's cold hand gripping mine gave me an idea.

"Hey! Brian!" That got his attention. "You think your dad'll hit you harder when he finds out you've been stealing?"

Brian Jerkboy turned around. "My dad?" The mention of his father halted his escape. His shoulders lifted, his gaze faltered, turning almost vacant. Maybe his dad did the same thing before he beat Brian.

He raised the huge knife and advanced on me. I dropped Dad's hand and stood to face him. Time did its dance again, slowing and blurring everything within and around me. Without looking, I grabbed something off the nearest shelf and hoisted it above my head. He began moving at full throttle now, closing the space between us, with his chopper aimed at my head.

The only sound I heard beyond my own breathing was a hoarse cry.

"No!" Dad howled, and the kid slowed down, like he'd gone over a speed bump. It gave me the second I needed to wind up for a throw that would have won any World Series. Only I didn't throw a baseball. I heaved a giant bottle of Herbal Essence Shampoo. Though heavier than the Listerine, this bottle fit into my hand as if it had been made for it.

Pure adrenaline put a force behind my throw equal to any Major League pitcher. The shampoo bottle tipped end over end, hitting Brian Jerkboy in the head hard enough to knock him down. He collapsed, his head slamming the old linoleum floor with a sickening *bonk*. The blade fell from his limp hand and clattered into the hairspray containers filling the low shelves. The garbage bag flew open and a shower of pill bottles sprayed over us.

I'd brought Brian Jerkboy down on the first throw, but my arms kept flinging bottles of hair-care products at his body as it lay sprawled on the floor. *Thump, thunk, thud.* Chopper attack trumped by Suave Conditioner for Flyaways.

"Twigs?" Dad's weak voice stopped me midthrow.

I looked at Brian Jerkboy's limp body and felt a combination of horror and relief.

I dropped the bottle in my hand and knelt next to my father. "Dad."

"Good throw," Dad said.

The shakes took over and I could barely speak, "I think I killed him." This thought dimmed when I looked into Dad's eyes. I felt as drained as he looked and shuddered at the sight of all the blood surrounding us.

"My cell," Dad said, and tried reaching for his front pocket. He couldn't lift his hand.

The call. I had to make the call. I gently pulled his cell phone from his jeans.

Jabbing at the buttons, I yelled, "Ambulance! Emergency!" and gave the store's address.

Cradling my father in my lap, I stroked his head. "Hang on, okay?" He was silent and his eyes fluttered closed. "Dad!"

I gave his head an urgent little shake. I wanted to see his eyes, the ones I'd missed so much over the last few years. Those eyes that could make me smile when I'd had a bad day and the world made me feel small.

Dad would put his face close to mine and peer into my eyes. He'd say, "I can see in there, Twigs. You know twigs are part of trees. You may be small, but you're a huge tree inside, one of those strong trees that grow taller than skyscrapers."

He always made me feel like a giant, capable of doing anything I wanted.

I tapped softly on Dad's face with my fingertips, something I'd do when he'd passed out from too many beers. I willed his eyes to open. They did.

"I love you, Dad."

He could barely whisper, but I heard every word, "Daughter Twigs, I love you, too."

A small, sweet smile lingered on his lips, even when his eyes closed again.

Chapter 32

I had to give Titusburg's finest their due. Seconds after I'd made the 911 call, two cops rushed in and helped staunch the blood draining from Dad. "Whoa, it's Dale Henry," one of the cops said, recognizing him. Dad had been the go-to mechanic for the local police and most everybody else in town.

Titusburg had no ambulance service, but several EMTs arrived from Hinkney. They concentrated on the bodies, nothing else. I'd given the cops the story of my *High Noon* showdown, but the EMTs didn't care who had started the fight. They worked quickly to keep a man from bleeding to death and carefully checked the young unconscious teen.

One EMT gave me a quick once-over, checking for injuries. "You hurt?"

"I'm not sure." I wore nearly as much of my dad's blood as he had lost, but as far as I could tell, I wasn't hurt.

The EMT looked like a surfer, tan and carefree. He placed his hand on my wrist, checking my pulse. His fingers were warm and firm on my skin and my pulse thumped with adrenaline. My legs wouldn't stop shaking and I felt cold all over.

"Is my dad okay?" I could see two more EMTs circling my dad, poking and prodding him like hungry vultures.

It was all I could do not to scream at them to make him live.

"Breathe," Surfer EMT said. "You're okay."

"Yeah." It didn't answer the question I'd asked, but the way he said it made me believe it was true, in spite of what had just happened, or maybe because of it. For the first time in a long time, I knew I'd be okay. I just hoped the same would be true for Dad.

The EMTs pulled Brian Jerkboy's T-shirt up to check him over. Bruises covered his body. My senses went numb, staring at his lifeless form. What had I done?

"Look," the surfer EMT said to the cops, who were busy collecting pill bottles. He pointed at the large black and purple blotches all over Brian's ribs.

Without hesitation, one cop recited an address, "Eighteen Deacon Street. Been to his house many times. Domestic crap. Fist-happy Dad, but the wife and kids won't spill. Too scared."

I wailed, suddenly overcome with the life this kid lived and what I'd done to him. "I didn't mean to kill him!" Brian could have taken all the pills in the store, but he shouldn't have hurt my dad. I huffed for breaths between sobs, and one of the cops came over and knelt next to me.

The EMTs and the cops spoke in unison, "He's not dead."

One of the cops gently patted my back, soothing me like a little kid who'd lost her puppy. "Sshh. Hey, hey. It's okay. He'll have a bitch of a headache, but you did that kid a favor. Those ER docs will report suspected abuse. Then we have a real shot of busting his pop."

So, by knocking Brian out, I had helped him? I sniffed and grabbed a bunch of tissues from a box someone offered me. I saw one of the cops pocket a Milky Way, but I didn't care. Pieces of rubbery licorice sat like lead in my stomach.

Both cops helped me up from the floor, and I swayed like I'd stepped onto land from a rocking boat. We moved out of the way so the EMTs could do their job. They hoisted my dad and Brian onto gurneys. The side of Brian's head had swollen to the size of a grapefruit. The shampoo bottle had done some damage, but falling on the hard floor had helped, too. If he hadn't stabbed Dad, I could almost have felt sorry for Brian. I didn't think of him as Jerkboy any longer. His father's brutality had pushed him to violence, as much as my dad's absence had affected me.

Dink returned from his lunch just as the patients were being wheeled outside. The few folks around the Titusburg town green on Labor Day wandered over to watch the commotion.

"Twigs!" Dink trotted up the sidewalk, panting as if he'd just been out for a jog. He'd either eaten lunch and/or spent the hour trying get into the pants of one of the TBGs waitresses. A half-chewed toothpick hung out of his mouth, peeking out from beneath his mustache. Dink stomped his foot and asked, "What did you do?"

His ridiculous question raised more than a few eyebrows from the cops and EMT crew.

"Sir, move aside," Surfer EMT spoke to Dink, clearly a command not a request. "This is an emergency."

Dink blustered, like an old bull, but moved aside and continued to glare at me.

An apology popped out of my mouth, "Sorry about this, Dink." I opened my mouth again and then closed it. Did I really have to explain myself to Dink? He'd never listened to me, so why did I expect him to understand what had just happened? I had another moment of clarity, just like I'd felt when the surfer EMT said I'd be okay. Dink didn't deserve any more of me, not even a smirk, so I turned away.

I followed the EMT guys as they loaded Dad into the back of the ambulance. His face and arms looked as white as the sheet they had wrapped around his body. "I'm here, Dad," I said, hoping for an eye flutter or some sign that he'd heard me, but he remained still. Still, as death.

Peaceful would describe Brian's face when they rolled him into the ambulance next to my dad. He looked harmless, like a sweet little boy taking a nap.

One of the cops approached Dink and his mustache nearly stood on end. The toothpick dropped from his mouth to the ground. He moved toward me, as if I would protect him.

"Hey, Dink, a few questions." The cop crossed his arms and blocked Dink's escape. "Why was your rear security door unlocked?"

"Huh?" Dink stuttered. I knew Dink left from that door when he locked up at night. If it was unlocked, it was his fault.

The cop continued, "Where were you during the robbery?"

"Robbery?" Dink looked over the cop's shoulder searching for me. "Twigs?"

"We've already talked to her," the cop told Dink. "I'm talking to you now."

Surfer EMT guy reached out a hand, guiding me. "You can ride with us, but you have to sit up front."

I nodded and he helped me step up into the front of the ambulance.

"Twigs!" Dink shouted. "You can't leave!"

I gave him one last look and made sure he heard me. "I quit, Dink!"

* * *

When Mom and Deaf Lou appeared in the waiting room at the Hinkney Community Hospital, I nearly fell over from shock. Mom kept hugging me, squeezing my arms and face. "Oh, Twigs. You're okay, you're okay." She checked me from head to toe, like she'd done once when I'd fallen off a slide at a park.

"Bob called," she said, referring to Mr. Platton. "He heard about the robbery on his police scanner."

I should have known.

Deaf Lou quickly signed something and gave me a little salute.

Mom translated, "Lou thinks you're as brave as any soldier to beat that robber the way you did." Mom paused. "Bravely stupid." She smiled and touched my face. "Just like your brother."

I liked being compared to Matt. A weird thought occurred to me, something I couldn't have ever imagined before. Mom was proud of me.

"Your dad will pull through," Mom said. "Dale's strong that way, like Matt."

I brushed away her hand. Her empathy confused me and rankled a bit. "Why do you care? You're not even married to him anymore."

"I loved the man, Twigs. Once." She gave Deaf Lou a sideways glance and then continued, "And he saved your life."

I disputed that, as I did most things with Mom. "He got in the robber's way. We both did."

"No, Twigs. Dale went there to see you. That's what I meant."

* * *

Dad needed blood. Gallons and gallons, the way the docs made it sound, as well as emergency surgery to repair the damaged artery in his leg. It thrilled me that my blood was a perfect match, even if it was the most common type. I told the vampire taking my blood my dad saga and said, "Make sure Dale Henry gets my blood first." I wanted Dad to have some part of me in him. He was in me, DNA or not. I could feel him in my heart.

Mr. Platton used his unique skills to round up my family, the neighbors, and anyone else he could wrangle to share their blood. Mom gave a pint, Marlee, Tower of Isaac, and a gang of cheerleader and football players from Titusburg High. Dad's friend Don Garkin and a bunch of strangers who I guessed were AA folks all showed up, too, offering their arms. They kept going outside to smoke cigarettes while waiting with us during Dad's surgery. Deaf Lou's blood wasn't a match, but he played gopher, getting coffee and food for everyone, even if we didn't want it.

"Twigs!" Helen arrived and squeezed me until I had to ask her to stop. She wore at least twenty colorful leis from the Labor Day Luau and tossed a green one over my head. "Like I said before. You're one wild woman."

It set me off. I grabbed her and cried, burrowing my face into her goodness.

"There, there," Helen said, rocking me in a big hug. "It's good to cry. You've got a heart full of love. Your dad's going to need that."

Helen's words made me smile. My love for Dad had been beat to hell over the past few years. But I loved him. That had never stopped.

Mr. Platton gave Helen a welcoming peck on her cheek and she put a bright pink lei over his head.

"Bob, show me where to give blood for the man. And let's call Pat and Chris. They'll want to help, too."

"Thank you, Helen." Mom had been sitting quietly on the waiting-room couch. "I'm sorry I didn't say this sooner. Thank you for caring about Twigs."

"How could I not?" Helen smiled and winked at me. "I hope they don't mind pink blood." She whisked out of the waiting room with Mr. Platton.

I paced nonstop around the small room, like a caged cheetah, desperate to run. Dad had lost so much blood that whenever we asked about him, the doctors or nurses replied, "It's too soon to say," or "We'll have to see."

Mom grabbed my hand after I'd paced a few miles. She patted a spot on the couch next to her. "Come and sit."

Somehow I ended up with my head on her lap. She began stroking my hair. It would be a lie to say it didn't feel odd to have Mom doing that, but it was wonderful, too.

Deaf Lou was signing madly to her. Finally, Mom sighed.

"Twigs, Lou and Matt won't leave me alone."

"Matt?" I sat up.

"Yes, Matt," Mom said. "We were on the phone earlier today—before all of this happened." She paused. Deaf Lou prodded her, signing a few words with his strong fingers. "Okay, Lou." She took my hands in hers. Everyone else in the waiting room quieted, like Mom was going to make some special announcement.

"Regrets and amends," Mom said. "Matt's been on me to talk to you. Lou, too. You know I'm stubborn—you get that from me." She began signing so Deaf Lou could follow along, "Anyway, I owe you a big apology, Twigs. I'm sorry for the way I've handled all this, but I wanted to protect you." She tilted her chin in a way that reminded me of Marlee. "What happened was a long time ago, and it's my fault. Dale's to blame, too, in a way, but I let his drinking push me away—to all those strange men. I hoped he'd be jealous enough to want me more than beer."

I held my breath, absorbing every word.

"He's never really forgiven me and sometimes I know I blamed you for that. That was wrong of me." Mom looked down and sniffed. "I'm so sorry. I hope your dad pulls through so I can thank him for being there today. If anything had happened to you, Twigs, I don't know what I would have done."

I took it all in, speechless. Mom took the blame. Mom opened up. Mom wanted me alive! The clock in the waiting room ticked so loud it could have been amplified, and my heart matched its beat.

Finally, I spoke, "Thank you, Mom."

"What for?"

"For apologizing."

Deaf Lou's hand was on my back, pushing me toward Mom.

"I love you," Mom said, and it hit me that both of my parents had said that to me today. After years of feeling alone and unloved, I felt loved today.

We hugged and sobbed, hugged and sobbed.

Then Deaf Lou began signing something, too fast for me to get. But everything in my life had been fast and furious lately.

Mom translated, “No more secrets, Twigs. Never again. Lou’s already asked Matt and Marlee, and he wanted to ask for your permission, too, before we make this official.”

Deaf Lou was smiling, and there was no need to sign a word. I reached over and hugged the deaf man, and he hugged me in return. The way Mom looked at us hugging made my heart swell just a little more.

“We’ll be bridesmaids, Twigs,” Marlee chirped up, from her spot on Tower of Isaac’s lap.

Mr. Platton and Helen walked in from the hall just in time to hear Marlee’s announcement. Her right arm was taped up with a bright pink bandage. “Pink is a perfect color for weddings.”

I pictured myself in a hot-pink pouffy dress with a gigantic bow covering my ass. The thought made me burst out laughing, so hard that tears streamed down my face.

“You okay, honey?” Helen asked.

“She’s okay,” Mom answered.

I nodded. Except for worrying about Dad, I was okay in every sense of the word.

I got up and let out a huge sigh. “I’m going for a walk. Just down the hall here.” I looked at Marlee. “If they finish Dad’s surgery, come find me.”

I turned and bumped into Coop as he entered the waiting room. “Whoa, there.” His hands grasped my arms, stopping me. “Leaving so soon?”

I swallowed my surprise. “What are you doing here?”

“Mrs. Raymond’s neighbors saw me sitting on her porch, waiting for you.”

Helen chimed in, “Pat and Chris. Are they here?”

“Giving blood as we speak,” Coop answered, but he hadn’t taken his eyes off mine. “I’m sorry about your dad. I heard that you fought off gangs of robbers.” He smiled.

"No gangs. One robber."

"Either way, you won. That's what counts, Twigs."

His voice hugged me, if that was possible. "You were waiting for me?"

Coop smiled. "I had to see you. You didn't come to the Radioneers. Did you hear the show this morning?" He grasped my hands in his, holding them to his chest. "When I proclaimed my feelings for you?"

I gulped, embarrassed at Coop's public spectacle. I pulled my hands, but he held tight.

Marlee spoke up. "We heard, didn't we, Twigs?"

Tower of Isaac grunted in agreement.

Coop squeezed my hands a little tighter. "Mrs. Raymond's neighbors told me that a crazed dope fiend tried to ax you. I had to make sure you were okay."

"I'm okay." I noticed the bandage on his arm. "You gave blood, too?"

Coop nodded. His eyes left mine and he pulled his hands away, moving them in the air. He was signing to Deaf Lou.

I couldn't believe my eyes. "You know sign language?"

Without missing a beat, Coop said, "Oh, you'd be surprised at the things I can do with my hands."

That got a laugh from everyone within earshot, but Coop was still signing. "I learned it to get a summer counselor's job but got fired for being too chatty. Imagine that."

"What are you two saying?" I asked.

Mom answered, "Lou's telling him to kiss you, Twigs."

I looked at Coop. He shrugged and gave me a shy smile. "I told him I didn't want to get slapped."

That's when I noticed his T-shirt. COOPER heart symbol TWIGS.

My face must have registered my surprise.

Coop's smile widened. "Why hide the truth? I can get you one, too. We'll be one of those annoying couples who wear matching clothes."

"We're not a couple."

"Yet," Cooper said.

Without another thought, I pulled him close and kissed him full on the mouth.

There may have been clapping from those watching us, or it may have been my heart bursting with joy.

When I opened my eyes and looked at Coop after what might have been the longest kiss in history, we were both silent. It was one of those moments that was too big for words.

Then he said, "Does this mean you want a shirt?"

Chapter 33

Dad made it through surgery. He'd opened his eyes briefly when they brought him out of recovery. "Twigs," he'd managed to say. The docs had him on enough painkillers to put down an elephant, probably the same kinds of pills that Brian had been trying to steal at the pharmacy.

They finally moved Dad to a room, and I settled in a chair next to his bed. About midnight, twelve hours since our showdown at the pharmacy, his eyes fluttered and he focused briefly on me before fading back into a medicated sleep.

I didn't want to leave his side, but the doctors and nurses expected him to sleep through the night.

"Get some sleep and go to school tomorrow," Mom had said, sounding more like a mom than ever. "He'd want that. Get that degree so you can get out of Titusburg or learn enough to run it."

"She's right," Mr. Platton said, and Deaf Lou signed the same.

Helen chimed in, "So true."

I knew I had a poli sci class that I couldn't miss again without flunking, so I agreed.

Before dawn the next day, I called the hospital. "Your dad's still sleeping," the duty nurse said. She promised to tell him I called when he woke up. I made it to school at 8:00, a full hour before class started. I found Room 4378A and sat in a desk in the front row. I wanted to meet this unknown professor the moment he appeared to apologize for missing two classes. I buried my nose in my book, skimming the first few chapters and hoping that had been part of the homework.

The classroom filled with sleepy students. When the professor entered the room, it was all I could do not to fall out of my chair. Stuart Raymond, arm still in a sling, holding a cardboard cup of coffee in his free hand, walked over to the desk at the front of the room and turned to face the class.

He dropped his coffee when he saw me. “Jesus Christ!” The cup hit the edge of the desk and the lid popped off. Hot liquid sprayed Stuart Raymond’s khaki trousers and brown loafers. Some coffee splashed his crisp white button-down shirt. “Shit!”

The quiet class let out a few giggles.

After surviving a life-and-death standoff along with my dad, I now faced the crazed eyes of a whore-screwing, one-armed political science professor. I released my grip on the edge of my desk. There wasn’t a shampoo bottle in sight, but as far as I could see, Professor Raymond didn’t plan on attacking me. Something about this realization was freeing. After every crazy thing that had happened in the past week, Stuart Raymond was a laugh. I let out a hearty “ha!” enjoying the moment. It was a powerful feeling, knowing I could handle this.

I jumped up and grabbed a handful of tissues from a box on the desk and held them out to Stuart Raymond. He stuttered, “Why are you here?”

He even took a few steps backward, clutching his re-casted arm to his chest. It made me feel like a giant.

“I’m in your class.” I dropped tissues on the coffee puddle, which was much easier to sop up than hair dye. “It’s Madeline Henry on your list there. You can call me Ms. Henry.”

He gave me a weak nod, cradling his arm closer.

Many things in life are uncertain, but at that moment, I understood with perfect clarity that Professor Stuart Raymond was afraid of me. Helen would be so proud.

* * *

When I arrived at the hospital a few hours later, Don Garkin was just leaving Dad’s room. He held a cowboy hat in his hands.

“Hey there, Twigs,” he said. “He’s been anxious to see you.”

I felt the same way. "Thanks."

Don Garkin slid the brim of his hat through his fingers. "That Helen woman came by earlier." Don smiled. "Told your dad not to hurt you again or she'd kick his you-know-what."

I reddened, but approved of Helen's protective words. "She's not lying."

"Nope. She strikes me as one honest lady." Don placed the cowboy hat on his head, getting ready to leave.

"Hey." I needed to know something. "Dad's always been a drinker. For as long as I can remember."

"You wonder if he'll stay sober."

I nodded.

"As long as he wants to. Make sense?"

Another nod. "Thanks."

"Better get in there." Don motioned to Dad's room. "Bye, now." He tipped his hat before striding away. Add a sunset and a horse, and he could step into any western ever made.

I went in to see my father.

Dad sat up in the hospital bed, with his bandaged leg elevated in some sort of harness. He still looked ghost white, but his eyes had life now.

"Hey," he said.

"Hey."

"Some day yesterday, huh?"

More nodding.

"Well, this gets me out of working." Dad gave a little smile. His voice seemed too bright, like the harsh sun streaming in through the window next to his bed. "I'm still fixing cars, you know. I work over at Hinkney Automotive. Twigs, you should see the wreck this guy brought in last week. One of those classic cars . . ."

Dad's voice faltered. I swallowed. I wasn't Matt. I didn't want to talk cars. Silence filled the room. As much as I wanted to see him, I hadn't moved from the door yet. That feeling of power I'd had with Stuart Raymond had disappeared. Shyness made my knees shake, but I managed to speak.

"I'm glad you made it, Dad."

Dad said, "I'm glad we made it."

More silence. He held out a hand to me. I walked over to the bed and took it in mine. His fingers were warm now. I gave a gentle squeeze and his eyes brimmed and he sniffed back tears.

"I'm a mess," he said, his voice cracking. "Still shocked that we made it out of there alive yesterday. But I'm better now, Twigs. I mean than when I lived with your mom. I'm not drinking anymore."

That made me smile.

"Doesn't mean I don't want to. I want to a lot."

We were both silent for a minute.

Dad cleared his throat. "I'll help you find him."

"Who?"

"Your real dad." When he said the word *dad*, he coughed.

With the craziness of the past few days, I hadn't even thought about searching for the sperm that had met Mom one night. The thought of meeting a stranger who knew nothing about me didn't matter right now.

I squeezed his hand and spoke the truth, "You're my real dad."

Tears and hugs, tears and hugs. Just like I'd shared with Mom yesterday.

"Hey," Dad said, "grab that bag." He pointed to a small shopping bag on the bedside table. "Don brought some stuff I wanted."

The open bag was filled with car magazines, a slim plastic CD case, and a deck of cards.

"Pull that table up here," Dad said.

A rolling hospital table covered the end of his bed. It held a laptop, a plastic water pitcher, and a small bowl of orange Jell-O. I pulled it up next to Dad and set the shopping bag within his reach.

"I saved that for you." Dad pushed the Jell-O in my direction. "Still your favorite?"

I smiled. I hadn't had Jell-O in years.

"You better eat it before it eats us," Dad said.

That phrase triggered a memory of sitting around our dining-room table when I was little. Matt sat next to me with Marlee on the other side of him in one of those booster seats. She had tomato sauce all over her face. Mom looked young and happy, leaning into Dad. He had a bowl of Jell-O in front of him, wiggling it with a spoon. "It's alive!" Dad exclaimed. "Attack of the killer Jell-O!" Matt had shouted, while stabbing the wobbling mound with a fork. We had all laughed together. Our family.

"Yep, I still love Jell-O." I spooned a wiggly orange square into my mouth.

Dad smiled at me. This man, related or not, had helped make me Twigs. The love I'd always felt for him had never wavered.

After I finished the Jell-O, Dad opened the laptop and powered it up.

"Get comfortable," he said. "I want to show you something."

I moved to the chair next to the bed.

"Nope." Dad patted the mattress next to him. "Right here, so you can see the screen."

"I don't want to bump your leg."

"You're not going to hurt me, Twigs. You saved me. Besides, the good nurse gave me some meds before you got here. I'll be snoozing in no time."

"You sure?"

"Yep." He patted the bed again. "Quick now, I want to show you this before I drift off."

I climbed up onto the high hospital bed. Dad looked older and pale, but healthy. Not bloated and drunk like I remembered. I settled in next to him and he pulled the plastic case from the shopping bag.

"I had this in the truck yesterday when I came to see you. But that sad kid changed my plans."

I thought of Brian. Mr. Platton had shared everything he'd learned from his police friends. After a night in the hospital, Brian had been taken to a juvenile detention center this morning. Social services would check his family. There'd be a trial, but maybe he and his family would get the help they needed.

Dad slid the disc into the laptop. A DVD icon appeared on the desktop window. I felt Dad's breath slow, or maybe it was my own. We always loved watching movies together and here we were, doing it again. When Dad pressed PLAY, I gasped at the black-and-white image that appeared on the monitor. Surprise and expectation flooded me, along with tears that began flowing down my cheeks.

"Want to watch this one with me?" Dad put an arm around me as the FBI warning faded into the opening of the film. "I've heard it's pretty good, especially the showdown at the end."

I leaned into Dad, and rested my head on his shoulder.

A lone gunman standing next to a huge tree, with a horse nearby, filled the screen. The theme from *High Noon* began to play. Gentle drumbeats followed by a soft strumming and Tex Ritter singing, as the opening credits rolled. The song floated out of the laptop's speaker, tinny but clear. Dad began to sing along, "Do not forsake me, oh my darling . . ."

When I found my breath, I joined him.

THE END